When Love Breaks Us

MONICA ARYA

To all the good girls, especially the ones whose favorite colors are morally-gray and red.

Author's Note

Dear readers, thank you so much for taking a chance on my books and me! Please know that there are content warnings listed at www.monicaarya.com.

Note: Damien Moretti is an "alphahole" male main character. He's possessive and will call you a "good girl". He may rub you the wrong way with his alpha behavior but he knows how to rub other things the right way. If you enjoy red flags, tormented and morally-grey men, then Mr. Moretti can't wait to meet you.

CHAPTER 1

Sophie

"Sophie! We need to go. We're late!" my older brother, Ezra, called out to me as he jogged down the stairs carrying the last cardboard box.

"I'm coming! I'm coming!" I yelled back. My footsteps echoed in the hallways as I let out a soft sigh. I couldn't help but feel the pit in my core sink lower as I passed the 'room.' The room that had made the warmth of the sunshine disappear even on the hottest summer day. The room that changed my life in every way, and made me feel lost to the point I knew no one could ever find me. The room that wrecked my life. But really, it was silly that I was holding a room accountable for a man's sins. The room didn't wreck me, *he* did. A shiver ran up my spine as my chest tightened at the memories I couldn't contain.

"Just take a deep breath," I whispered to myself. Inhaling and exhaling, I ran my hands across my face. I'd never have to come here again.

This was the first time I had come back into this house after a year of it sitting empty, just like my heart.

My older brother had bought this pale blue townhouse for me my freshman year of college because it was a good deal, and Jesson University, the small private school I went to, was referred to as a 'suitcase' college. Most students lived off-campus because of how tiny the school was and how the dorms hadn't been updated in probably the last century. But it was the best pre-dental school in the state. Sure, becoming a dentist wasn't something overly exciting, but both of my parents were dentists. Now that they weren't alive, it made me clutch onto anything I could in order to feel closer to them.

"Sophie! Seriously, kid, I'm going to be late for work." My brother's voice ricocheted through the emptiness of the place I once called home. Running down the last few steps, I exhaled.

"I'm right, here. Geez." I tilted my head with my eyes narrowed at him. Ezra Shah was ultra-bossy but seemingly, was also always right. If I had listened to him about my ex-boyfriend, I could have saved myself from the impending doom that came soon after.

"You okay?" He eyed me carefully as he was trying to finagle the boxes in his sports car like a rubix cube.

"Mm-hmm. I'm okay." I nodded and sank into the passenger seat. I could tell by the way his lips curved down that he knew I wasn't okay. But what choice did I have? It had been one year, and after intensive therapy and two different anxiety medications, I was finally finding a balance and way to keep pushing forward.

"Want to grab a bite to eat?" Ezra was seated next to me and pressed the button to start his car. Leaning against the headrest, I looked at him. We didn't look completely alike, yet similar enough to know we were siblings. He favored my dad, and I was my mother's replica. His eyes were a pretty shade of hazel, where mine were dark brown. His hair was lighter than my black hair, but our skin was a creamy bronze, thanks to the beautiful blend of Indian from our mom and everything our dad was. We always joked that our dad was a melting pot, because he was half-Greek and half-Persian. My dad was adopted at a young age, so we didn't really have all the details beyond an Ancestry 21 result.

Our mom was a true beauty, but not just on the outside—it was also the beauty of her soul that reflected outward. She was also my best friend in the whole world.

My dad was the quieter counterpart of their duo, and I loved the way my dad would look at my mom every time she lit up a room with her vivacious and vibrant laugh.

They were volunteering at a dental and medical camp in Ecuador when a deadly earthquake rampaged through the country and left countless dead, including my parents.

I was only ten years old, and my brother was twenty. He was in college, and I had to live with my grandparents, far away from where he was in Illinois. *Where home was.*

Finally, when I got into college at Jesson, I couldn't wait to be closer to my brother, who did his best to constantly fly back and forth to check on me.

"Sophie, I asked if you wanted to grab a bite to eat?" Ezra repeated. This happened a lot. I often felt like I'd get so lost in my own thoughts that I didn't even feel present. I suppose that's how my brain was wired. My parents died when I was ten, and then my world was shaken up again when I was eighteen.

"Sure, I'm starving." I offered a small smile back.

"Okay, kid." My brother grinned back. Since Ezra was ten years older than me, he really took on the role of a parent more than a sibling after our parents died. Overprotective, check. Overbearing, check. Over the top, check, check, check. But I didn't mind; I was grateful, even though he was annoying with his nosiness and constant state of panic, especially if I didn't answer my phone on the first ring.

Pulling into Le Petit Bistro's parking lot, I opened my door and headed in beside my brother, who towered over me. Unlike him, I was a member of the elite group of individuals who made sure the half counted in my height. The small bistro was bustling since it was in the dead center of the well-loved and tourist central, 'Magnificent Mile' with Jesson University only a few blocks away. I grabbed us a small booth in the corner while Ezra got in line to order us lunch.

Pulling my phone out, I started scrolling through social media until the seat in front of me creaked. Looking up, my eyes froze on the man in front of me. My lips parted as I stared at him in shock.

He was hot. I'm talking on a scale of one to ten, he was easily a three hundred. *Easily.*

Except while I was drooling over him and wondering if he was here to prank me, he was looking at me like he wanted to eat me.

And not in a sexy way.

The gruff guy in front of me—scratch that, growly man in front of me—was looking at me, annoyed, as if my breathing was irritating him.

"Um, can I help you?" I raised my hands and widened my eyes at him, even though I could feel my cheeks heat just by his heavy gaze on me. He didn't break eye contact. *Talk about awkward.*

Averting my eyes, he scoffed.

"Okay, so I'm not sure if you're just new around here... like on planet Earth, but when someone is sitting at a booth or table in a restaurant, then it means that seat is taken and if it's empty, that means you have to *ask* if you can sit there." I crossed my arms over my chest, secretly cursing at the low cut of my blouse that this prick's eyes lingered on a second to long. He sat there with his icy eyes as he glared at me to the point I had to look away. What the hell is his problem?

CHAPTER 2

Damien

"I don't ask for anything," I replied hastily at the feisty girl in front of me. I had to bite back the small smirk that was teasing my lips because it had been a long time since anyone had spoken to me that way. Most women simply fawned over me or stammered through batted eyelashes trying to get my attention.

"Well, you obviously don't have manners. If you'll please move, that seat is taken." She nodded at me and looked toward the exit sign.

"There's no other empty seats besides this one that you have reserved for your imaginary friend, sweetheart," I said flatly, brushing my fingers across my jawline, anticipating what this petite spitfire was going to say next.

"Oh really, Sherlock?" She planted her palms on the table separating us and scooted closer, which was very,

very inconvenient considering it was making her cleavage tighter. My gaze dropped shamelessly to her breasts.

She gasped, "Oh my God, seriously, perv?" She tugged her shirt up, but it didn't do much.

"Maybe you should wear more material." I shrugged, pretending to be bored, though I was far from it.

"You are despicable. You know, as a friendly reminder, I hope you schedule your colonoscopy soon." She stood angrily.

"Colonoscopy?" I cocked my head at her, completely confused but eager to watch her perfect, thick pink pout fire something else at me.

"So, the doctor can pull your giant, inflated head out from your ass." She flicked her long, raven-black hair over her shoulder, then spun on her heels, giving me an opportunity to grin but also have an excellent view of her peach-shaped ass that was hidden under stretched denim. She started walking away, but stopped in her tracks in front of the person I was waiting on.

My best friend. I cringed for him. If he hit on her, he was going to crack in thirty-seconds. He was the much nicer, straight-edged counterpart to our friendship. He was also engaged, which made this even more intriguing. I'd never seen him take a second look at a woman who wasn't his fiancée. Granted, this girl was worth every damn second-look.

The firecracker glanced over her shoulder, looking at me in shock as my buddy spoke to her. *Nice. He's putting in a good word for me.* I grinned back at them and gave him the nod. You know the nod; the one that says, 'Thanks for my next lay.' I leaned back in the booth with my fingers laced behind my head.

"Hey, man." Ezra slid into the seat in front of me, and peach-ass followed behind. "I heard you met my little sister." He lowered his brows, carefully watching my reaction. The cocky smirk I had on my face washed away as quickly as windshield wipers against a downpour beating down on the car.

"Your... little sister?" I gulped, and choked on the last word, but made a mental note about the word *little*.

"Yeah." Ezra smiled, without any idea of the very dirty thoughts that had crossed my mind while looking at said little sister's cleavage and ass.

I flicked my gaze to her, but she averted mine at all costs.

"Want to introduce yourself, or do I need to?" He opened his palms and shrugged.

Clearing my throat, I straightened my spine and looked at her in a completely different light. I'm talkin' angel halo over that pretty little head of hers, kind of light.

"Hey, I'm Damien Moretti." I tightened my leather

jacket inward and waited. She kept her eyes on the menu in front of her until Ezra elbowed her.

"Ouch!" she screeched at her... *big brother's* face.

"I'm Sophie." She glared at me. I had to clamp my teeth into my bottom lip to refrain from the stupid smirk that, for some reason, kept begging to break free when she spoke.

"Cool," I replied with zero excitement. Her doe brown eyes that resembled something like creamy hot chocolate stayed pinned on me. *Two can play this game, sweetness.* I stared right back as if we were both fighting with nothing more than our eyes.

"Sophie is studying pre-dental at Jesson," Ezra boasted like a proud dad. Uh-oh, by little sister, my mind wondered how little. Sure, she looked young as hell, especially with those long thick lashes and eyes that had never seen pain. Her skin was bronzed naturally, yet a flush of pink highlighting her cheeks from what I could only assume was my presence. But then the way she was dressed in the tight denim and even tighter, low-cut shirt had me thinking not so little.

"You're a senior?" I took a sip of my black coffee, trying to be civil, even though war was the only thing painted across her pretty little face.

"No. I'm a junior." She looked away again.

"I'm hoping she gets into Jesson's dental program. I

just moved her closer to your place, actually," Ezra added.

"Well, good to know you're not heading into medical school." I scoffed.

"Why is that?" she spat back.

"I mean, your knowledge of medical conditions seems... *amateur*." Shrugging, I looked over for our waitress. Sophie sucked in a small breath of air, and the sound made my dick jerk. *Fucker.* I adjusted myself under the booth.

"Am I missing something? Please tell me you've never met before." Ezra's voice and face were laced with concern as his eyes widened at me.

"Nope. Just had the pleasure of meeting your bestie today," Sophie said, popping the 'p,' which only showed her age all that more. Speaking of... how old were juniors in college again? *Fuck, young.*

As if my 'bestie' knew what was roaming wildly in my mind, he added, "Sophie is nineteen." Okay. Fuck, really young. She was seventeen years younger than me. *Seventeen.* Not only that, but she was my best friend's little sister. *Abort mission you asshole, traitorous cock.*

"Great," I replied, acting as if I didn't give a shit. By tomorrow I'd forget this girl all together and be on top of another. Hell, tonight I'd have someone to be buried deep inside of.

"Ezra, what is it that you called me here for? Please tell me you're not asking me to help move this little sister of yours into her new place." I kept my eyes on Ezra and not the temptress squeezing her tits together next to him. Okay, she was probably cold considering she didn't have a jacket and the air conditioning was blasting over her. But suddenly, I felt too warm and far too annoyed.

"I had some files to give you, for the Brunson case. I need... you to take care of it." He let his eyes trail around us.

Leaning back, I brushed my hands together. "Done."

"Shit, I left them in my car. I'll go grab them. Keep an eye on Sophie, please. Too many creepy tourists in this area." Ezra shook his head and left without a second thought. I began drumming my fingers against the edge of the table as Sophie stared at her phone. I heard obnoxious snickering. Cocking my head, I looked to the side.

A group of college-looking assholes were eyeing her from their stools at the counter. My jaw ticked as my fists instinctively clenched.

"Here, take this." I peeled off my leather jacket and tossed it over to her.

"I don't want it," she fired back while rubbing her arms.

"I can't believe your brother let you out like that." Aggravation was clear in my words.

She let out a small laugh. "Oh, I'm sorry. I forgot you're old as balls, so you must not know we are in the year 2023 and not 1950. My older brother doesn't tell me what to do or who to do." As soon as the words fell out her mouth, she dropped her jaw. "I mean, *what to wear*," she stammered as her cheeks filled with pink.

My lips curled up. "What's on your mind, Sophie?" First, you're talking about my balls, and now you're talking about your big bro not having a say in who you fuck," I said, my voice low, pressing against the table to fill the space between us as much as possible.

She pulled back further on her side, as if she was scared to be in my presence. Before she could answer, I heard some asshole near us talk about, and I quote, 'her big rack.'

Standing, I pulled my arms back and stretched my head from side to side as I walked over the jock, who was neatly cutting into his sandwich like the fucking moron he was.

"What did you say?" I growled at him.

He spun around on his stool and widened his eyes as I towered him. He smiled with arrogance, and then leaned back into the counter. "I said the chick you're with has a really nice rack."

I nodded slowly and cracked my knuckles. "Fuck, I didn't hear you. Say it again?" Just as he opened his mouth, I swung straight into his jaw. His friends gasped, falling back as if they had no interest in being next. *Wimps.*

He wobbled on the small steel stool with my impact. Cracking my knuckles again, I repeated myself, "Say it again!"

His hand flung to his face as blood pooled out of his mouth. "I'm calling the cops. I hope that slut was worth it."

Okay, now he's dead.

I punched his nose so hard that the noise that followed made me concerned I had bashed his skull in. He flung back into the counter so hard that the waitresses screamed and scurried away.

I grabbed the not-so arrogant jock off his stool and dragged his ass over to our table. "Now, tell me again what you said about her."

Sophie's eyes were so wide, I swore they'd pop out of her head.

"Man, I'm... I'm so sorry," he stammered with blood seeping all over his Ralph Lauren oxford.

"Nope, that's not right." I gave him a little shake.

"I'm sorry, ma'am," he cried out to Sophie, who was definitely younger than him but he had me laughing.

"That's right. Good boy." I gave his head a little pat

before throwing a wad of cash onto the table and reaching for my jacket.

"Time to go," I said to Sophie as I wiped my blood-stained hands with a napkin. She was frozen and staring at me without words—which was impressive since she seemed to have plenty of those before.

Sliding out, she stood beside me. Hell, she was short. Meanwhile, at six foot four inches, I was like the damn Eiffel tower next to her.

"Put this on. *Now*," I commanded her.

Letting out a sigh of defeat, she turned around and I thought she was testing me. But no, instead, she held her arms out so I could slide my leather jacket over her thin frame.

I don't know why, but the simple act had my bastard of a cock hardening, again.

All I knew was I needed to stay far, far away from Sophie Shah.

CHAPTER 3

Sophie

"He's a psychopath," I shouted as my brother drove down the busy Chicago freeway.

He shook his head. "He's not a psychopath, Sophie."

"Fine, sociopath, at the bare minimum. He would have killed this guy, Ezra. I swear. You didn't see the blood. Then, Damien just wiped his hands on a napkin like he finished a meal, threw a stack of money on the table—a hefty stack, may I add. Before we left, he forced me to wear this jacket and sent me home with you. What in the actual hell are you doing calling that lunatic your best friend? I mean, Reese is my best friend and you don't see her bashing skulls in," I rambled as my brother drove in silence with his eyes fixed on the road in front of him.

"Sophie, Damien was looking out for you. I got caught up in a call from the firm, and I'm glad he was there." My brother paused. "And for the record, that shirt is way too low to be wearing in the middle of Chicago, especially if you're alone." He gave me a quick side-eye.

Rolling my eyes, I let out an annoyed sigh. "Men." I rested my head on the seatbelt strap until we got back to my new apartment.

Once we got inside my new place, Ezra sat down a few boxes. Most of my stuff had already been moved in from where I had been living with Reese for the past year. And while I loved living with my best friend, to be honest, I was more of an introvert when it came to living situations. I liked peace and quiet, and Reese loved bringing home a new guy every other night. No judgment from me, but the paper-thin walls weren't helpful with all the moaning and groaning my best friend was doing. Meanwhile, I hadn't been touched since the... incident. I didn't think I was capable of letting a man be trusted with my body... with my love anymore. I wanted it, though. I wanted to have sex and feel the adrenaline coursing through my body as his teeth brushed my skin, as his hands gripped my hips, and when he whispered dirty things into my ears. I didn't want to be a glass doll; I didn't want the past to predict how I enjoyed things in my present or future. I just didn't know how I'd ever feel safe again with a man when the one I thought I was safe with shattered me.

"I really wish you would have just stayed with Reese. I hate that you're living by yourself. You refused to live with me, which makes no sense considering I live in a huge condo." My older brother started unpacking some kitchen items.

"Ezra, I love you, but you and Amira need privacy. The last thing I want to do is hear my big brother and his fiancée doing things... that one cannot unhear nor unsee." I stuck my tongue out and fake gagged. Amira was my brother's beautiful, sophisticated fiancée, who I swear, was a saint. She was an interior designer, and they were high school sweethearts. She even knew my mom and dad, which made me hold her even closer to my heart, and deep down, I knew Ezra loved her all that more. She had been around as long as I could remember —she was the one who called me when I got my first period because she knew my grandma would make it awkward.

She was there to talk about boys and heartbreak, and also... the incident that made me not even want to be in the same room as my brother because I hated the pity in his eyes. I hated the way he blamed himself for not protecting me. I hated the way everyone looked at me. But Amira was always there for me.

Sometimes, I was envious of the fact that Ezra's soon-to-be wife had met our parents. I'd never have that. Any man in my future—if I ever ended up settling down, which was highly unlikely—would never have the chance to meet my mom and dad.

Ezra broke me out of my wallowing. "I like how this place is walking distance to Jesson but don't walk alone. Call me anytime, and just so you know, Damien happens to live five minutes away." Ezra busied himself, neatly stacking plates in my cabinets. This is what he did—he worried, he made sure I knew I was taken care of, and then he worried some more.

"I never ever want to be in the same room as Damien Moretti." I sank into my new couch that Amira had bought for me. It was a beautiful blue velvet couch that had no right being in a college girl's apartment, but she saw the way I stroked it in the store and she knew it needed to be mine.

I suppose I was extremely blessed. Sure, my life had been a series of unfortunate—scratch that, shitty—events, but the few people in my small circle were truly the best.

Reese, Amira, and Ezra held me up when I thought I

was drowning. They extinguished the fire that scorched me and saved me from turning into ashes.

I was still wearing Damien's leather jacket, which I'd never admit but felt smooth like butter on my skin, and the way he put it on me...

Clenching my thighs together, I thought about how his finger brushed against my arms before the smooth leather covered it. The white V-neck he had on underneath provided a small peek of what was clearly a large tattoo on his very buff and defined bicep.

The smell of expensive leather mixed with a deeper scent of sandalwood and sexiness. Yeah, yeah... I know sexiness isn't a scent, but if it could be bottled up, it would be this scent that was wrapped around me.

"What exactly is it that Damien does, and if he's really your best friend, how come I never met him?" I let my feet rest on the coffee table in front of me.

"Damien is an attorney like me. He was constantly traveling and you never visited me in Chicago; I always came to you in Texas since you were busy in school." He paused and came around to sit in the accent chair near me.

"Oh. He works with you? I can't believe he's a lawyer. I mean, he looks like one of the criminals you'd put away."

"Sophie..." my brother said sternly. "To answer your

question, he runs his own firm, and is probably the richest thirty-six-year-old I know. I mean, he legit made the Forbes Forty under Forty Richest list." My brother sank into the chair further, and I could tell he was tired. Between me, his job, his fiancée, and life in general, I felt kind of guilty. He was basically raising me during his entire twenties, even from afar. Now that I was in the same city, he took his role on with even more pressure.

"Damien Moretti was on that Forbes list?" I dropped my jaw. "How does a lawyer have that kind of money, and why did you need him to help you with a case if you guys don't work together? What did you mean by him needing to take care of it? What exactly is *it*?" I asked my brother as everything began piecing together into questions.

Ezra's face dropped slightly but he still didn't crack to show enough of a reaction. "Sophie, Damien has a bit of an unusually unique take on his job as an attorney. He likes to balance the scales on his own terms. I can't tell you more, and you really don't need to know more. Just please, be good, and don't have me worrying about you more than I do. Please promise me you'll reach out if you ever need me." He brushed his hand across his tired scowl.

I knew what he meant. He was scared he would lose me like he almost had.

I nodded. "I promise you won't have to worry, Ezra. Go home to Amira. I'll call you tomorrow." I smiled at him.

He stood slowly. "You're absolutely sure you don't want to come home with me?" he asked again over his shoulder.

"I'm sure. I'll be okay." I started closing the door on him.

"Sophie, I love you, kid," he said softly, and it made my heart tighten. The way he said that simple sentence always made me miss my dad all that more. My dad used to always call me kid. It was the thing I cried the most about when they died, and since then, Ezra used the term and it always made me happy.

"I love you too, brother." I shut the door quietly, then slowly turned back around to the eerie silence of my new apartment. As much as I loved living alone, I didn't necessarily enjoy *being* alone.

Releasing a long breath, I tugged Damien's jacket tighter around me.

I'd usually have felt emptiness and depressed in this moment, but for some reason, this jacket made me feel less...alone.

CHAPTER 4

Damien

After the slight inconvenience at the bistro, I came home with an erection that could have penetrated a damn brick wall. Feeling a sliver of guilt that the culprit of this pulsing and aching status of my cock was my best friend's much younger sister, I decided I'd have to hope the cold water pounding on my head in the shower would help it subside.

Both heads.

Running my hands through my hair, the water pellets crashed down in harmony as flashes of her face popped into my mind every time I closed my eyes.

"Fuck!" I hit my hand against the shower wall. This was not good. I couldn't remember the last time a woman had ever made it into my thoughts beyond the sheets.

The self-control I had to have to not jerk off at the thought of her perfect ass was one that honestly, should have won me an Olympic gold medal.

Peeling myself out of the shower, I wrapped the towel around my waist and picked up my ringing phone.

"Is it done, Mathison?" My voice dropped low.

"Yes, sir. He's been taken care of."

I hung up the phone without any further words and called Ezra. "Brunson is done. He overdosed."

"Shit." He let out an exhale. He knew Thomas Brunson hadn't overdosed—more so was forced to overdose in the bougie prison he was living happily in. That motherfucker had kidnapped, assaulted, and killed countless innocent women, but because he was a well-known congressman, his sentence was twenty years with the possibility of parole. He was sent to a prison, which was more like a white-collar camp, where he was busy taking art classes and watching tv.

That wasn't sitting okay with me and surprisingly, it didn't sit well with Ezra, either. He was the prosecutor on the case, and unfortunately, because even judges can be bought, Brunson got away with the most outrageous and watered-down sentence.

Luckily for me, in my line of work you meet plenty of innocent individuals, but even more guilty criminals. Some of which I've kept close; those who reside in the surrounding prisons because occasionally, I need to balance the scales of justice and make sure it's served right.

People like Thomas Brunson are men who've always had money, status, and connections handed to them. They don't care who they hurt because they know they'll get away with it. Ezra is an excellent attorney, but he doesn't have the darkness inside of him that I do. He can't stomach or live with the way I easily pull the trigger or have the triggered pulled.

That's what makes Ezra the guy you marry, and that's why I'm just the guy you fuck.

After a brief chat with Ezra, his fiancée Amira stole the phone and demanded I come over for dinner over the weekend, and to be quite honest, Amira made the best damn Indian food you could imagine. I'm not talking about the jarred shit that you throw a tomato in and call it curry. I'm talking every spice, every seed, every leaf all blended to sheer perfection.

"Yeah, fine. I'll come," I said to Ezra and Amira, who annoyingly had the phone on speaker like all couples of their tenure do. I had to be in court tomorrow, but I was finally taking some time off over the weekend. Weekends were when I liked to do what I referred to as going out into the field and cleaning up messes and filth that our judicial system failed to do, but I seriously needed some time off.

I sank into my couch and flipped the T.V. on just to fill the silence of my penthouse. As much as I didn't enjoy company, I also didn't enjoy the lingering stillness that was the constant in my life. I couldn't help but think about Sophie. A stupid smile formed on my face, and I wanted to slap it off myself.

Why did she impact me so much? Why did I like when she opened those thick lips? Fuck, what I'd give for those thick lips to be wrapped around my thick—

"Fucking hell." I shook my head. I needed to get laid. I needed to just find some hot blonde at one of the exclusive clubs I frequented, bang her in the alleyway, and be done.

I had been so caught up at work, my balls were bluer than sapphires, which was probably the only reason I was having obsessive thoughts about Ezra's little sister.

Yeah, that's it. Just some sexual tension built up combined with stress. This had nothing to do with Sophie Shah. Nothing at all.

CHAPTER 5

Sophie

I tugged the straps of my backpack tighter and made my way down the street. My skirt was blowing up slightly with the breeze rippling against the Chicago River. It was nice to be within walking distance from Jesson University. My first night in my new apartment went better than I had expected. I did my nightly meditation, turned my noise machine on, took my anti-anxiety medication, a melatonin pill, and was knocked out. I only woke up once around two a.m. because of a creaking that I was absolutely certain was indeed a serial killer named Noah Wimberly that I read about in a thriller book I had picked up, but it turned out to be a neighbor coming home and simply shutting their door.

Crisis averted.

Well, and this should most definitely not be public knowledge, but when I thought it was about to be my untimely death from the creaks and squeaks of my new apartment, I decided to tug on Damien's leather jacket and sleep in it. If that's not a face-palm moment, then I don't know what is.

Tourists shoved past me as I walked down the bustling sidewalk, and I kept pushing my skirt down with my free hand, cursing the taunting wind. My long hair was in tousled waves, and I felt like this move had really made a world of a difference in my mood. I felt... okay, and sometimes okay was more than enough. It was a hell of a lot better than the depressed, sulking, sleep-deprived emo maniac I was last year.

I stopped by the small coffee stand and smiled at the old man behind the cart. "May I have a vanilla latte, please?" I tugged my wallet out.

"Make it two." A gruff voice behind me rose. I turned slowly, and immediately stumbled over my own foot, quickly catching myself as I put more distance between us.

"Oh, great. You're stalking me now?" I slanted my eyes at the dark, intense gaze in front of me.

"Damien! How are you?" the old man behind me said cheerily.

Oh, shit. This was *his* coffee stand.

"Doing good, sir. You?" Damien broke his stare from me and handed the old man a twenty. The old man handed back change, but Damien shook his head with a lifted eyebrow, causing him to chuckle and put the money in his small register.

Did Damien just call this guy, *sir*?

Damien looked down at me and handed me my latte. "Shall we?"

"Shall we, what?" I followed behind him only because I didn't want to hold up the ever-growing line.

"Walk you to the strip club?" He took a sip of his latte and kept his eyes forward.

I froze in my spot. "The. Strip. Club?"

"Dressed like that, there's no way you're going to classes. I just didn't know you had a part-time job at The Wet Dream." He turned and stepped closer toward me, sharing the same oxygen as me. I was wearing strappy heeled wedges, a white but loose short skirt, and a cute pale pink blouse that was slightly cropped. My backpack was tightened and heavy with textbooks. I absolutely looked like a college student because I was a college student, *not* a stripper!

"You are appalling, and here I thought you weren't a wild animal and actually civilized when you called the coffee guy sir. But *clearly*, I was mistaken." I rolled my eyes and pushed past Damien. Except, I felt slightly dizzy from the scent that wafted in my nose from him—sexy sandalwood, but as intoxicating as that fourth shot of tequila.

A strong grasp tugged me back slightly and spun me around. My coffee almost spilled had I not used my free hand to steady myself on his chest.

"What are you doing?" I seethed.

Leaning into me, his breath grazed my neck sending chills throughout my body. "Roll your eyes again, sweetheart, and see what happens." His grip tightened as my entire body flushed with heat.

Swallowing, I looked up at him slowly, and his eyes grew darker as he looked into mine. "Oh yeah? And what are you going to do about it, Damien?" I taunted with my voice low. My heart was pounding against my chest so hard, I swore he could hear it, and the way his lips curled slightly, I'm pretty sure he definitely could.

"How would you want me to punish you, Sophie? Bend you over my knee and spank that tight ass of yours?" he whispered against my ear, and I swore, the world started spinning at one hundred miles per hour. I was seeing stars. The muscles between my thighs clenched as he jerked away, releasing me, and he smiled at me the way the devil does.

With sheer satisfaction.

Shivers ran through me even though the sticky

August humidity was hovering. "I'm telling my brother what you said." I cringed at how young I sounded.

Letting out a light laugh, he came closer. Brushing his index finger and thumb against my jawline, his smile faded. "No, you won't, because you *want* me to punish you. But, sweet Sophie, you'd never be able to handle me. So, stop looking at me with those big eyes like that. You are Ezra's little sister, and that's all you'll ever be." My eyes widened with his presumptuous statement.

What an arrogant asshole.

I didn't want him.

"Give me that." He pointed at my backpack strap.

"What? I need my backpack for classes. Get a life, Damien. You don't need to be such an ass." I sighed and started to walk again.

"I'll carry it for you," he said. A chill went up my spine as I turned back to see he was standing in the same spot.

I didn't want him. I didn't want him... Oh shit, I *really* wanted him. I wanted my brother's best friend. Not in a romantic, love-sick way, but in a horny co-ed being tempted by a fine piece of ass kind of way.

Damien Moretti, all six foot and four inches of his stunning self, was carrying my blush-pink backpack. He was wearing a white dress shirt with the top two buttons opened, perfectly fitted gray slacks, a cognac-brown leather belt around his waist and shoes that matched. His dark hair was slightly messy while his face was... perfect. His thick brows knitted together as he looked down, catching me staring and probably drooling.

Suddenly, he reached for my hand and tugged me on the inside of the sidewalk as cars sped by. Looking up at him, I sank my teeth into my bottom lip. He wanted to make sure I didn't get hit or hurt...

"Stop." His voice rasped.

"What?" I asked, suddenly nervous.

"Sophie, seriously. Find someone your own age to drool over. I saw you on the sidewalk and walked you to class. Don't look at me like I'm some sort of prince charming." He said the embarrassing truth so blatantly, I was positive my cheeks were red.

"You are way too arrogant for your own good. I'm not into you, and I'm definitely not drooling over you." I let out a forced laugh.

"And for the record, Damien, I know you aren't prince charming." I opened my hand, and he slid my backpack into it as we reached campus. "You're a fire-breathing dragon." I narrowed my eyes at him and left him behind me. I heard him let out a small laugh, causing me to bite my lower lip harder. I blew out a breath of air once I reached the quad. This man was clearly delusional.

CHAPTER 6

Damien

I was acting reckless. What was I thinking? I told Ezra's nineteen-year-old sister that I knew she wanted me to spank her? Rubbing my hand across my face, I sat back in my chair. My office overlooked the Chicago River and was a block away from my penthouse—and conveniently way too close to Jesson University.

She was now going to my daily coffee stand? I knew I did some shady shit, but this was really way too far. *Karma, you bitch.*

"Mr. Moretti, you have a personal call on line one." My secretary buzzed in.

I lifted the phone and answered, "What?"

"Hey bro. Is that how you answer all your calls?" Ashton replied.

"Ashton, what's wrong?" Worry plagued me. My younger brother never called me, and if he did, it meant one of two things.

One, he was in trouble.

Two, he needed money.

"Talk about having faith in me. I'm fine. I just wanted to check in. Damn."

"I'm busy, Ashton. Everything good?" I asked once more.

"Yeah. I was thinking about visiting..." His voice lowered.

"That's not a good idea." I let my head fall into my palm. The day had only just started, but I was ready for it to end.

"Chicago is my home. I hate it here," Ashton whined like the ungrateful twenty-two-year-old that he was. He didn't know what hard work was; all he knew was that I would bail him out of anything and everything.

"Not anymore. I have to go. Get your ass to work. I am checking in with James." I hung the phone up.

My younger brother Ashton was a pain in my ass. Well, he was technically my half-brother. We shared the same mom but beyond that, we shared nothing else. Polar opposites. He was lazy while I was driven. He was laid-back, and I was always on-edge. He enjoyed life on everyone else's dime, but I was the one who made those damn dimes.

I rolled my shoulders back and stood up, walking over to the wall-to-wall windows that made up the other half of my expansive office. The river below was rippling, and large boats holding tourists made their way up and down the waterway.

Chicago. It was the city I loved to hate and hated to love. Hell, but also heaven. The memories here scorched me but also built me. I wasn't born with a silver spoon; hell, I wasn't born with a plastic spoon. My dead-beat dad was a drunk who preferred to use me as a punching bag. And then my mom had an affair with Ashton's dad, who shockingly, was also a damn dead beat. I guess humans really do have a type. My mom's preference was apparently losers who drained all her money on booze, prostitutes, and cigarettes.

He was an abuser. He beat my mom daily, and I was too young, too weak to do anything about it. *About him.*

But then, I grew up. I got taller than him, I got stronger than him. I would run miles after school, and I'd use lingering scrap metal at the dump near the trailer park where we lived as weights. I made it my goal to make sure he paid.

The police came to our house just as often as the mailman, but they didn't do shit. In the ghettos of

Chicago, a 'domestic dispute' was a usual occurrence, and they had bigger problems. Gangs were rampant, drug dealers were on every street corner, and murderers lurked in dark alleys. Men, like my pathetic excuse of a father, got to roam the earth freely with no consequence.

One day, during my senior year of high school, I got home and before my feet even hit the shitty green carpet, I heard him screaming at my mom. My mom's choice in men was the only bad thing about her. She worked two jobs, sometimes three. She fed us, and sure, most days it was either the electricity bill or the water bill—sometimes neither—but she tried her best. For us. Every bit of money she made was usually taken to fund my dad's alcoholism and strip club visits. My dad thought Ashton was his, and once he found out that he wasn't, he decided to unleash his wrath even harder than the flames of hell allowed.

I remember opening the creaky door to our trailer and seeing my mom crumpled in the dark corner—the lights were off, and probably not by choice. Her loud cries tainted my soul, and my knuckles were white from how tight my fists were.

"Where is he?" I asked calmly, unlike the speed of my heart.

"Damien..." she cried into her hands.

"Mom, where is he?" She looked up at me and a

glimmer of the sun that was setting gave me enough light to see the darkened, blackish-purple bruises that covered her otherwise beautiful face.

"Where. Is. He?" I shouted. But before, she could answer, her eyes flicked behind me and I spun around.

My dad sneered and wobbled in a stained white tank, letting out an arrogant laugh.

"You lookin' for me, boy?" he let out in his Southern drawl that never went away, even after living in Chicago for decades. He was born and raised in some trailer park down in Alabama, and he met my mom when she was visiting family.

He followed her to Chicago and ruined her life. She claims he didn't ruin it because he gave her me, but that hurt even more. I wasn't something to be thankful for; I was a reminder of him. When she got pregnant with me, he didn't let her leave. He claimed he would have made sure the courts knew about her brief drug use—the drugs *he* got her addicted to.

"Did you hit my mom?" I asked him, even though I knew the answer.

He tossed his head back and let out a laugh that made my skin prickle. "Stop defending that dumb slut. You're my son," he barked at me while popping open another can of beer. The smell of cheap beer was one I'd always relate to that trailer.

Especially that evening.

"What the fuck did you just say?" I cornered him in the small L-shaped kitchenette. The dishes were overflowing, and the trash was spilling over with frozen meal boxes and lingering beer cans.

"I hope you ain't talkin' to me like that, boy." My dad, who was shorter than me by at least four inches, looked up at me without fear.

The last time that would ever happen.

Gripping his shirt, I pulled him and slammed him into the wall. The sound of his head hitting it echoed off those four metal walls.

"You son of a bitch!" he yelled as his arms flailed around me. The whites of his eyes were tinged with red.

Letting my hand go around his neck, I dragged him upright against the wall. My knuckles paled as I clasped harder, and his feet lifted off the floor. My mom screamed, "Damien! Honey! No!"

"What. The. Fuck. Did. You. Call. Her?" I paused between words, speaking through clenched teeth.

"I'm going to kill you!" he choked out.

Clocking him in the jaw, his head turned so fast a crack emitted, and not from my fist but the motion of his neck.

"Son! Honey! Don't!" My mom stumbled over as blood dripped from her nose.

I looked at her briefly. "Mom, go to the room." A moment in my life where it felt like I was the parent protecting my child. I hated it, but I had to do it. I slammed my dad's body once again into the wall.

"I asked you a fucking question, you piece of shit," I yelled in his face with spit spewing from my mouth.

"I'm sorry! I didn't mean it, Teresa!" he yelled out.

"That's what I thought you said." Releasing him from my hold, he piled at my feet from the copious amount of alcohol he drank and the face pounding he just got.

"You little punk!" He jerked up quickly and tackled me to the floor. My mom began crying and started to slap his back as he pinned me down. He elbowed her in her mouth, and she was flung back.

Final straw.

Pushing him off me, I swung my fists into his face until you couldn't see his features in the pile of blood that coated it. I no longer heard the screams coming from his mouth or my mom's. Everything blurred, everything disappeared, and I didn't feel anything. And I knew from that moment on, I wouldn't.

But most of all, after that night, he left when he regained consciousness and never showed his face again.

He knew if he set foot in Chicago again or anywhere near my mom, he'd be dead.

That evening was the worst and best night of my life. It was the best because after that my mom never lived in fear. But it was the worst because I had unleashed a side of myself that I had suppressed for so long. The violent, dark side that I didn't want to have to bring out but was forced to. I also learned that loving someone makes you ignorant, powerless and silent. Ignorant to the truth, powerless to the wrongs, and silent to the words you know should be said but can't.

I had no interest in loving someone. Loving someone meant losing yourself. It meant making yourself weak and vulnerable. I had too many damn enemies in this city, and I had too much blood on my hands. Loving someone would mean I'd have a weak spot, and that's something I refuse to ever have.

Sophie

Tapping my pen against the smooth wood table in front of me, I looked around. The lecture hall was packed with eager students. Junior year was here and soon, I'd be applying for dental school. My grades meant everything to me. Ever since I was ten years old, my brother had been supporting me. My parents' money was all tied into their new dental practice, our house, and cars, so the inheritance helped my grandparents get my medical insurance, first car, and just little things. Beyond that, it was always Ezra making sure I wasn't without all the things he knew my parents would have given me.

Professor Ko, my new biochemistry professor, was notorious for failing students. He was in his mid-thirties and from what I had heard, was perpetually in a shit mood.

It was the first day of classes, yet he was firing off questions and eyeing us like he was praying he'd find the weakest link.

That isn't going to be me, professor. I straightened my back and typed away while listening to his lecture.

The next ninety minutes of class felt like a lifetime as we went through the lesson.

I squinted as soon as the double doors opened, and we all staggered out into the beautiful day. The sun was shining, the sky clear and bright blue. The vivid green grass in the quad swayed slightly with the cool breeze.

"Hey!" a voice called out behind me. Turning around, I saw a handsome, blond-haired, blue-eyed guy coming out from the same lecture hall.

"Hi." I scrunched my nose. Socially awkward with people I didn't know? *Check.*

"I'm in biochem with you." He gripped his back-pack straps and pointed his thumb at the closing doors behind him.

"Oh, really? I couldn't guess with you coming out of the same class," I said jokingly. His face shifted slightly as his cheeks flushed with red. "I'm joking!" I clasped my hand over my mouth. "I'm sorry. I have a wicked sense of humor and barely much of a social life outside of my three friends." I clenched my teeth and slammed my eyes shut, officially embarrassed.

"Wow, you totally just roasted yourself," he said with his hand outstretched. "I'm Zach." He smiled and his pale blue eyes shimmered against the sun.

"I'm Sophie." I scrunched my nose again and shook his hand. Clutching my textbooks to my chest, we began walking side-by-side toward the quad.

"So, I figure with us having Professor Ko, it would be useful to have a study buddy?" Zach offered a lopsided grin at me.

Pinching my lips to one side, my heartbeat raced, and not in the sweet crush kind of way. Being around college guys especially made me anxious and fearful. After all, it was just a charming and sweet college boy who took advantage of my trust and vulnerability, changing the course of my life forever.

But I didn't want my past controlling my present; I didn't want pain to withhold my happiness. "Sure. I usually study in the library daily after dinner." I offered a polite smile.

"Great. That works for me! Do you live around campus?" Zach asked me while roaming his eyes down my frame.

"Mm-hmm."

"Oh-kay. Got it. Don't want me knowing where you live?" He grinned at me.

"I just met you, Zach. We can just study on campus if that works for you," I answered before glancing at my phone.

"I respect that." He pulled his phone out. "Swap numbers at least?"

"Yeah, that works." I let out a sigh of relief as we exchanged numbers. To be honest, Professor Ko's class was one I'd need all the extra help with, and a study partner would be nice. Besides, studying in the library around tons of other students was the safest place, and Zach looked harmless.

But so did he...

After a quick goodbye, Zach and I headed in opposite directions. My phone rang and I answered. It was a universal rule to not call me unless you were one of four people in my circle, and even that had some requirements.

Ezra always called because he wasn't much of a texter. "Hello, big brother," I said teasingly.

"How's your first day going?" he asked, and I could

hear muffling behind him. He was definitely at work, and probably heading to a meeting.

"BioChem is going to be the death of me. Make sure everyone wears pretty colors at my funeral?" I sighed.

"We can get you a tutor, but I highly doubt you'll need it. You're a smart girl, Sophie. Don't doubt yourself," Ezra replied and I couldn't help but smile.

"You know you're going to be the best dad one day."

"One day, but not anytime soon. I have to take care of you first. Anyway, have a good day, and I'll see you for dinner at my place tomorrow, right?"

"Definitely. Amira confirmed that samosas and mango lassi milkshakes were on the menu, so I'm skipping lunch tomorrow to have extra room."

My brother's fiancée was talented at many things, but her culinary skills in Indian food could earn her a Michelin star, and I was always happy to be her guinea pig for all the new recipes she enjoyed trying.

"Don't skip lunch, but we will see you tomorrow. I'll pick you up. I don't want you riding with some random driver or taking the train in the evening." Before I could protest, he said he loved me and hung up.

Throwing my hands in the air, I shook my head. This guy was going to baby me until I was fifty or at least married.

. . .

Heading to my next class, I kept my focus on making sure I made a good first impression with all my professors and to sit next to someone who looked friendly enough, and most definitely a female. After Zach, I think I hit my quota for being around the college male species for today.

While in class, I couldn't help but drift off into the sandalwood bad-boy world of Damien Moretti. I didn't really believe in the concept of butterflies swarming someone's stomach, but I supposed if that feeling existed, it was what I felt the moment he demanded I give him my backpack. Even after we went at it back and forth, he noticed how the straps dug into my shoulders from the weight and insisted he carry it.

No college man—correction, boy—would do that. Chewing the tip of my pen, I couldn't help but feel flushed picturing his magnetic deep, dark eyes pierce into mine and holding my gaze without a sign of wanting to stop.

"Miss Shah?" My Sociology professor's voice rang out and made me immediately sit up. "Yes?" I said meekly.

"Do you have any thoughts on to what extent an individual is shaped by the society they reside in?" she asked, eyeing me and fully aware I was lost in a different society of my own.

My brother's best friend's.

* * *

"I cannot believe you're waiting to tell me about your brother's hot friend until now?" My best friend, Reese, crossed her arms over our smoothies.

"Reese, he is..." I hunched my shoulders and took a long sip of the smoothie in front of me. "He is so damn aggravating, and honestly, I kind of hate him. But then, I also want to rip his pants off. Maybe I'm just so damn screwed up after... you know, last year. It's probably unhealthy to be on this long of a dry spell." My lips twisted and I closed my eyes.

Reese brushed my hand gently. "You're not screwed up. This is a good thing. You're clearly excited about this guy." She smiled with hesitation.

Reese Hart, my best friend since freshman year, was everything you could ever want in a best friend. Not only was she beautiful, with her long legs, shiny golden curls, and bright blue eyes, but she had a heart of gold and patience I didn't understand. She took me in when I really didn't want to live with my brother, and quite literally helped piece me together. She held me when I cried, she helped me shower when seeing my naked body scared me. Unlike many female friendships that eventually erupted and broke down due to competitiveness and for lack of a better word, bitchiness, Reese cheered me on, rooted for me, and I did the same for her.

"I'm *not* excited about him. He's not just a guy. He's old," I huffed.

"He's thirty-six; I'd barely call that old. I mean, and he's not just a guy." Reese mimicked me and laughed so hard she started choking on her smoothie.

"Will you stop!" I flung my napkin at her. "Reese, he's Ezra's best friend, and I'm telling you, he's a certifiable psycho. He's obnoxious and..."

"Sexy, hot, with majestic eyes that melt you every time you look his way?" Reese squeaked out in what I'm assuming is her attempt at a phone-sex operator voice.

"I seriously am going to move to the Taj Mahal so I can get away from everyone."

"Will *Raja* Damien be joining you, mi'lady?" Reese giggled.

"That sentence makes no sense. When did Shakespeare come to India?" I covered my face with my palms. She erupted into laughter, and I had to hide my own smile because I, for one, was not giving my ridiculous best friend the satisfaction that she won.

I knew she was over the moon happy to see me this way. I was barely functional beyond forcing myself to study and keep up with classes. I was a walking, emotionless zombie. It wasn't the physical toll that seared into me; it was more of the emotional toll. The hardest bruises to heal aren't the external ones... they are the internal ones.

"You know I love you." Reese tilted her head and peeled my hands from my face.

I nodded at her and squeezed her hand. "I know. But I swear, if there was something to tell, I would have told you. Damien is on my shit-list and not only that, even if he was my type, which he totally isn't, he's Ezra's best friend and thirty-freaking-six years old. He's seventeen years older than me. Which, not to mention, and redirecting, but my brother would probably never ever speak to either of us again." I pointed at Reese. "So, no more joking about him. He's totally off limits, and I don't care to push those limits." I shook my head dramatically for added effect.

"Mm-hmm... got it." Reese slurped up the rest of her smoothie with mischief dancing in her bright blue eyes.

"All I know is there's worse things for you to be doing," she shrugged her shoulders.

"Like?" I scrunched my nose in anticipation.

"I think you're better off doing Damien rather than bursting with sexual tension and doing something worse like cutting your bangs." Reese said with pursed lips.

And just like that, we both laughed so hard until our stomachs ached.

She had a point. Cutting bangs was far worse than banging Damien. *Right?*

CHAPTER 8

Damien

Pulling into Ezra and Amira's parking deck on my motorcycle, I quickly parked and tugged my helmet off, clipping it onto the seat. I grabbed the bottle of Dom I brought and walked into the building, making my way to the elevator and hitting the button for the penthouse floor.

"Damien!" Amira swooped over wearing a bright yellow dress, her dark locks pinned up. She planted a swift kiss on my cheek and hugged me.

Amira and personal space were opposing forces.

"Hey man, come on in." Ezra waved me toward their formal dining table and the aroma of spices grazed my nose.

"This looks great, Amira. No thanks to Ez, I'm sure."

"Sit down, we're just waiting for—" Before she could finish, the elevator chimed, marking the arrival of whoever they were waiting for.

"Sorry! Sorry, I'm late!" a frazzled voice called out. That voice tightened my chest as quickly as the footsteps landed in the dining room. I turned my head slowly, and my breathing hitched. Sophie came in like a damn tornado, tumbling into the dining room before tripping over her own foot, and quickly steadying herself. A moment later, she was laughing and hugging Amira. She wore a floor-length emerald green dress that emphasized her natural tan, her long dark hair was in waves, and her big brown eyes were darker and more enhanced with whatever unnecessary makeup thing she put all over her eyelids.

She looked beautiful.

She is beautiful.

"Hey sis. You look great." Ezra leaned in for a hug. She was clearly wearing heels because shortstop could actually hug almost at eye level.

I stood and shoved my hands deep into my dark wash jean pockets.

She finally noticed me, and froze. "Oh... I didn't know you were coming," she stammered letting her eyes scan me in one quick sweep.

"Good to see you, Sophie," I said coolly, flicking my

gaze up as Ezra watched us intently. Amira paid no attention to any of us as she busied herself by grabbing and setting plates.

"Good to see you as well, Damien." Sophie straightened her back and sank into the chair across from mine.

Fuck. I'd have to watch her open and put things in that perfect pink pout while sitting next to her big brother.

"Let's all sit. You know I hate for the food to get cold. Eat up!" Amira said cheerily.

Sophie and I reached for the spoon in the curry dish at the same time. Her hand brushed mine and when I looked at her arm as it jerked back nervously, I saw the tiny little goosebumps racing across her soft skin.

Looking at her, our eyes met for a brief moment before she anxiously tucked a strand of hair behind her ear and faced Amira, who was seated next to her, pretending to make small talk.

Chewing my lip, I served myself some of each item and began to eat as Ezra and Amira discussed their upcoming nuptials with an overly-excited Sophie, who I did everything in my power to avoid looking at directly.

"Damien, you'll be walking Sophie down the aisle," Amira said nonchalantly.

I stopped mid-bite and looked at Amira. "That won't be necessary. She's not a dog."

Amira choked on her wine and looked at Ezra, who squinted at me before letting out a small, awkward laugh.

But it was Sophie's reaction that stirred excitement within me.

"You're absolutely right, Damien. If anyone's walking anyone, it would be me walking you... but you're not just any dog; you're a rabid stray." She leaned back into her chair and crossed her arms, pushing her perky breasts upward that had no business taunting me.

"Sophie!" Ezra and Amira said simultaneously. Another one of those gag-me moments couples like them often did.

"What? I'm just saying the truth." She rolled her big brown eyes and shoveled rice into her mouth.

"What is up with you two?" Ezra looked at me.

"Don't ask me why your little sister is a pest." I wiped my face and stood, grabbing my plate off the table and carrying it to the kitchen.

Footsteps echoed behind me, and I turned.

"What is your problem?" She pushed past me and cleared her plate before washing it off.

"You," I said flatly.

Clicking her tongue, she dropped her jaw. "I haven't done anything to you." She placed her plate into the sink and walked closer to me. Pressing her chest into the plate

I held between us, she looked up at me through her thick lashes. This girl was the only human on planet earth that had me thinking about my words.

I tilted my head, eyeing her. "Maybe that's the problem."

"I don't understand..." Her voice dropped.

"You haven't done anything to me, but I really want to do something to you." I let one hand brush her thick bottom lip that parted as my thumb swiped against it.

"The problem is...what I really wanted to eat wasn't on my plate." Dropping my eyes down her body, I smirked.

Stepping back, I winked before walking around her. I left Sophie Shah there in the kitchen, completely speechless.

CHAPTER 9

Sophie

The rest of the night I stayed far, far away from Damien, which wasn't much considering we all sat around on the patio, talking through the wedding details. I was so excited for Ezra and Amira. They were having this perfect, intimate winter wedding. It just also occurred to me that I was Amira's maid of honor and unfortunately, Damien was my brother's best man. That meant we would soon be forced to do quite a few things together.

Gulping, chills raced my arms as I thought about doing anything and *everything* with Damien.

What did he mean earlier? He wanted to do something to me? Like, with me? On me? How rude was it that he chose to not explain?

"Sophie, are you staying tonight?" Amira stood and carefully lifted the dessert plates.

"Um, no. I have plans on campus tomorrow," I replied as my brother and Damien carried on their conversation near us.

Amira's forehead creased as she looked at me. "It's Saturday?"

"I kind of found someone to study biochem with at the library, and Professor Ko already assigned a quiz next week, not to mention I have a million lectures to get through." I shrugged. "I know I'm a complete nerd," I added with heat rising in my cheeks.

"You are far from a nerd. You are smart, beautiful, and I'm so proud of you." Amira squeezed me in a tight hug. Yep, my brother lucked out, and so did I. Amira filled in that maternal void I had always felt.

"Okay, well, I'll drop you off." Amira went to grab her purse.

"Actually, Damien can. Sophie's place is right on the way to his. That's cool, right, Damien?" Ezra asked a clearly annoyed Damien, who didn't even care to hide his displeasure.

"I'll call a car," I quipped.

"No. I don't like you going with random strangers. Damien?" Ezra's voice spiked.

"Yeah, sure. Whatever," Damien huffed as if he had to take Lord Voldemort back to Hogwarts.

Rolling my eyes, we said our goodbyes and made our way down the elevator, standing on opposing sides. Sharing the same air as this man was intoxicating and suffocating all at the same time.

I hated how the scent of his aftershave made my heart pulse recklessly. I hated how his presence both intimidated and comforted me. I hated how he couldn't stand me, yet he did these little things that showed me he had some sliver of a heart inside that ridiculously fit body.

What the hell is wrong with me? Had to be my hormones.

"Where's your car?" I asked as he continued two steps in front of me in silence.

"Here." He stood behind a shiny black motorcycle.

I looked around anxiously. "When are the cameras coming out, telling me that I'm being tricked?" I asked, because clearly, this man had to be delusional if he thought I'd ever get on the back of his stupid, sexy bike. He didn't say anything.

Instead, he simply took the one and only helmet attached to his bike and handed to me. "Put it on," he demanded with an attitude.

I pushed his hand and helmet away. "I'm sure this whole hot, bad-boy motorcycle vibe gets any girl you want on the back of your dumb bike, but I, for one, am not risking my life just so you can feel young, wild, and free." I crossed my arms and backed away.

He took two steps and got so close to me that the heat of his body warmed mine. Lifting his hands, he put the helmet over my head as my mouth fell open.

"Excuse me!" I shouted, my voice echoing in the parking deck.

"You're excused." He shrugged while fastening the straps tighter. I stood there in my maxi dress, strappy heels, and his bulky helmet over my head.

"I'm not going anywhere with you!" I fumed. Pulling out my phone, I tried to pull up the app to get a car here.

Shutting the eye cover of the helmet, he grinned. "It's cute how you think you're going to win this." He jumped on the bike and said, "Get on, Sophie. Now."

"No." I said with my tone breaking.

Sliding back off, he caged me in and looked down at me. My breathing hitched immediately as the warmth of his body brushed against mine. "You're riding my bike or me. Your choice, sweetheart." Tapping his fingers against the helmet he shoved on, he smiled deviously.

He winked as he jumped back on his bike.

Swallowing, I stuffed my phone into my purse and slowly climbed on behind him. I clung to the sides of the back and knew this was it; I was going to die. I was going to die on Damien Moretti's bike.

Reaching behind him, he pulled my arms around his waist, taking me by surprise. "Don't worry, Soph, I don't bite. Well, only sometimes..." he purred over his shoulder.

"You're absolutely disgusting." I was thankful his helmet was covering what was definitely beet-red cheeks.

"Really? The last time I checked, you thought I was a hot, bad-boy." He let out a cocky laugh and revved his bike, which made me jump closer to him. My arms clutched around his tight chest and my fingers dug into his abs over his thin shirt.

"Don't you need a helmet?" I asked. *Only to be polite.* Not that I cared if his overly large head exploded.

"You need it more," he replied and began driving. My heart pounded against my chest as we zoomed through the parking deck with the noise of the bike bouncing against the concrete walls.

Inhaling and exhaling, I slammed my eyes shut as the fresh, evening air slapped against my bare arms. I clung to him tighter as adrenaline coursed through every vein in my body. It was exhilarating and terrifying at the same time.

Just like Damien.

Parking in front of my apartment building, the abrupt stop had me dizzy. Damien got off first, then reached his hands around my waist, helping me off his bike. Wearing pencil heels, I wasn't a fool to refuse his help, but as soon as my feet hit the ground, I slapped his hands away—but not before noticing how he let them linger a moment longer than necessary.

Tugging the helmet off, I handed to him and looked down as I fixed my wild hair. "Thank you for the ride, and for not letting me die," I said in a soft whisper.

"You're welcome," he replied without emotion.

There we stood, me in his shadow, nervous, and awkward as ever, knowing I'd regret this next statement, but I needed to fill the uncomfortable silence.

"Uh, um... do you want to come up?" I fidgeted my fingers and drifted my eyes upward slowly. His lightweight cream sweater clung to his body perfectly, the same way his dark wash denims did.

"Fine," he replied in that gruff voice that seemed to cause the hairs on my neck to stand and heat to spread to places that most definitely should have remained cool and calm.

I didn't expect he'd agree to come up, and now I anxiously tried to map out my entire apartment, worried I had left dirty laundry splayed out or dried cereal bowls on the counter.

Shit.

CHAPTER 10

Damien

Why the fuck did I agree to come up to her apartment? *Damn it, Damien.* She walked up the stairs slowly, her perfect peach ass way too close to my face.

Turn around. Just turn the fuck around and go home. That's what the little animated angel would have whispered on my shoulder, but just as luck would have it, I had zero angels near me. Both shoulders only carried devils. The ones taunting me to test the limits and indulge into my temptation.

Unlocking her door, she pushed it open and flicked on the light. I paused before walking in to allow us some distance. The scent of her apartment was sweet and innocent, just like the aroma that was embedded in her. Her living room walls were decorated with framed pictures, and a blue velvet couch sat in front of a marble coffee table that had a stack of books piled high.

"Would you like a drink?" She peered at me, pressing her hands into the barstool by the kitchen counter. "I have wine and some coolers." Her cheeks flushed a tinge of pink.

"I don't drink," I replied and sank into the couch, crossing my leg over my knee.

"Like ever?" She lifted her eyebrow and slowly sat on the small accent chair across from me.

"Very rarely. Alcohol doesn't benefit you in any way; it only impairs you. You shouldn't be drinking, either. You're not even twenty-one."

She sighed with irritation and kept staring at me as if she were trying to solve a puzzle. "How did you and Ezra meet?" She peeled off her heels and threw them to the side before piling her dress up to her knees and pulling herself fully into the chair. She fit perfectly in that small chair.

So delicate, so sweet, and so damn innocent.

"Law school," I replied.

"How come I've never met you before? I've lived in Chicago for two years now?" she asked curiously.

"I was traveling a lot, and when I'd see Ezra, I don't think it crossed his mind to invite his *kid* sister over to hang out with us."

She cringed as soon as I emphasized the word 'kid.'

"I'm not a kid; I'm nineteen." She pouted.

I shook my head with a laugh. "That's exactly what all kids would say. You are nineteen, Sophie. You haven't learned shit yet. You have no experience in *anything.*"

Her eyes widened. "What does that mean, exactly?" She clearly took offense to my statement.

"Nothing. Where's your bathroom?" I asked her while standing and brushing my hands that were slick with sweat against my jeans. This girl was triggering something inside me that most definitely shouldn't be triggered.

"Oh, just through my bedroom." She pointed behind her. I made my way to her bedroom and flipped the light on.

She had a queen-sized bed, with this bohemian-looking headboard that was laced with sparkling lights. Wincing at her choice in décor, I glanced around and froze at my reflection in the oversized mirror that was centered in front of her bed.

Agitation pooled in me. There was only one reason someone put a mirror in front of their damn bed.

Was she seeing someone? Suddenly, her conversation with Amira crossed my mind. She was supposedly meeting someone to study with tomorrow... on a Saturday. Bull fucking shit.

I went into her bathroom, clutched the counter, and shook my head.

But why did I care? Running my hands through my hair, I looked at myself.

After tonight, I needed to stay away from her. She wasn't my problem. I could find a new coffee stand; I could avoid dinners with Ezra and Amira. Sure, we'd cross paths for their wedding, but we'd be around many others.

Nodding at my rationale, I exhaled. This was a good idea. Besides, she *should* be seeing someone her own age. A college guy... Who would probably run his slimy little hands all over her perfect, toned, soft body...

My cock twitched at the thought of her bare body but was quickly replaced with violent thoughts about any other man touching her.

She deserved a man; a real man who would appreciate every curve, every mark, every imperfection. Who would lick her, bite her, kiss her in every fold of her body... not forced to endure rabbit sex from some frat-boy.

"Damien?" her soft voice called out. I flung my head up and opened the door.

She had changed into shorts and a fitted tank top. Her hair was piled high on her head with her face bare.

Fuck, she was even more beautiful like this.

"Everything okay?" She tilted her head and looked at me carefully.

"Who are you seeing tomorrow?"

Her forehead creased. "What?"

"You told Amira you were studying with someone on campus."

Her forehead relaxed and her eyes filled with satisfaction as a small grin curved her lips. "Why do you care, Damien?"

I couldn't think of what the hell to say. Just as I was about to make up some stupid comment to piss her off, my eyes fell to her unmade bed. More so, what was under the blanket.

My leather jacket.

The one I had given her the night we met at the bistro. She followed my line of vision to the jacket and immediately looked at me.

"Um... I meant to give that back to you. I washed my bed sheets, and it must have gotten tangled in the clothes or whatever..." Sophie stammered out quickly.

She moved backward as I moved forward, and she stumbled into her bed. I quickly steadied her with my hands gripping her thin waist.

Her chest rose and fell rapidly as I brushed her flesh where her tank top didn't meet her shorts. "You're sleeping with my jacket?" My voice dropped.

Her breathing was the only sound between us, and the way it quickened made my entire body fight the urge to lay her across the bed.

Slowly, she stood on her tiptoes, filling the space between us. My eyes dropped to her perfect, lush, pink lips that were begging to be bitten.

Her warm breath grazed my skin, and just as she began closing her eyes, I pulled back, breaking myself from the high. I was stunned that I had even considered letting my mouth align with hers.

This girl was a nineteen-year-old college student, and she was my best friend's much younger sister. Ezra knew how much blood I had on my hands, and he would never forgive me if he knew I was fooling around with Sophie. That's all it would have been, anyway—having a taste of her before cleansing my palate and moving on to the next woman. Except, Sophie wasn't that kind of girl. Her big brown eyes looked desperate for human interaction and touch—a touch that would linger, not leave.

I would *never* stay.

"I told you to stop drooling over me, Sophie. Go look for another guy's initials to doodle in your notebook." I cringed at the coldness of my words, and when she flattened her feet and red filled her cheeks, I felt surprisingly shitty.

Turning down women wasn't hard for me, and the

ones I did pursue knew damn well they'd be in a hotel bed with me and never welcome in my own. There wouldn't be any cuddling or breakfast the next morning, I'd be tugging my jeans on before they could even sit up.

I wasn't a savage; I paid for the nicest of rooms and let them charge room service or whatever they wanted, but I wasn't there to hold them. Fuck that.

I left, and never spent the night with any of those women. That would only lead to unexpected expectations.

Women wanted their prince, their protector, their partner, and I would never be any of those—especially not to this doe-eyed, nineteen-year-old, college student in front of me.

"Get out of my apartment, Damien. You're an arrogant jerk." She turned immediately and for a brief moment, I saw the slight glisten in her dark chocolate eyes, which only furthered why I needed to keep away from her.

I followed behind her and cornered her into the wall. Planting one hand by her face and the other on her waist, I tried to be civil. "Sophie, I'm only going to hurt you. Even if you weren't Ezra's little sister, you're too innocent and delicate for a man like me. Don't take it personally."

"You don't know a thing about me, Damien. I'm far

from innocent and delicate. But you know what, you wouldn't be able to handle a real woman anyway, because you're too scared," she fired back.

"Scared?" I let out an agitated laugh. "There is nothing I'm scared of." I pushed off the wall and eyed her.

"You're a liar. You are scared." She walked closer to me, poking my chest. "You are scared of connection and emotion. You're scared of love." She smacked her lips together.

"You're just too sweet, Sophie," I said knowing I was pushing her over the edge.

"I'm not sweet," she hissed at me.

Leaning in toward her, I couldn't resist as I whispered against her ear, "But I bet you taste so damn sweet."

The way she sucked in her breath made me know I had her body wanting mine even more. I knew I was being cruel to leave her this sexually tense.

Ducking under my arm, she opened the door. "Leave my apartment and leave me alone, Damien. I'm not yours to worry about." She pushed past me, leaving me without words for the first time in a long time.

Because she was *wrong.*

Just as she began shutting the door on me, I held it opened. "Who are you seeing tomorrow?"

She let out an annoyed laugh. "I am not *yours* to worry about."

Slamming the door in my face, I realized she wasn't wrong. She was fucking right, but not about me being scared of connection and love. I was scared of something else.

I was scared of the way I felt when she said she wasn't mine to worry about. Why did that sting more than the insults? This girl was getting under my damn skin and driving me insane.

CHAPTER 11

Sophie

I peeked through the peephole and saw he was still standing there. What was his deal? He was beyond infuriating. How dare he ask me who I was seeing tomorrow after literally turning me down when I attempted to kiss him?

Speaking of which... nice going, Sophie! What the hell was I thinking? Trying to kiss the devil in a leather jacket? I mean, this man was the most annoying human being I had ever met.

Except he wasn't in his leather jacket anymore, considering he knew I was sleeping with it at night like a damn teddy bear.

"Ugh!" I yelled out with my fists clenched. Damien Moretti was officially on my shit list. Never again.

Before I knew it, I was fast asleep, embracing his

damn jacket because clearly, I had more issues than *Vogue*.

Walking to the coffee stand by campus, I looked around. In some sick way, it bothered me that Damien wasn't here. Clearly, I was attracted to toxic men.

However, my ex-boyfriend didn't start out as toxic; he was charming and engaging. He made me fall for him faster than lightning in the sky during a storm. But then, just like a tornado wrapping me into his wrath, all I was left with was destruction.

He ruined me.

He broke me.

Now, here I was, having some sort of magnetic pull toward a man who had red flags flashing above his head. Meanwhile, I was smiling stupidly, implying that red was my new favorite color. Wiggling my shoulders and blowing out a breath of air, I walked to campus.

I was meeting Zach at the library, and when I saw his bright blue eyes and even brighter smile, I couldn't help but beam back at him.

The last thing I was looking for was a relationship—which was why I didn't understand why I wanted Damien.

Wanted being the key word. Past tense. Definitely past tense. I just needed to manifest the thoughts and they'd come to fruition.

"Hey, Sophie!" Zach stood at the table in the center of the library. I think he could sense my uneasiness of studying together, which was strange considering I had no issue being around and alone with Damien. Maybe the fact he was Ezra's best friend helped. If my brother trusted him, especially around me, then that alone put me at immense ease.

"Hi, are you ready to have some biochem fun?" I groaned as Zach laughed.

"I'm just hoping Professor Ko doesn't kill us with this quiz." Zach pulled out a stack of papers. "I printed an outline for you, too." He slid it over to me.

"Ah, you're the best!" I tugged out my bag, full of every colored highlighter imaginable, and lined them up neatly. Zach grinned at me.

I wiggled my finger at him. "Don't laugh at me."

"Girl, I have nothing but respect." He reached over and plucked the blue highlighter.

Two hours later, we both felt prepared for our next biochem quiz and finished the assigned lectures. Jesson University was one of the top four universities in the nation, meaning the professors made sure to weed out any of the weakest links, especially if you were heading to their graduate programs. I really wanted to get into their dental school because being close to Ezra and Amira was something I needed more than ever. Reese was planning on applying to the medical school here, so it would be perfect.

"My fraternity is having a party tonight at the Beta Tao Alpa house. I'd love it if you came, Sophie." Zach opened the library door for me.

Chewing my bottom lip, nervousness immediately pooled inside me. I hated how my anxiety flared up at the idea of fun. "Oh, I don't know, I might—"

"Well, hello there stranger!" I flung my head and saw Reese about to walk inside the library.

"Reese!" I wrapped my hands around her. "You're studying, too?"

"No, just need to print some stuff off. I'm not wasting my ink." She shrugged and flicked her eyes between Zach and me.

"Oh, sorry. Reese, this is Zach; he's in my biochem class." I held my textbooks tightly against my chest.

"Hi, Zach..." Reese stretched his name out with a devious smile and looked back at me curiously. I shook my head with my eyes wide at my presumptuous best friend.

"Hey, Reese, it's nice to meet you." He put his hand out and she happily took it.

"What are you two up to?" she asked as we moved to the side as to not block the door.

"Well, I'm trying to convince Sophie to come to the annual back to school party at Beta Tao, my fraternity." Zach sighed.

"Oh, hell yes, we are coming! I'm actually friends with Matt, and he already invited me. I was planning on dragging Sophie there anyway." Reese wiggled her shoulders excitedly. I parted my mouth to argue, but there was no point by the looks of how thrilled she was.

"Well, that's perfect. I'll see you both there. Have a great day, ladies." Zach flashed his charming smile and turned away.

Waiting until he wasn't in an earshot, Reese dropped her mouth. "You little seductress."

As much as I wanted to keep a straight face, I erupted into laughter. "That's a very strong word compared to study-buddy, Reese Cup." I nudged her shoulder.

"I mean, I thought you were crushing on zaddy, and now you've got yourself a fratty." She leaned against the brick pillar.

"Zaddy?" I pinched my lips to the side, not sure I wanted to know.

"You know, hot older dude? Ezra's friend, Damien." Reese opened her palms and her eyes got huge.

"Ew. He's not a zaddy, and no, for the record, I will never be speaking about him. He's actually intolerable. Nauseating, really. Anyway, I'm going to head to the gym. I'll see you later?" I gave Reese a quick hug.

"Yes, you will. I'll pick you up for the Beta Tao party at eight." She paused and lifted her hand at my dropped jaw. "No, don't even think about it. You need to have some real college fun again. I know he took a year of that away from you, but... don't let him take anything else, sis. You're far more powerful than any man." Reese squeezed me tightly and rubbed my back.

The thing I loved about Reese was how she could be light and funny, but then sneak in something deep and make a huge impact.

"See you at eight." I hugged back and we went our different ways.

CHAPTER 12

Damien

I sat in front of Theo Barkley, who wore skinny black jeans and a black tank, which showed off his neck full of tattoos. Sitting across from me in my office, he reeked of cigarette and cheap beer, which had me fighting the flashbacks connected to the scent.

Theo Barkley worked for me—not for my firm per se, but for me directly. Chicago was brimming with criminals, especially rich ones. Often times, these individuals got a slap on the hand and then were sent away with community service.

As much as I enjoyed finishing my cases, it was hard for me to take care of certain aspects and serve justice without help. But that's where Theo came in. Theo was a reformed drug dealer. He never hurt a woman or a child; he just got a shit hand of cards dealt to him in life and was thrown into a gang at the age of fifteen. I tried to get him a job that didn't carry violence or reminders of his past, but he told me and I quote, "I'm no damn pussy. Either give me a job I'm going to want or I'm out." By out, he meant he would head straight back into a gang and definitely get himself killed.

Now, here we were. He was a trained form of 'security,' and he also helped me make sure people paid for their actions when the judicial system failed the innocent.

Speaking of innocent, a certain brown-eyed girl's words looped in my mind and agitated me.

I'm not yours to worry about.

Who was she seeing today? And more importantly, why the hell did I care? I even avoided my daily coffee stand, which I went to because not only was it the best coffee in Chicago, but because the old man, Leo, expected me. Let's just say one cup of four-dollar coffee turned into an easy twenty for him every morning. Leo was one of the few people I could actually tolerate, minus whenever he shoved pictures of his grandchildren in my face and insisted I wasn't getting any younger.

Sophie just had to move a block away from me. She's taking over my breathing space, but didn't have the audacity to tell me who she was seeing today? I gave her my favorite fucking leather jacket, let her have my helmet and risked my own life taking her home...

She clearly doesn't know who she's defying.

I'm Damien fucking Moretti.

I lifted my phone and one ring later, she answered. "Hey, Amira. So, I was thinking, we should make these dinners a weekly staple. I don't mind hosting the next one." I rubbed my hand against my face.

"Wow! Really? I would love that. I'll tell Ezra." Amira paused. "Wait a second... Why are you suddenly so eager for weekly dinner parties? Oh my... does this have anything to do with a short, feisty brunette?" Amira gasped with her realization.

"Who?" I pretended to have an early bout of amnesia.

"Damien, you know you're playing with fire. Ezra would actually burn you to an untimely death if he found out about your crush on his *little* sister." Amira lowered her voice.

"Amira, contrary to what you have crafted in your *little* imagination, I have zero interest in that girl. I'm just thinking we will have to learn to get along for your wedding," I said flatly.

"Mm-hmm. Well, I'll talk to Ezra—and not about your crush because I really don't want to mess up the bridal party and my wedding over your funeral," Amira said coolly.

Hanging up the phone after a quick goodbye, I sank back into my seat. Theo came back into my office after meeting with my secretary to discuss his extra payment.

"Wow, bossman, you lookin' real stressed. You need to fuck one out of you," Theo said, clasping his knuckles together with a thick silver ring on each one. Those weren't there just for style; he enjoyed leaving an imprint on the faces of his targets.

"Fuck one out of you?" I eyed him, my voice fully irritated.

"The only reason someone looks that pissed is when a woman did something to him." Theo pointed at me with a half-toothless smile.

"Theo, shut the fuck up and get to work. Tell me what Bryan Stewart is doing these days?" Bryan Stewart had met both of my fists one year ago. He promised he'd do no more wrong and would never lay his hands on his wife again. Unfortunately, I was his attorney, and I, for one, did believe in second chances, but a third....? *No way.* He was once the mayor of Chicago until he was caught screwing his assistant on his desk; meanwhile, he'd be knocking his wife around without any thought.

"You know I got you, bossman. Take my advice and fuck one out." Theo chuckled in his raspy, smoker laugh.

"Yeah. Thanks for the life-altering advice, Theo." I opened my laptop and began to finalize a few things before heading out. I needed to distract myself.

* * *

A few hours in the courthouse, and I finally got outside, the humidity sticking to my face as I jogged down the steps. I was heading to dinner with Carmen. Carmen was what I'd like to call an old friend, but nothing was friendly between us.

Basically, we had sex and then didn't speak, and she knew I never spent the night—*ever*. There wasn't any hate, or love, or like... just fucking. She was an equally busy attorney and completely Type-A, and it was the perfect balance.

Most women I'd sleep with would sometimes wake up while I was tugging on my pants and would be furious or in tears because of my swift departure. I didn't always have time or the energy to handle those women, so Carmen was the go-to.

Amira was absolutely right; if I ever acted on the dirty thoughts coursing through my mind about Sophie, then my friendship with Ezra would not only be over, but our professional relationship would be tainted. He'd also murder me, making sure my corpse rotted on the Magnificent Mile, my least favorite part of Chicago.

I tugged at my tie. Loosening it, I stuffed it into my pocket and unbuttoned my dress shirt at the top. I wouldn't have time to change, and we were dining at Bella Amore, which was one of Chicago's best Italian restaurants—not ranking wise, but coming from a true Italian. It was the closest thing to my mom's cooking, which to me, made it the best.

I jumped on my bike and headed over to the restaurant. Another rule was that I never gave Carmen a ride to the hotel we'd agree to fuck at. I refused to have women over at my place since it complicated the whole 'leave at two a.m. aspect.'

Pulling up, I parked and locked my helmet on. Walking into the restaurant, I immediately spotted Carmen. She was easily five-eleven, with short blonde hair, and always in some kind of cream-colored sleek suit, designer heels, with a bag worth more than most people's rent.

"Hi, handsome," she purred and stood, meeting my eyes and leaving a sticky kiss on my face.

"Carmen." I grinned at her with a small laugh as her eyes scanned my body hungrily. Carmen wasn't just fun for sex; she was actually somewhat of a friend in the sense that we could talk about work with ease. She often knew details of high-profile cases that were coming up and had ins with a different crowd from mine.

We spent the next hour eating and talking. Maybe discussing murderers and criminals and how we'd destroy them all was our sick form of foreplay.

Maybe she was into some vigilante kink. I don't know, and I don't care. Taking Theo's unsolicited advice, I just needed to fuck one out.

Carmen's arm laced into mine as we walked out and crossed the street to the hotel.

Getting into the penthouse, Carmen peeled her jacket off, tossing it onto the chaise seductively. I mimicked her and kicked my shoes off, unhooking my belt as a smile curved her face. She had a thick layer of makeup on; meanwhile, I couldn't stop thinking of the way my thumb brushed against Sophie's bare skin as her big, brown eyes begged me to give in to her temptation.

My cock hardened under my black briefs, but it wasn't because of Carmen's strip tease and touch...

It was hard from the thoughts of *her*.

"I'll be right back." I turned and walked into the bathroom, needing space to breathe. What the hell was happening to me?

Suddenly, my phone rang. It was Ezra.

"Oh fuck," I whispered. Amira probably told him her assumptions and now he probably had a hit on me. I glanced down at my chest for a red circle, hoping a sniper wasn't outside.

It didn't stop ringing. Strumming my fingers against the smooth counter, I knew I couldn't ignore him forever.

"Hey, Ez," I said under my breath.

"Hey man, I have a huge favor. Amira and I are at her friend's engagement party, and Sophie just called from some frat party. She sounded upset and asked if I could pick her up. I'm almost an hour away from campus and wondered if you were home... could you get to her first?" He sounded stressed out and panicked.

My heart pounded against my chest, and before he had even finished his sentence, I was out of the bathroom, sliding on my pants and shoes without a second thought.

Carmen's eyes slanted as I held a finger up. "Text me the place and I'll get her home... to her house," I clarified to Ezra.

He let out a sigh of relief. "Thanks, Damien. Seriously. She sounded really upset. She doesn't do so great at these huge parties, and I am shocked she's even at a frat party, considering." He paused. "Text me when you guys are back at her place?"

"Yeah, I will." I hung up. What did he mean by *considering*? Parties were the normal thing to do for most college students, so why didn't Sophie like them? Most of all, what had her so upset that she needed to call her brother at almost ten p.m.?

"Carmen, I've got to go." I handed her the hotel room key. "Charge anything you want." I shrugged. I didn't owe her an explanation, but her parted lips and heavy sigh didn't agree. I had to get to Sophie—that was the only thing on my mind.

Her.

CHAPTER 13

Sophie

I walked into the frat party with my arm looped in Reese's. She was wearing a denim mini skirt and a white tank top, where her pink lace bra shined through purposely. Her long legs dipped into heels, and her golden blonde hair was pulled in a sleek, high ponytail. Blue eyeshadow covered her lids and made the deep azure of her eyes stand out and sparkle.

"Oh my god... Reese," I blew out as the music blared around me, shaking the framed pictures of fraternity brothers through the years as college students all swam.

Yes, swam. *Indoors.*

They were frolicking through the foam that had flooded the entire bottom floor of the house. I glanced down at my thin, black body con dress and layered gold necklaces.

"Reese! You didn't tell me this was a foam party!" I shrieked as students started yelling and dancing around us, throwing foam on our heads.

Reese tugged her white tank off, revealing what was not a pink bra, but a pink bikini top. "You'd never have come!" she called out over the noise, laughing and spinning in the thick white foam.

"Reese!" I cried out but it was too late. She was floating through to the keg that was in the back corner and suddenly, a tap on my shoulder had me turning around.

It was a guy I didn't know. His shirt off and he was holding two red solo cups before he shoved one into my face.

"Hey, what's your name?" he asked me, though his eyes fell to my boobs. Clearing my throat, he looked back at me with an arrogant smile.

"Sophie," I said, filled with regret that I had agreed to come out. People say leaving your comfort zone is a good thing, but I don't agree with that. Leaving your comfort zone only does one thing: makes you uncomfortable.

I glanced around and saw Reese giggling over her drink with some other guy. "Well, Sophie... I'm Tanner. Wanna dance, gorgeous?" He leaned in. The music blared with Doja Cat, and everyone was slinging their solo cups in the air, screaming like they were at Coachella. The lights turned off and neon lights flashed around in random corners.

"Um... okay." I started swaying awkwardly to the beat. Tanner's hands dropped to my waist, tugging me in closer. I quickly took a long sip of the bitter purple punch that was Jesson's signature frat party drink. I had no idea what was in it, but it made you feel like you were floating after one cup.

Tanner's hands ran up and down my hips, and he slowly turned me around, pulling my ass into his crotch. He was hard and was clearly making it known as he rubbed himself over me.

I started to wiggle out of his grasp, but his fingers dug deeper into my hips and my heart rate skyrocketed. "Do you wanna go somewhere private." He blew his hot breath into my ear.

"No. I'm actually about to head out." I pushed his hands off me, but between the music, the crowd, and the movement, everything started spinning.

It was too hot. I ran my hand up my neck, scratching it anxiously.

"Come on." Tanner grabbed my hand and tugged me to a room down the hall.

"I just need water," I blurted out, my head spinning and my chest tightening.

This whole situation was giving me a panic attack.

"Come here. I'll make it all better." Tanner pushed me onto a worn-down futon in the room and hovered over me.

My vision felt fuzzy as my mouth grew drier. "No... I'm going home." My words were shaky as he unbuttoned his pants and leaned down to me. I leaned up, trying to stand, but he shoved me down.

"Come on, don't be that girl, Sophie." He grabbed my arms, and as soon as he got closer, I stood with all my strength and kneed him so hard in his crotch that he screamed like the little bitch he was.

"No means no, motherfucker," I yelled and pushed past him, racing through the damn foam to the front patio. My entire body felt prickly and heated. All I wanted to do was get away from all this and shower. My body folded in half as soon as the cool air hit my skin, and I gulped in the fresh air.

My nerves took over, and I pulled out my phone, knowing my panic attack was still flaring, considering even with the cool air, I still felt like I was suffocating.

I tugged my phone out with tears streaming down my face. Reese was probably upstairs, having fun with the guy she met; meanwhile, fun and me didn't mix. Clearly, I just had a sign on my head to attract entitled college boys who intended to use and hurt me.

"Ezra..." my voice shook, "I-I need you to come pick me up." I softly cried into my elbow as others walked around me, eyeing me like I was crazy.

Ten short minutes later, he pulled up. Except, it wasn't my brother.

It was Damien. On his motorcycle.

Pulling his helmet off, he clipped it to his bike and looked at the house in front of him, not able to see me in the dark corner I huddled in. Throwing my head back, I muttered, "Oh, this is just great."

Some girls around me on the porch saw him and giggled together. Blowing out a breath of air, I wanted to call my brother back and demand to know why he sent Damien. But it was the weekend, and I remembered Amira telling me about an engagement party. I knew I couldn't keep bothering them; eventually, they would want to just live their lives. They already did so much for me.

My heart rate slowed as Damien walked up to the house. I stayed seated on the small porch swing, and the panic and anxiety began to dissipate with his presence growing closer. He began rolling up his white dress shirt sleeves as he jogged up the steps.

The two girls on the opposite side smiled stupidly at him. "Do you know where Sophie is?" he barked.

"Forget Sophie, I'm Katrina... and I'll give you

anything you want." One of the leggy, tipsy girls grew closer to him, which made the pit in my stomach drop.

"Oh look, you dropped something," Damien snarled as the girl looked down to the ground and I snuck a peek as well.

"What?" she asked in her squeaky, high-pitched voice.

"Your fucking dignity." He turned as the girl gasped and the sliver of the streetlight shining on her face showed her embarrassment.

Damien was about to tug the door open, but I stood. "Damien," I said almost inaudibly, quickly wiping my tears. My dress was soaked, clinging to my body, and I immediately regretted not wearing a bra. He jerked his head in my direction and his eyes ran over me wildly.

Walking closer into the shadows of the porch, he waited until the light caught my eyes so he could see what was probably smudged makeup and tears.

Lifting his hand, and without any words, he swiped his thumb under my left eye before drawing his finger downward and cupping my chin. "Are you okay?" His voice shifted as his jaw ticked.

"I just want to go..." I looked down and crossed my arms over my chest. "please."

His eyes dropped to my arm, which had reddened

from Tanner's tight grip. He squinted as he asked darkly, "Who did this to you?"

"No one. Can we just go?" I whispered.

"Don't lie to me. If someone touched you, tell me." His voice grew possessive and raspy.

"There you are! Damn, you sure move quick. Dude, you're cockblocking me." Tanner stumbled out of the front door and onto the porch.

Damien flung around and looked between us. "Did he hurt you, Sophie?" he growled while pushing his sleeves up further. I nodded slowly.

"Come here, babe." Tanner laughed, completely ignoring Damien's presence as he came closer. I instantly walked back with fear pooling in my stomach.

But before I could even blink, Tanner's collar was grabbed from behind, and Damien dragged him away, putting himself between us.

Pinning him against the house, he lifted him up where his feet dangled. Tanner's eyes widened like a small animal facing their worst predator as he cried, "I'm going to kill you! Put me down, asshole!"

"Did you touch her?" Damien roared.

"She wanted me to," Tanner spit out, and that's when a crack echoed, Damien's fist smashing Tanner's face to the side. The girls who were standing nearby shrieked and ran off the porch.

"You fucking bitch!" His eyes met mine.

Damien let out a sound that could have cracked the windows. "What the fuck did you say?" Damien growled, and in one swift motion, he slammed Tanner's body to the ground like a ragdoll. Damien continued to smash his face over and over without a second thought.

"Stop! Help!" Tanner yelled while choking on his own blood.

"I didn't hear you, fucker!" Damien yelled into his face.

"I'm sorry... I'm sorry!" Tanner began crying. *Actual tears.*

My breathing quickened as I stood there, frozen.

"I'm sorry *who*?" Damien shook his body into the dirty porch floor.

"Sophie! I'm sorry!" he cried out.

Damien released him and wiped his bloodied knuckles on Tanner's shirt. "Touch her, or any girl, again without their consent and I promise you, it'll be your death sentence." Damien stood and looked at me.

Pulling his hand out, I grabbed it as he helped me step around Tanner, who was playing dead but shot me a look, then immediately closed his eyes when Damien glared at him.

We got to Damien's bike, where he studied me carefully before his eyes dropped to my chest. My nipples were poking through the thin, wet material, while my arms shook from being cold.

Slowly, he started to unbutton his dress shirt, exposing his bare chest. A large tattoo decorated one of his pecs and snaked down his arm. My eyes fell to his carved abs as he tugged the shirt off and pulled it on me.

We didn't speak as I slid my arms into his sleeves that pooled around my thin frame, but we didn't need to. The heat between our bodies and the possession radiating from him and into me was warmer than anything I'd ever felt. He started buttoning the shirt over my chest and looked at me once more. "Sophie..." he tilted my chin up with his index finger, "where do you want me to take you?"

My chest rose and fell quicker than ever as I whispered, "To your place." His dark brows tightened and his jaw clenched. "I want to go somewhere I feel safe, and for some reason, that's with you."

Nodding slowly, he helped me onto the back of his bike and handed me his helmet. I wrapped my arms around his body and let my head fall into his bare back. I melted into Damien Moretti, closing my eyes and never feeling safer in my life.

CHAPTER 14

Damien

Pulling into my parking deck, I kicked the brake and paused. Sophie's smooth cheek was planted against my flesh and her hands were gripping my abdomen. She felt so damn good against my body that I didn't want to move.

"Sophie?" I said gently as she slowly pulled her hands away, her fingers trailing across my chest and that simple act made my muscles tighten against her soft touch.

"You should let Ezra know you're okay. Or I can." I got off my bike and helped her down, and she tumbled into my arms.

Looking up at me from under her thick lashes, her beautiful face was streaked with makeup and tears.

"I'll text him. I'm sorry, Damien," she said softly, breaking our gaze.

"Don't apologize for idiots behaving poorly and someone stepping in to help you. Don't apologize to me, Sophie, because it'll make me think I did something wrong. All I know is if anyone ever touches you, I'll fucking kill them, and to me, that's right." I turned quickly, pushing the button to my elevator.

She followed behind me with her breathing heavy. We stayed silent in the elevator—the tension between us palpable—until the doors opened to my penthouse.

"Wow," Sophie breathed out as we stepped out. I glanced at her in my button-down, which was the sexiest thing I had ever seen.

"Damien, you have the best view ever." She walked toward the wall-to-wall, floor-to-ceiling windows that made up half of my penthouse. The Chicago River and skyline shined through.

"Are you hungry? Thirsty?" I asked as she stayed by the windows.

"It's so beautiful," she said in awe, lost in her own thoughts.

"Yeah... so beautiful," I replied, and she slowly looked over her shoulder. Her eyes met mine and the pink in her cheeks grew, making it clear she knew I wasn't talking about that view, but about my current view directly in front of me.

"I'm starving," she said nervously.

"I'll order Bertolli's?" Her face lit up in a big smile, making the ice in my body start to crack. Breaking our stare, I turned to the kitchen.

"Damien?"

"Yeah?"

"Can I take a shower?"

"Use my shower, it's better than the guest one." I pointed toward my bedroom, and she rolled her lips together.

"Thank you..."

"Sophie..." I started, and she stopped without turning toward me. "If he... Did he... I can take you to the hospital if you—" I choked on each word, but I had to ask. *I had to.*

"He didn't. You saved me from that," she said shakily and walked away.

As soon as she walked into my bedroom, I clutched the counters and leaned down, taking deep breaths.

"You saved me..." I muttered under my breath.

The pizza delivery arrived before Sophie was done showering. I figured she'd enjoy the massive double-headed rain shower. I quickly changed into a T-shirt and gray joggers, then went to set out plates and drinks.

The door creaked open. "So, I think I may just need to move in." Sophie sounded much happier, and I looked at her from the coffee table.

Her long, dark hair was even darker when wet, and it draped over her shoulders, soaking into the T-shirt she was wearing.

My T-shirt. It swallowed her in size, and her thin legs wiggled as she laced her fingers together.

"I hope it's okay..." She looked down at herself and back at me.

I quickly tightened my lips. "Yeah... of course." Clearing my throat, I looked away as my chest grew tighter.

"This smells amazing. Bertolli's is my favorite!" She came and sank into the couch next to me, curling her legs up and pulling the plate into her lap. She smelled like my soap and looked absolutely gorgeous with her face bare and eyes clear again.

I turned on the T.V., hoping it'd help me stop acting like I had never been in the presence of a woman before.

But I hadn't... at least, not like Sophie. She was airy and bright. She wore her heart on her sleeve, and this vulnerable side of her hurt me in a way I didn't know pain could exist.

"Mmm..." she moaned loudly. I let out a laugh and looked at her enjoying her pizza.

A dribble of sauce tainted her chin, and without thinking, I swiped it and licked it off my finger. Sophie sucked in a breath and parted her thick pink lips.

Clearing my throat, I looked back at the movie, hoping I could steady my erratic breathing.

Moments of silence came and went as we both pretended to be engaged in the random movie we were watching.

"How long have you lived here?" Sophie asked me after finishing her pizza and taking a sip of water.

"I bought this place when I was in law school," I replied.

"It's beautiful. Could use a few lighter touches..." she eyed the massive room, which was decorated professionally in navy blue and gray. "Like a woman's touch." She laughed but quickly sunk her teeth into her lower lip.

"Don't do that."

"Do what?" Her eyebrow arched as she turned toward me.

"Suppress your laugh. It's the most beautiful sound I've ever heard," I said lowly.

Her cheeks flushed, and somehow the small space between us filled.

"You're not who I thought you were..." Sophie licked her bottom lip, and my eyes didn't break from her mouth.

"And who did you think I was?"

"The devil..." She laughed lightly, and the sound alone made my chest clench.

"That's where you're wrong, Sophie. I'm worse..." I whispered as her eyes dropped to my lips.

"I want you to kiss me," she breathed out.

"No," I replied hastily.

Her eyes lifted to mine. "Why?"

"Because I won't be able to fucking stop there, Sophie. If I taste your lips, I'll want to taste every part of you. I'll need to taste you here." I brushed my fingers against her trembling lips, "and here," I dropped my hand over her breast, her nipple hardening under my touch. "Then I'll need to taste you here..." I let my hand fall to her exposed thigh. "and then..."

"Here?" She drove my hand under my shirt and up her thigh, all the way until my fingers touched her bare flesh.

Fuck. She wasn't wearing panties.

My cock hardened and the air from my lungs escaped as she brushed my hand against her pussy.

Her soaking wet pussy... for *me.*

"Please, Damien," she pleaded, her big eyes filled with lust.

"Sophie..." I tugged my hand out from under the shirt and planted both palms against her cheeks, drawing her face closer to mine.

Our breath collided and a force pulled us together, but I didn't kiss her. I took in her breath. Her air. Grinding my teeth, my internal demons taunted me.

"Damien, please..." she begged.

It took every ounce of my strength to move off the couch and over to the cognac leather chair to the side. Picking up the remote, I flipped channels as she groaned and stuffed her face into a pillow.

"Is it because of Ezra?" she asked quietly.

I looked over at her. Her cheeks were pink as she quickly averted my eyes. I didn't really know why I was controlling myself. Then again, I had a mental list that only had infinite cons of sleeping with her, which only had one pro. The only pro being immense satisfaction of burying myself inside the gorgeous girl in front of me.

"Is it because of Ezra?" she repeated, her voice agitated.

"No. I'm old enough to be your dad," I replied flatly. She winced and threw a pillow at me.

"I don't mind calling you daddy." She swiped her tongue across her thick bottom lip. The lip I wanted to sink my teeth into. "I mean, you're seventeen years older than me... so maybe if you were a teen dad."

"Sophie, watch the damn show and go to bed."

She rolled her eyes, and I swear, my hand twitched, wanting to spank that perfect ass for being defiant.

My jaw clenched. "Don't do that."

"Do what?" she fired back.

I flicked my eyes to hers. "Roll your eyes at me."

A small, devious smile curved her thick lips. Standing, she bit her bottom lip and cut in front of the screen. Her small frame was covered in my T-shirt, but then she decided to send me to an early death.

Turning away, she stretched her hands over her head and feigned a yawn. My shirt crept up higher, and she flashed the bottom curve of her perfect ass.

Groaning and smashing my face into the pillow, I mumbled, "Go to bed, Sophie."

She let out a sweet, yet mischievous, laugh before looking over her shoulder. "Okay, *daddy*," she sang out mockingly.

I peered over the pillow. "You can sleep in my bed."

"Ew, no. That's where you choke your..." She paused and looked away. Now, it was my turn to have fun.

Standing, I threw the pillow to the side and walked behind Sophie. She had her back turned toward me and I leaned in, brushing her hair away from her shoulder.

I knew my breath was grazing her neck, and the way she sucked in the air had my chest tightening.

"Choke my *what*, Sophie?" I taunted. She shook her

head slowly. "Say the word." I padded my fingers against her collarbone.

"Your cock," she said lowly.

Releasing a long breath, I pulled away and turned her to face me. Lifting her chin with my index finger, I knew arrogance was painted across my face. "Oh, sweet Sophie... the only thing that would choke on my cock is this pretty little mouth of yours." I brushed my thumb against her bottom lip.

Her eyes widened at my words and immediately dropped down.

"Goodnight." I moved my hand, and she took a step backward.

"Goodnight," she mumbled and spun back around, sprinting to my room. My cock was pulsing in my joggers just hearing Sophie say the damn word. Rubbing my hand across my face, I looked at the couch.

Fuck that... I wasn't sleeping there.

CHAPTER 15

Sophie

I was counting my breaths as my mind raced like a hamster on its wheel with Damien's filthy words and how his fingers felt against my skin. Tracing my collarbone, I blew a breath of air out.

My emotions were tangled up with my entire body being set to flames. Everything, and I mean *everything* was tingling.

The door creaked open, and I quickly clenched my eyes shut, tugging the soft blanket higher... My heart constricted and annoyance built inside me as the bed shifted and Damien laid down next to me.

"How is there only one damn bed in this entire penthouse?" I hissed from under the blanket, which Damien was laying on top of.

"I don't have overnight guests, so what is the point of a guest room?" he replied flatly.

"Go sleep on the couch," I demanded and looked over the blanket at him. Seriously? His shirt was off and he wore only thin boxer briefs. "And for God's sake, put some clothes on!"

"Stop looking," he replied hastily.

Rolling my eyes, I tugged on the blanket, but it wouldn't come over enough since Adonis over there was laying on it like a statue.

Suddenly the room felt too warm and I felt too flustered.

"Why wouldn't you kiss me?" I asked, licking my lips as I sat up.

Damien's eyes slowly opened, with one hand tucked behind his head. His entire abdomen was exposed—muscles carved perfectly into his body—his chest rising in falling in perfect harmony, unlike my erratic heartbeat.

Without looking over at me, he blinked a few times. "Because you'd want more."

"Well, usually when two consenting adults kiss, it leads to something like se—"

"No, not just fucking; you would want some bullshit cuddling, morning kisses, and make something physical into something emotional. Someone would fall..." Damien said coldly.

"I wouldn't fall for you," I scoffed, though I knew I sounded unconvincing.

"Okay," he replied without a hitch.

"Okay, so kiss me."

"No."

"Why?" I whined.

"Because... What makes you think I meant you'd be the somebody to *fall*." And just like that, my heart stopped and Damien closed his eyes.

I tossed and turned all night, staring out the gorgeous windows that had Chicago on display. I blinked as the sunlight seeped in from the windows and glanced over. Damien was no longer beside me.

I knew he wasn't sleeping well either, but we didn't speak after our conversation. If I thought I wanted him then, now I wanted him more; but at the same time, we were a disaster waiting to happen. Nothing good would come from us hooking up. Because that's all it would be, a hook up.

The one man that got under my skin, annoyed me more than anyone I knew, suddenly was the one man I wanted to quite literally be under, or on top off, or in front of, or bent over for.

Crawling out of the excessively comfortable bed I barely slept in, I swiped under my eyes and walked out to the living room.

Pinching my lips to the side, I looked around. He wasn't there. Suddenly, a voice rose from down the hall.

I tip-toed toward the closed door.

"Damien, honey, you are the best... Are you sure I can't repay you? I know exactly what you like," the voice echoed—a *woman's* voice. I swallowed the lump in my throat.

I hated how my heart hurt; I hated how my mouth grew dry, and I hated how tears burned my eyes.

Walking backward, I turned and jogged down the hall, then pressed the elevator button to leave.

I hated Damien Moretti. He couldn't wait for me to leave before fucking someone after I practically begged him to kiss me?

I hated him.

"Thank you for picking me up..." I put my face in my hands, peeking at Zach through the cracks of my fingers.

"Sophie, it's no problem." He glanced at my outfit—well, lack thereof. I was still wearing Damien's T-shirt and had no shoes on. I hadn't brushed my teeth or my hair, so I basically looked like a train wreck. Well, not just looked... I felt like one, too.

"Reese didn't answer..." I added, feeling guilt course through me. I knew Zach may have had a small crush on me, and I felt rude sitting here, asking him to pick me up from another guy's house.

"Sophie, we're friends. If you need me, I'll be there." Zach offered a smile. Sinking back into his passenger seat, I looked out the window. Why couldn't I just like someone normal? Someone stable, and maybe my own age?

Oh, that's right, because I did and that blew up in my face.

"By the way, I didn't see you last night at the party, but I saw your friend Reese." Zach flicked his eyes to me.

"I... Yeah, I didn't go." I looked out the window to hide my lie.

"Want to grab some breakfast?" Zach asked, sensing my discomfort.

"I'd love to, but it'll need to be drive-thru because I've somehow forgotten my clothes and shoes." I slapped my hand over my face as Zach let out a laugh.

"McDonald's drive-thru has seen crazier things, my friend." He tapped my hand sweetly.

My phone rang as we pulled into the line. Looking down, my eyes widened as the devil emoji flashed on my screen.

Damien.

I hit ignore, and immediately, it started ringing again.

Zach looked over at me sheepishly and shrugged. "Maybe just pick it up?"

"Hello?" I snapped.

"Where are you?" Damien asked unemotionally.

"Obviously not there. I wanted to give you and your whore privacy," I fired off. Zach's eyes widened as he bent his head out of the window to order us food.

"Who the hell are you with?" Damien no longer sounded calm; he sounded pissed.

"None of your damn business." Slamming my finger against the red end button, I turned my phone off completely.

"Oh-kay. Definitely not going to ask..." Zach made a goofy face that made my frustration melt away.

Shaking my head, I grabbed the egg and cheese biscuit from his hand and peeled the wrapper off. Taking a big bite, the greasy biscuit felt heavenly in my mouth, especially chased down with a hot sip of coffee.

"Can I pay you back for my food when I get home?" I wiped the crumbs from my mouth.

"Sophie, it's McDonalds." Zach cringed, and I laughed harder than I had in a while.

Yeah, screw you, Damien.

CHAPTER 16

Damien

I stormed over to Sophie's apartment. The voice I heard in the background of our brief phone call was definitely some idiot guy who was probably picking her up and going to take advantage of the fact that she was already vulnerable from that Tanner motherfucker basically assaulting her.

Something I was working on taking care of.

This is exactly why I could never touch Sophie or get involved with her. She was already on an emotional roller coaster of being nineteen and in college. She had her share of assholes, and I was the king. A man with morals and a soul would stay away from her.

But the problem was, I didn't have either.

My soul was dark, and my morals were non-existent.

Waiting outside, I kept calling her. I couldn't call

Ezra; he'd freak out and go all helicopter-mom-mode on my ass.

Once someone opened the building door, I slid inside and opened the small note I had written.

One kiss. Tonight. My place.
D.M

I slid the note under her apartment door, forcing myself not to break it down. One kiss. I'd give her that much, and after that, she'd get over her little schoolgirl crush and move on with her damn life, and I'd do the same.

* * *

The rest of the day was spent at my office, yet I couldn't focus. I left and tortured myself at my penthouse instead. Sophie didn't pick her phone up, but Ezra called and mentioned she was hanging out at their place. He called just in time, considering I was about to burn Chicago to the ground trying to find her.

I didn't know if she had seen my note. I didn't know if I wanted her to anymore, considering my best friend called and talked about her like she was an innocent teenager. I flinched. She was nineteen, and that made her a teenager. *Fuck.*

But I was unsettled with how we left things this morning. I figured she had heard Lana, who was nothing more than my assistant. Sure, we had a sexual relationship at one point, but now it was only professional. Lana always wanted more, and she was more than happy to provide it too, but I didn't want her. I didn't want anyone. Except for...

I paced around until I heard the elevator. The doors opened and there she was. She was wearing a short skirt and tucked-in, fitted tank top. Her tits were pouring out. Walking closer to her, I paused. "Did you take an Uber in that?" My eyes drifted down.

"Mm-hmm," she replied with defiance in the simple word.

"If you had answered your phone, I would have picked you up." I tried to keep my voice calm. "Who was the guy you were with this morning? While you were wearing *my* shirt?" I took one step closer, leaving a sliver of space between us.

She lifted a brow not even trying to conceal her amusement. "A friend."

"I hope you don't have plans this weekend with him..." I eyed her.

She tilted her head to the side and slanted her eyes. "Why?"

"He'll be unavailable, since he'll be in the fucking ground," I rasped as I brought her face in between my palms. Her lips parted, and I swore I could hear her heart beating rapidly.

"And for the record, he might give you the shoulders to cry on, but baby... I'll give you the shoulders to put your legs on."

Sucking in a breath of air, she exhaled, "You'd have to kiss me first."

"How can you not see all the fucking red flags around me?" I asked while slowly tracing her mouth with my finger.

"I do. It's just... red is my favorite color," she replied without a second thought.

Groaning, I leaned in closer. "I'm only going to hurt you."

Her lips shook as her eyes stayed fixed onto my lips. Inching closer, I waited as her chest heaved rapidly. "If it hurts, that means you're doing it right. I can handle it," she whispered.

I lifted her up into my arms with her ass pressing against my forearms. Pressing her back against the wall, I swiped my tongue along her bottom lip. "To be honest, I wanted to kiss your other lips, more." She gasped before

I pushed my tongue into her mouth and pressed my lips against hers. The small moan that escaped her body had fire rampaging through my veins.

She rolled her head back, and I began kissing the length of her neck. "Damien..." she moaned.

"I knew you'd taste so fucking sweet..." I brushed her face and looked into her eyes before putting her down. She opened her palm and looked at me with desire planted deep in those deep brown eyes.

I let my palm connect with hers, following behind her as she walked without hesitation to my bedroom. I slid the light switch lower, making the lights dimmer.

She turned her head and looked over her shoulder, biting down into her lip, "Fancy pants..." she mocked in that cute fucking way that made my entire being shake.

"It's just a light," I replied as she lifted my hands into hers and brought me to the edge of my bed. Sinking down, she sat at the foot of it. "Open," my eyes dropped to her thighs. My mouth slowly dropped as she spread her legs slowly, inviting me in between.

"Soph..." I breathed out.

Her eyes flicked up to mine and something in her face shifted from desire and lust to something else entirely. "That's the first time you've called me Soph..." She smiled and licked her lips. "I like it."

I ran my hand through my hair and stared at her. "I'm not going to be your boyfriend," I said blankly.

She nodded. "Good, because I don't want a boyfriend."

"I'm not going to hold you after," I added.

"Luckily, I don't like being held." Her voice grew jagged.

"I'm not going to be gentle. I don't make love." I dropped my eyes between her legs.

"I don't want you to be gentle; I'm not a glass doll. And I sure as hell don't want to do anything that entails *love* with you," she mocked.

Damn, this spitfire was tempting me.

"This is a one-time thing. Just to get it out of our systems. And we will never speak about this again."

"I won't want it after this once..." She narrowed her eyes, taunting me again.

"Don't even think about catching feelings."

She pursed her lips, "I'd rather catch the flu." Her eyes twinkled with mischief.

"That's it. Get on your fucking knees. Now," I boomed. The smile that curved her perfect lips made my cock pulse. She crawled off my bed and onto her knees right in front of me. Peeling my shirt from over my head, I threw it to the side. Her hand shot up to the outline of my cock and ran it over my bulge, squeezing and tracing its length. Her eyes connected to mine when her hand and mine aligned, and she realized something.

"Oh damn... you're really big," she squeaked.

My body tensed.

"Are you sure you want to do this, Soph?"

"Yes. This is my choice, Damien. I want this. I want you."

"Baby, once I'm inside you, I own your body." I ran my fingers through her lush hair, wrapping a fistful into my palm before tilting her face upright to look me straight in the eyes. Her cheeks were tinged pink, but her chest was rising and falling rapidly as she took my words in.

Crossing her arms over her chest, she pulled her clothes off, revealing her smooth, golden skin and perfect round breasts with hardened pink nipples that were begging for my mouth.

I took my time relishing in her beauty, like how the flat of her stomach melted into her flawless bare pussy. This gorgeous woman on her knees in front of me had crossed my mind and clouded my thoughts. I tried to push them aside, and fuck, did she infuriate me with her constant ability to make any conversation a debate or how she always had to defy me.

Now, I'd show her...

"Tonight, baby girl, your body, mind, and soul are

mine. I tell you what to do, and you will obey. The only thing in your mouth will be my cock, and the only thing coming out will be when you're screaming my name and leaking my come." I dropped my joggers and let my cock spring out in front of her face. Her eyes grew wider and her lips parted. "Do you understand, Sophie?"

Her eyes didn't move from mine. "Yes. You know you could have just written this all out in a contract so I didn't have to hear you talk so much. I'm just really here for a good lay. Something I'm not even sure you're going to be." She swiped her tongue across her bottom lip with mischief dancing wildly in her eyes.

"Open your mouth, now. You're going to suck my cock like a good girl," I growled.

She opened her perfect pink lips and my hands wrapped around her long hair—something I had envisioned countless times. Sophie paused but didn't take me in her mouth; instead, she smirked at me deviously and gripped my length, tilted her head, and licked me from my balls to my tip. Pre-cum oozed out instantly at the touch of her tongue against my flesh.

I couldn't help but grin. She was proving her defiance in this slight gesture, but I didn't give a fuck because the way she was licking every vein in my cock had me fighting every urge to lift her and plunge inside her. I was desperate to feel the warmth of her pussy that I knew would tighten around me. Finally, after teasing every crevice of my cock, she took me into her perfect mouth.

I pushed her head and shoved my cock deeper into her throat. She gagged, and it only made me repeat the action. She didn't quit sucking me like it was the best damn thing in her mouth, even though she was gagging at the size and force of my movements.

Fuck, she felt good. "Sophie…" I breathed out as she suctioned my tip and swirled her tongue around it, tasting me. "Come here."

She slid my cock from her mouth and stood in front of me. Lifting her up, I placed her on my bed gently, gripping her knees and spreading them as she laid back. "Keep them wide open for me, and feet on the edge of the bed, sweetheart." I commanded.

I went around to my bed and grabbed two pillows, then slid them under her head.

"What are you—"

"You're going to watch me taste you, and eat you like the fucking sweet dessert you are." I dropped to my knees and she let out a long moan as my tongue swiped through each of her folds. Her perfect, pink pussy dripped on my tongue as I bit her clit and sucked it. "I want you to sit on my face, baby girl." My voice grew hoarse with desperation while looping my arms under her thighs dragging her further onto my mouth.

Grabbing a fistful of my hair, she cried out, "Damien!"

"Your pussy belongs to me." I pushed one finger inside her and she threw her head back. Gasping for air, she bit into her hand to stifle her moans.

"Sophie... if you think that feels good, you have no idea what my cock will do to this tight pussy," I rasped while tasting every single bit of her.

I swiped my tongue across her one more time before kissing the inside of her thigh and trailing my teeth higher to bite near her soft flesh. Standing up, I couldn't help but grin at how she was panting.

"Wait!" She cried out and dropped her jaw in shock.

"Don't worry, I'll be right back. You'll come when I let you. Keep your legs wide open. You're going to want to move up and hold onto the headboard."

Two minutes later, I came back with an unwrapped cherry popsicle. Her eyes widened. "Are you serious? You left me like this to go get ice cream?" She shouted with frustration.

"Open your mouth, Sophie." I rasped, as she immediately parted her lips. Her forehead crinkled with confusion.

"Suck it." I pushed the cherry popsicle into her

mouth as her lips suctioned around it. My cock twitched in envy.

Shoving it deeper into her mouth, I pulled it out and dragged it down her lips, onto her toned abdomen until finally, I lifted it and pushed it inside of her desperate pussy.

Gasping, she let out a small scream as I pumped the ice-cold popsicle in and out of her. "Dam—" she whimpered. Pulling it out of her, I sucked on it and could taste her all over it.

"Fuck, you made it so much sweeter..." I moaned before putting it down and climbing over her body. "Now, anywhere this popsicle touched, so will my mouth." I kissed her lips and let my tongue drop all the way down her body following the cherry trail before lifting her legs up and pressing my mouth against her pussy.

"Hold onto the headboard, now." I demanded. Swirling my tongue against her pulsing clit and fingering her as she screamed out. Her hands slapped against my headboard and I could hear her nails dragging into the fabric.

"Damien, I'm going to..." She swallowed in air and choked on her words. Her toes curled and her back arched. She let herself go, shuddering as I swirled my tongue around her. "Damien!" she screamed out.

"That's right, baby; my name is the only one you'll ever be able to think of as you come. I've ruined you for anyone who even thinks they'll ever be able to please you." I licked up every bit of her and groaned. "Fucking delicious." I swiped my thumb on the corners of my mouth.

Her lips parted in shock as I kissed her pussy. Her breathing was fast and sweat glistened across her beautiful face.

I stood, my cock still pulsing and begging for release. I was too hungry for her delicious pussy to let her finish sucking me off.

"Are you on the pill?" I looked up at her. This was a first for me in years; I never trusted the women I slept with to be honest.

Sophie, well... I knew she wasn't like the women I usually slept with.

She swallowed and nodded. "Yes..."

"Sophie, I want you to come all over my cock. Because if this is a one-time thing, which it is, then I want to feel every single bit of you wrapped around me. I want you to suck every last drop of my come into your perfect pussy.

"I've never..." She dropped her eyes.

I paused and processed the look across her face.

"Fuck, Sophie... you're a virgin?" I ran my hands through my hair, immediately stumbling back.

"No, I'm not a virgin... I've just never done it without a condom," she whispered almost inaudibly.

Done it? Fuck, this girl could barely say the word sex in front of me. She was nineteen. She was in college. Oh, fuck... she was my best friend's little sister. The best friend who'd probably tie a noose around my neck and hang me from the balcony if I didn't clean my hands of this... her, now.

I pulled my pants from the floor and tugged them back on.

"Wait? What happened? I thought... I mean, you haven't even..." she stammered and looked at the bulge that was now screaming in my pants. Why my moral compass decided to kick in at the worst moment was beyond my understanding.

"I'm tired, Sophie." I picked my T-shirt off the floor and handed to her, averting my eyes.

"What just happened?" She pulled the T-shirt over her head and climbed down, following me as I walked out of my room. "Don't do this..." she called out.

"Do what, Soph?" I poured a glass of water and slid it to her.

"Shut me out. I want you to..."

"Want me to what, Sophie?" I planted my palms on

the counter that separated us. She ran her index finger across the rim of her glass, understanding exactly why I stopped.

I had to stop.

"You're nineteen. I'm so much older than you, and… you're Ezra's younger sister. I lost control tonight and I shouldn't have." I sighed.

She batted her lashes and looked down into the glass of water. "Can you take me home?"

Damn it, she was crying. *I made her cry.*

CHAPTER 17

Sophie

I can't believe I was crying in front of Damien Moretti after he just made me come on his tongue and I sucked his dick. I mean, come on. What the hell? So what, I didn't say fuck or sex in front of him, but he didn't have to be a total douchebag and embarrass me.

Maybe I just wasn't good enough, like the women he was used to. The ones who probably showed up in black leather straps and five-hundred-dollar lingerie.

"Will you please take me home, Damien?" I repeated as tears rolled down my cheeks.

"No," he said coldly. "You don't have anything proper to wear, it's one a.m., and you need to go to sleep."

I squinted at him. "Are you serious right now? You're not my dad. I want to go home."

Anger replaced the lust I felt for this ridiculous man. So what if he was the most gorgeous man I'd ever laid eyes on? His entire body was carved like a Greek god, and he had muscles defined that I didn't even know existed. The way he didn't think twice before showing the stars to the two guys who had done something wrong with me. The way he unleashed a wrath of fury with possessiveness.

He was bad.

I was good.

"Do you really want to go home?" He walked around and came closer to me. The closer he came, the more steps I took backward until my back hit the kitchen counter.

"Yes." I swallowed. "Clearly, I'm not your type." I sniffled, humiliating myself further.

Damien took a deep breath in before releasing it slowly. His eyes darkened as his brows lowered and his gaze stayed steady on mine.

Brushing my lips with his thumb, I turned my head away, knowing if we shared the same air, I'd only become intoxicated all over again.

"You're so very wrong, my beautiful Soph." He paused. "I thought I didn't have a type until I met you."

He turned my jaw with his hand and pressed his forehead against mine. "The problem is, you *are* my type. Only you." His Adam's apple bobbed and my heart fluttered.

I closed my eyes, too scared to look at him. "Then why did you stop?"

"I'll only destroy you. You are going to give me your heart, and I'll do nothing but burn it to ashes. You're too trusting, and I'm not to be trusted. I'm doing myself a favor, but I'm also protecting you from me," he said without skipping a beat.

Tears streamed down my face, and I didn't know why emotion had overcome me.

Damien swiped my tears. "Go to sleep, Sophie." His voice shifted, again into the usual icy tone he always used.

I was a tired, blubbering mess. Maybe Damien was right. If I was already crying like this, then what would happen if we slept together? I didn't think I was the girl who could keep emotions out of sex, but I wanted his hands on me. I wanted to feel him inside me, doing the things in the heat of the moment that he had promised.

Nodding, I turned to walk back to his bedroom. "I'm sleeping in your bed. You can sleep on the couch." I cleared my throat and I swore, he bit back a small smirk.

* * *

Two loud voices woke me from the sweetest and steamiest of dreams.

"You are dead, Damien!" The cozy, sleepy smile on my face melted as I stretched my arms in Damien's bed and heard his voice.

My brother... Ezra's here.

Pushing the fluffy blanket off my body, I ran out into the living room and dropped my jaw. Ezra was fuming, and Damien was keeping a safe distance. Damien looked at me and squinted like he was in pain, while scanning my body. I was still in nothing but his T-shirt.

Shit. Shit. *Shit.*

Ezra followed Damien's line of vision. "Sophie! What the fuck are you wearing?" he asked through clenched teeth. "And you're saying you didn't do anything?" He shoved Damien's bare chest so hard Damien stumbled back, even though he was bigger than my brother, but he didn't even try to defend himself.

Ezra lifted his fist, and I screamed so loudly that I was fearful the windows would shatter. I ran over to my brother and tugged at his raised arm. "What are you doing?!" I screeched.

"I trusted you with her. She was in a vulnerable place

from that damn frat party a few nights ago, and you took advantage of her, Damien. You fucking took advantage of my baby sister and fucked her!" Ezra flung his arm into Damien's face.

He didn't even block. A *crack* echoed and Damien's face turned slightly.

"Ezra!" I grabbed at my brother's back. "We didn't sleep together!" I cried out.

Ezra flung around and looked at me with disappointed eyes. "Why would I believe you? You're coming out of his bedroom wearing his T-shirt," he said with anger fueling each word.

"You know why I couldn't do that... After last year, do you honestly think I have any interest in a man touching me right now?" Tears teased my eyes. It was the only way to make Ezra believe we didn't do anything. Sure, we hadn't slept together, but Damien's cock was in my mouth and he was between my legs—two things I'm sure would put my older brother into an early grave if he found out.

"Sophie, Damien is the last man on earth you should be with. I need you to hear me on that." My brother's words were so cold that my lips parted in shock. I peeked around him and saw Damien's eyes drop to the floor.

"That's rude to say, especially in front of him, Ezra," I fired back, sadness pooling in my belly.

"It's not rude if it's the truth. Damien knows it, too. He has too many fucking demons inside him to ever be good to a woman." Ezra turned back and looked at Damien. "And for the record, if you ever touch or look at my little sister the wrong way, Damien... every ounce of our professional and personal relationships will be set on fire."

He lifted his head. "I can fuck any woman I want to. Why would I pick some college brat who cries over everything and wouldn't know what to do with me, anyway?" he scoffed arrogantly.

There he is. The real Damien. My heart cracked with his cruel words.

"Enough, Damien," Ezra warned. "Get your clothes, Sophie. I'm taking you home. I'm going down to my car; meet me there." My brother stormed into the elevator, shooting daggers at the both of us until the doors shut.

The silence between us was more uncomfortable than having my brother see me in his best friend's shirt, assuming the worst.

"I need my clothes." I hated how I had to say something to him.

I can fuck any woman I want to? The words rammed into me like a slap of cold air on a winter day.

Damien walked away and I followed him. He opened a door that led to an extremely nice laundry room. He pulled my dress and thong out of the dryer, handing it to me.

He did my laundry? He probably had to have done it past two a.m.

I jerked it out of his hands, not missing the way he stared at my thin lace thong. Storming away, I went back to his room and shut to door, locking it behind me as I angrily tore his shirt off and tugged my tight dress on. I wish I had some sweatpants and my hoodie. I went to his bathroom and turned the light on.

It was the most over-the-top bathroom I'd seen in my life. I was almost tempted to take another shower in his massive, dual-head shower with the best pressure in the universe. I looked at his enormous soaker tub and wondered how many gorgeous women—who knew how to fuck Damien the way he wanted—laid in it with him?

It was true; he and I were on two different playing fields.

I hadn't slept with anyone in a year. I didn't even have any interest in doing it until I met Damien. It wasn't just because he was unnaturally hot; it was the fact that he made me feel safe. He didn't treat me like a fragile doll just because someone else chose to break me.

Safe... something I hadn't felt in a year. But now I knew how he felt. He thought I was some cry-baby college girl who couldn't keep her emotions in check, and after I leave, he'll probably invite someone he had on his frequent flyers fuck-buddy list to come help him with the blue balls I had left him with last night.

Splashing cold water on my face, I turned out of the bathroom and exhaled. Just as I was about to unlock his bedroom door, I froze. I could hear his raised voice, talking to someone on speakerphone.

"Theo only did what I asked him to do. That man didn't deserve a beating; he deserved death. He doesn't have the right to walk the earth," he roared. I couldn't hear the other voice on the phone, but my entire body broke into a cold sweat.

What the hell? Damien had someone murdered? Goosebumps covered my arms, and I looked around his massive bedroom. Should I escape through a window? I'd probably fall to an untimely death, but hey, being stuck in a space with a murderer was a little worse. My phone rang loudly, and Damien immediately stopped talking.

It was Ezra. "Hey—" my voice cracked.

"I've been waiting for fifteen minutes. What the hell is going on up there?" He was pissed, which was unusual for my overly calm older brother.

"Ezra, I think Damien killed someone," I whispered, covering my mouth over the phone with my trembling hands.

"Sophie, you have no idea what you're talking about. Just come down." He hung up, leaving me with my mouth opened in shock.

He was definitely not winning any older brother of the year awards this year. He was leaving me in an apartment with a man, who just talked about having someone killed. *Killed!* Sinking onto the floor, I panicked for what felt like two seconds, but actually became another fifteen minutes, as I paced behind the closed door.

"Sophie?" Damien's voice echoed. I jerked back. I had to face him; I had to run to the elevator and go down to Ezra. Damien wouldn't hurt me knowing my older brother was right downstairs. Blowing out a breath, I slowly opened the door. Damien moved back and his eyes widened as he scanned my body. My nipples hardened at the way his eyes froze over them.

Traitors.

"Ezra's waiting for me." I pinched my lips to a side, hoping the tremble in my body wasn't apparent.

"He just left. Amira got locked out of her car. I'm taking you home," Damien stated.

That's it, Ezra's never getting a Christmas gift from me again. I just told him that Damien may have killed someone, and he brushed me off.

Why did no one take me seriously? When I was dead with Damien next to my body, he'd feel really terrible.

"I'm calling an Uber," I squeaked out, unable to look up at him. I dashed over to the elevator, holding my breath.

A strong grasp around my arm startled me and I turned slowly. "I'll drop you off. You're barely wearing clothes, Soph." His eyes dropped and outlined my entire body.

I wiggled my arm free from him. "Don't call me Soph. I don't need you to protect me when I clearly need to be protected from *you*." I cinched my brows and rolled my lips as I pushed the button for the elevator.

"Whatever you think you heard isn't the truth... because the truth is even worse. This is why I want you to stay away from me. But you're not going anywhere like that." He waved to the opened elevator doors as I forced myself to move inside it.

My entire body was shaking. How could it be worse? I looked over at Damien, who kept his eyes forward. I stood as far away as I could from him, because now the crush I had on him was crumbling in front of my eyes.

Now I was scared of Damien Moretti.

CHAPTER 18

Damien

I watched as Sophie's leg slid over my bike. The way she splayed her legs apart and straddled my bike had my cock jerk. Her perfect ass perched out as I slid in front of her after handing her my helmet.

"I wish you would have just put my damn jacket on," I growled since her entire body was on full display.

"I don't need a collection of your jackets, or you telling me what to wear," she fired back.

"That's right, you already have the one you're cuddling every night." I grabbed her hands from behind and slammed them onto my waist. "Hold on tight, Soph. It's going to be a quick ride," I said, irritated.

"Well, I guess I saved myself the trouble, then," she taunted. My lips twitched and I was thankful I was facing forward.

Smart ass.

I turned my bike on and Sophie's grip tightened around my waist. She leaned in and clung to me, and fuck, if I wasn't tempted to take the long way back to her house.

The conversation she heard...? Well, it should scare her. I just had one of the men involved in Chicago's largest human trafficking rings shot dead in the middle of his dinner. While I defended some criminals who I knew deserved another chance, I also served justice to the ones who didn't deserve it.

And I got a hefty paycheck, too, from the men who had been trying for the past two years to get that mother-fucker off the streets. My line of work was shady, it was dangerous, and most of all, it was deadly.

I couldn't afford to have a weak spot. When your enemies come after you—and they always do—they came for that spot. The spot that folded the easiest. I had plenty of blood on my hands, but Sophie's wouldn't be one of them.

I sped over to her place, which was the world's shortest ride. She jumped off my bike quickly and started walking to her building.

"Sophie..."

"Don't." She waved me off and opened her door. I threw my helmet on and waited until the door shut behind her before I sped off. This was it; I was wiping myself clean of Sophie Shah. Better yet, she was wiping herself clean of me.

I got to Ezra and Amira's place, and thankfully, it was Amira who greeted me.

"Damien…" she trailed. "You said you weren't interested in her; she's nineteen. She's his little sister. She's been through so much." Amira shook her head as I followed her into their living room.

"He's not home, but he's furious with you… with you both," she added and sat across from me.

"Amira, nothing happened. Your fiancé is a fucking drama queen, just like his sister. I saved her from some slimy guy at a frat party and then gave her my bed to sleep in. I didn't touch her."

Lie number one.

"I am not interested in some scrawny, college girl who is buried in her little dental textbooks and studying on the weekends."

Lie number two.

"She's a sweet girl, Damien. It'd be in both of your interests to keep away from one another in that sense. Ezra would never forgive you if you did anything with her, or to her. Damien, you… you only leave destruction behind."

"Yea. I know. Not capable of love, blah, blah, blah," I

said flatly, sinking into the chair and looking at the ceiling.

"Damien, you…" Amira shook her head and looked away. "Forget it."

"What has she been through?" I quickly sat back up and looked at Amira, who immediately stood. She walked to the kitchen, and I stood and followed her. "Amira. What has Sophie been through?" I licked my lips and waited.

"I'm going to get the answer from you or her. So, it might as well be you," I pointed out.

She turned around from the sink. "Damien, I shouldn't say this, but truthfully, the way you looked at her during our dinner made me see something different in your eyes. I know you like her, and I know you want her," she said softly. "I shouldn't be telling you this, but last year, Sophie was…" She stopped as her eyes flicked behind me. "Ezra?" Her voice spiked.

"Moving from my sister to my fiancée, Damien?" Ezra spat out.

"Ezra!" Amira gasped. Ezra's forehead was creased and his fists were clenched. The one man I considered a brother was looking at me with disappointment and fury.

"Can we talk?" I nodded toward their balcony.

"Fine." He walked out and I followed behind. Once we got outside, the warm August air swarmed us.

"I swear to you, nothing happened between your sister and me. I swear, Ezra. I can't believe you are pissed when you're the one who asked me to get her from some shitty frat party; and let me just say, I was about to be knee-fucking-deep in Carmen. You know Carmen, the hot as hell model-turned-attorney? But remind me again why I'd be into your pesky sister? She was over the second night because she was shaken up and didn't want to bother you and Amira." The words tasted bitter on my tongue—the same tongue that was inside Sophie hours ago, making her scream my name. The same tongue that pushed inside her perfect mouth and tasted her, leaving me desperately wanting more.

"I know you didn't. I just... You know, she's had it rough, man. She struggled a lot after my parents died, and then when she finally got to college, I thought her being close to Amira and me would help her, but things really got bad with her. A lot of shit went down and honestly, she's finally got some color back in her life. I just want her to do well, stay healthy, and you know, not have me worried sick." Ezra sank into the patio furniture.

What was he talking about? Besides her snark with me, Sophie seemed like she was all sunshine and butterflies. She was the girl going off to study on a weekend; she was drinking vanilla lattes and carrying a pale pink backpack with a bunch of those cheesy iron-ons all over the canvas. Her wrist always had a stack of those beaded bracelets and the ways she lit up when talking about wedding stuff with Amira made me see her in a different light. She wanted all of that. She wanted the dress, she wanted the romance and the prince charming. She wanted the fairytale. She needed it.

"What happened to her?" I sat next to Ezra and looked at him. The bags under his eyes had deepened. He was rubbing his face the way I'm sure most parents do for their children—and that was Ezra to Sophie. He was the one having to make sure she was okay and taken care of.

"Not my story to tell, man." He slapped my shoulder, and we sat there for the next hour, side by side, staring off at Chicago in front of us.

It had only been four days, but it felt significantly longer. I had to fly to New York for a meeting and had texted Sophie a few times, but she didn't reply. It was embarrassing, but part of me wanted to make sure she was okay. Apparently, Ezra cleaned up my mess after she heard my phone conversation. He didn't want his baby sister thinking his best friend and best man was a sociopath. *Or a murderer.*

I walked to the coffee stand two hours earlier than I was supposed to be at work, but I knew it was when she had class. "Hey, Leo."

"Where you been, brother?" Leo poured a large coffee for me—black, with no cream and no sugar. The first time I found Sophie here, I drank what she was having—a vanilla latte—and I thought I was going to be admitted for a diabetic attack.

"I went to New York for work," I replied running my hand across my face.

Leo nodded. "Your girl just got her coffee with her boyfriend."

My chest tightened.

"Her boyfriend?" I repeated. "Sophie came here with a guy?" My fist clenched tighter.

Leo laughed and shook his head. "Yes. Now move, brother, there's a line behind you." He pointed to the caffeine-deprived customers behind me.

CHAPTER 19

Sophie

Reese, Zach, and I walked to campus with Leo's delicious vanilla lattes in hand. "Did you hear Tanner transferred out of Jesson?" Reese took a sip and looked at me.

I had told them both everything that went down at the fraternity party. Reese felt horrible that she had left me alone to hook up with some guy, but it wasn't her fault. Tanner should have known better. I hate how, as women, we are groomed to think we shouldn't have dressed a certain way, we shouldn't have danced with a certain guy, we shouldn't have flirted. It's not our fault when some men make the choice to be egomaniacs and attackers.

"Wait... he transferred?" I stopped in the middle of the quad and looked at her.

"Yeah. Apparently, he was given two options: transfer or be murdered," she whispered over her steaming coffee.

"What?" Zach and I said simultaneously.

"Okay, so the murder part was a presumption, but plausible." Reese shrugged.

"Who... who made this all happen?" My mouth felt dry. Zach looked between Reese and me.

"I don't know. Maybe Ezra's scorching hot bestie?" Reese lifted her brow but didn't say anything further as Zach gripped his backpack straps.

"I have to get to class, but I'll see you both later." He caught on that we were entering best-friend-confidential-level conversation.

"Bye, Zach. I'll definitely be up to studying this evening at the library if you're around." I waved my fingers at him.

"Yea, of course. See ya, ladies." He flashed his perfect smile at us and walked off.

When he was no longer in an earshot, Reese looked at me. "Damien made a call to the dean—like, the fucking Dean of Jesson University—and said if he didn't expel or transfer Tanner out, then he'd blast the school on every media outlet and file the biggest lawsuit possible." She was talking so quickly, and my heart rate matched her urgency.

"What?" I whispered. "I didn't know." I licked my bottom lip. "Why would he do that?" I rubbed my arms and looked at Reese.

"Girl, please. He clearly has a thing for you." A mischievous grin emerged on her face. "When you guys fuck for the first time, please use the daddy kink. I'm talkin' 'Ooh, spank me hard, daddy!'" she bellowed, and a few students turned their heads at us.

"Reese!" I screeched and grabbed her arm to tuck mine in. "Shh!"

She erupted into laughter, taking my mortification to the next level.

"We are *never*... having sex," I whispered. "He's Ezra's best friend and also a complete ass." I nodded.

Reese's laugh started to fade as her eyes widened to something behind me. Turning my head swiftly, I swallowed the lump in my throat.

It wasn't a something... it was a *someone*.

A very angry-looking Damien Moretti was cutting through the quad in a full three-piece suit. Girls froze with their mouths hung low, and guys stopped and stared, probably questioning their khaki shorts and polo button-downs.

Reese let out a low whistle behind me. "Not going to have sex, my ass... He's coming for you, baby girl. Just remember to tell daddy to spank you real good because you've been so *naughty.*" Reese shoved me toward Damien and darted off.

"Sophie." Damien stood tall in front of me, his shadow consuming me in the middle of campus.

I tilted my head back to look up at him. "Damien."

"Who's your boyfriend?" he asked, his voice gruff and ragged.

"What?" I squinted at him. Letting out a small laugh, I turned, waving him off. "You have to be kidding me." I started to walk away but felt his hand wrap around mine as he turned me around. "Damien! What are you doing here?"

His eyes dropped as he shamelessly studied every bit of my body, stopping at my breasts and then back up.

A ditzy student came up to us with her cheeks flushed. "Are you single?"

"No. I have a girl." Damien didn't even look her way.

A girl? Was he talking about me? I couldn't help but bite back a smile.

"What?" he eyed me carefully.

"Most guys say, *'Sorry,* I have a girl.' I like how you just said no, even though I don't know who your girl is..." I taunted.

A small smirk grew on his face. "I didn't know you wore glasses." His face softened as if my Warby Parker's had extinguished a blazing fire around him.

Fidgeting with them, I looked away. I was wearing ripped jeans and a Maroon 5 concert T-shirt with a giant image of Adam Levine across my chest.

"I usually wear contacts, but I was in a rush this morning to meet—" I stopped when I noticed the fire in him was relit.

Damien's eyes dropped to my lips, and I swore they grew darker. "Finish the sentence, Soph. To meet who?" His voice was so low, it sent a chill up my spine.

"Reese. You just saw her running because she clearly thought you were a mobster cutting through campus." I pointed to the perfectly-tailored, deep navy suit that fit the man like a damn glove. The airheads behind us in the quad had their eyes parked on what I assumed was his ass.

"Just Reese?" he said it like a question, but really, it was more like a test.

"Mm-hmm..." The last thing I needed was him putting a hit on innocent Zach. "Well, if you'll excuse me, I need to get to class, and you need to go film the next *Godfather* movie." I bit my bottom lip as a smirk curved on his.

Leaning in closer to me, his hand brushed against my arm. "I have never been more jealous of Adam Levine in my entire life." He pulled back as my mouth parted, and

I looked down at my T-shirt, where Adam's face was all over my chest.

He turned around and left, but I swear, that man took the air from my lungs with him.

* * *

I had back-to-back classes for the next five hours. By the end of my last class, I considered dropping this whole pre-dental gig. My brain was fried. I had so much studying to do, and I really needed to talk to my advisor about shadowing dentists and whatever else I was already behind on.

Walking toward the side exit of campus to head back to my apartment, I stopped and clutched my textbooks closer to my chest. My glasses were sliding down my nose, I had thrown my long hair into a messy bun, and my face felt sticky from the end of August humidity.

Damien Moretti was still in his suit, leaning against his motorcycle with black aviators on and his arms crossed.

He straightened when I walked closer. "Hey, need a ride?" He came closer and opened his hands.

I looked down at them and arched my brow. "I'm not giving you a hug."

He let out a loud laugh and shook his head. "I was

trying to help you with your textbooks." Then, if my heart couldn't beat any faster, he reached forward and pushed my glasses up on my face.

I stepped back. "I'm just going to walk."

"Sophie, please. Let me give you a ride."

"Oh, my goodness... Mr. Moretti are you actually *asking* me? You usually just try to tell me what to do."

"Very funny, now get on." He grabbed my textbooks and slid them into the seat. Students walking by slowed their paces to just watch us. I mean, we probably looked absolutely ridiculous together. I was a walking ad for a college nerd, and he was the walking ad for Versace's next cologne line.

"I'm starving," I said as I climbed onto his bike and put my arms around him. Oddly, it felt normal, and the anxiety I usually had started to float away. It felt... right, even though I knew it was so damn wrong.

Handing me his helmet, I slid it on as he turned his bike on and off we went.

The sun was starting to set as we pulled up to Bellucini's. "Okay, you're actually crazy. I am beyond underdressed for this place." I watched women in stunning dresses and men wearing basically what Damien had on walk through the golden doors of the upscale restaurant.

"You're perfect. Let's go eat." He reached his hand out, and something about the way he said that statement with ease, and with no hesitation, made me believe his words. I slid off his bike and pulled my glasses off my face. Before we got to the front door, I tripped and nearly fell, but Damien quickly broke my fall.

"Sophie, are you okay?" He steadied me as I blinked, my vision too blurry. Taking my glasses out of my hands, he slid them back on my face.

"Stop worrying about how others perceive you. I told you, you're perfect. It's time you actually listened to me for once." He bent his elbow, and I looked up, lacing my arm into his.

Walking through, I tried stopping at the hostess, but she simply nodded as Damien and I walked past.

We got to a table in the corner, lit by a candle with a single peony sitting in the center. "Did you already have this reservation for yourself?" I asked as I sank into the chair he had pulled out for me.

"No." He unbuttoned his suit jacket and sat across from me. His stunning eyes pierced into mine. "I made the reservation for *us* after I left campus." He lifted his menu and began to read it as my breathing hitched.

Us. One simple word that altered the entire course of our relationship.

CHAPTER 20

Damien

We ordered our meals and drinks in silence that felt misplaced. Usually, Sophie didn't have a problem with finding some snark-filled thing to say or some random story to spiral into. Sophie looked beautiful. She barely had any makeup on, her natural tanned skin had this glow to it, and her raven-dark hair was splayed all over her shoulders. I couldn't help but grin at the ridiculous baggy Maroon 5 T-shirt she was wearing with ripped jeans, or how her wrist was stacked with the usual colorful, tiny-beaded bracelets.

Meanwhile, I was in a Dolce & Gabbana tailored three-piece suit with my Rolex wrapped around my wrist.

"Are you liking Jesson?" I laced my fingers together

and tried to fill the silent tension that floated between us. The air felt different, almost suffocating.

"Yeah, it's fine. This year is better than last year. I just need to stay on top..." She paused at my grin. "On top of things, *like school*, you perv," she added with a small grin.

"I didn't say anything," I replied, rubbing my chin.

"Oh please, you didn't have to." She waved her fork at my expression. I let out a laugh and shook my head. Sophie brought out a side of me where laughter was possible.

"Can you believe Amira and Ezra are getting married so soon?" Sophie wiped her mouth after taking a bite of her meal.

"No. I can't believe your brother is that stupid."

"What?" Sophie's brows furrowed as she looked at me with irritation.

"Marriage is useless. It's a legal contract, binding you to someone until you get sick of them or they get sick of you," I answered, my voice laced with the harsh reality.

"Well, you won't have to worry about that, since every woman probably gets sick of you before you even have the opportunity to drop down on one knee. No woman would want you on your knees, anyway," she fired back.

I had to bite back the smirk to her quick wit. No, I couldn't give her that satisfaction.

Drawing in closer, I licked my bottom lip. "There's only one reason for anyone to drop down to their knees and usually, I'm not on mine."

Sophie's cheeks flushed and her eyes plummeted down to her almost finished plate. "I had you on your knees..." she whispered with a wink. I couldn't help but let out a laugh, shaking my head at the fire in her.

"I want to get married one day, I think..." she murmured, as if she was speaking to herself.

"I know," I answered. Deep down, my blood curled, imagining another man on his knees in front of her, promising her things I knew with certainty he'd never keep.

"Can I ask you something?" She looked up at me after finishing a bite of pasta.

I placed my fork down and eyed her carefully. "Depends."

"Why does it depend?" she asked.

"I'm an attorney. I have client-attorney privilege, so I can't always share things. Then you throw in the mob life I'm living according to you..." I kept my face straight.

"Ha. You could do stand-up." She rolled her eyes at me.

I leaned in, placing my elbows on the table and filled the large gap between us. "Keep rolling your eyes, sweetheart, and daddy will have to spank you." I pulled away and winked at her as her cheeks flushed.

I loved the lust in Sophie's big brown eyes that she desperately tried to hold back whenever something sexual came up between us. It was fucking palpable.

"The phone call... the one where you said some guy deserved *d-e-a-t-h*."

"Sophie, I'm certain one hundred percent of the restaurant guests here know how to spell the word death." I looked at her as she pursed her lips.

"Stop being a smart ass." She took another bite.

"If you think I was a part of something like that, then why are you sitting with me and eating dinner? Shouldn't you be scared?" I raised an eyebrow and watched as she kept her eyes fixed on her plate before lifting those chocolate brown eyes at me.

"Do you know what fear is, Damien?" The way my name rolled off her tongue had something tighten in my chest. Before I could speak, she parted those thick pink lips again. "It's a negative emotion caused by the belief that someone is dangerous and likely to cause you pain." She clasped her hands together. "And you'd never do that to me," she said confidently.

"How are you so certain about that?" I asked as curiosity coursed through me.

"Because you don't just care about me, Damien; you want me. You *need* me. That's why you can't stay away."

My jaw ticked. "That's where you're wrong, sweetheart. I don't need or want anyone. You sucked my cock once, and you don't see me begging for more, do you?" The words tasted bitter as soon as I said them, but I couldn't have her believing I'd ever pursue her. I couldn't, for so many reasons.

This time she placed her elbows on the table and kept her face emotionless. "You don't fool me with your bad boy front. You like me."

Breathing out, I looked at her carefully. I knew what was spinning inside that pretty little head of hers. I knew how she was the girl you hooked up with, did things for, and she felt all the damn feels. I knew she was the girl who closed her eyes and saw the white dress, the kiss, the dream.

The only problem was, I didn't make dreams come true—only nightmares. But I also wasn't a liar and couldn't say I didn't care for her or like her because in this black heart of mine, I did. I liked Sophie Shah far more than I should; I cared for her enough to test the limits of my best friendship and potentially shatter it.

Except, I wouldn't cross any more boundaries. Dinner was different. I'd never touch her the way my fingers and body craved. I'd never know what she felt like wrapped around my cock.

"What happened to you last year?" I spat out, hoping to divert her attention from the psycho-analysis she thought she was doing.

The confidence and feistiness she usually had embedded across her face melted as soon as I asked. "What? Who said something happened to me? Did Ezra tell you something?" Her voice shifted with anger and panic. It was my job to read expressions and find the truth between the façade. Usually, Sophie had a damn good poker face, but right now, every emotion was painted across her face.

"No, he didn't tell me anything, which is why I'm asking you." I shook my suit jacket and straightened my spine.

"I don't owe you a thing, especially not anything about my personal life." She took a long sip and looked away.

"Did someone hurt you? Sophie, I'll kill them if they did. I'll fucking ruin them. Just tell me," I demanded. Her eyes locked on mine and filled with tears. "What's his fucking name?" I clenched my fist.

She shook her head as a tear dribbled down her soft skin. Reaching across, I wiped it away with my thumb and she pressed her face into my palm.

"I don't want to talk about this here. Please."

"I care about you, Sophie; and hell, I might even like you a little bit." I tried to lighten her mood, and the small half-smile that grew on her face made the brick wall around me crumble slightly. *Really, I need to know so I can make sure the motherfucker never shares the same air as her again.*

"It's just... I need to know who the reason behind the tears are so I can make sure he sheds more before I take his last breath." My jaw clenched as she stared at me.

Tilting her head slightly, she sighed. "Damien..."

"Sophie, just tell me. Please."

"Take me home, and I'll tell you the second worst thing in my life." She sniffled as I immediately waved down the waitress for our bill. *I know the first was losing her parents.*

The waitress brought over a to-go bag, and Sophie looked between our basically clear plates.

"What's in the bag?" she asked curiously, wiping underneath her eyes.

"The first time we met at Bistro Le Petit, you were eating their triple-layer chocolate cake. This is a seven-layer chocolate cake. You deserve the best Sophie. Only the best."

Her eyes shot up to mine and her chest rose and fell faster. "Damien..." She swallowed and stood.

"Let's go home," I replied and bent my arm for her to take.

Time stood still as we drove back to Sophie's apartment. She wanted to go back to her place, and I figured she wanted to feel in control of the environment when she told me a story that clearly happened outside of her control.

She clung to me tightly as I weaved in and out of traffic as her cheek rested against my back. The simple gesture made my breathing unstable. I didn't know what I was opening by asking Sophie to tell me everything that had happened to her last year and how it changed her. Ezra said Sophie used to have a huge group of friends when she started at Jesson; she was even on the cheerleading team, which I couldn't imagine because she seemed so consumed by her books and school. She changed. But she didn't choose to; some asshole chose for her.

I wanted to know everything I could about what had happened so I could make sure I chose what I was going to do with him.

It'd probably involve me killing him with my bare hands or ripping his spine out... if he even had one.

I parked my bike and took my helmet off. Sophie slid hers off and looked at me for a moment.

"What?" I tilted my head and ran my hand through my hair.

"You have two helmets." She didn't break our stare.

"I figured since I was basically your Uber driver now, I didn't want my head to crack open. Because then who would drive you around?" I shrugged it off, but the way she looked at me, I knew she was diving so damn deep into it all. Smiling, she slid off with my help. And shockingly, she didn't slap my hand off her.

CHAPTER 21

Sophie

I changed into my soft PJ shorts and tank top, then washed my face before coming back into the small but cute living room. Damien was sitting there with his suit jacket off, slowly untying his tie.

His eyes flicked to me, and my nipples hardened as I felt them drift to my white tank and lack of a bra. "It's cold." I pointed to the air conditioning above my head, trying to use it as an excuse to why my nipples decided to harden as soon as his eyes touched them.

"So cold," he said flatly with a cocky grin. "Sophie, come here." He brushed the spot next to him on my couch. "I don't want us to do what we always do. Banter, go at it, and bicker... I want you to tell me about last year." His voice shifted completely. He wasn't the usual Damien who mocked me, drove me crazy, yet made my body basically convulse. He was calm and concerned.

I swallowed and tugged the fuzzy blanket over my legs and curled in. Damien didn't take his piercing eyes off me.

Exhaling slowly, I swiped my tongue across my lip. This moment felt far more intimate between us than anything else. I wanted his lips on mine, I wanted him to hold me... but ultimately, it was so intimate because I was about to open my soul to Damien Moretti.

"I was dating a guy from school for a while. We met during my freshman year, and he was..." I paused and closed my eyes. The memories I had tried my best to erase and eradicate from my entire being were surfacing and causing anxiety to pool inside me.

Until I felt Damien's hand on mine, holding it.

"I thought you didn't hold hands with anyone?" I whispered with my eyes still clenched shut.

"You're not just anyone. I want to hold yours, Soph. It's an honor to hold yours." His voice was so buttery smooth, and I was certain he could tell how rapidly my heart was beating.

For him.

"He was sweet at first. He meshed well with my friends, seemed ambitious enough, respected my goals and dreams. Ezra and Amira even approved of him, initially. But then there was a shift in him. Once we moved in together, he flipped a switch. He got more comfortable with yelling at me over the smallest things, and I'd notice his fist clenching whenever we'd fight. I just never thought it would get to the point it did..." I shuddered but didn't stop. If I stopped, I wouldn't be able to finish this story I never thought I'd tell again.

"Reese was over, and we were studying for our upcoming exams. He came home from work and classes, and he started bickering with me. Reese was used to our bickering at this point and thought nothing of it. She had begged me to break up with him, but I couldn't. I was scared to break up with him because I thought I loved him. I thought loving someone meant loving them during their worst and their best. I just didn't know that when love breaks us, we're supposed to let go." Tears started to trickle out of my eyes, and without hesitation, Damien wiped them away.

"Soph..." he started, but I shook my head and held his hand to my face, not wanting him to move away.

"Reese left to go grab some food for us, but as soon as she did, my ex-boyfriend started yelling louder and then... he hit me." I rolled my lips together as my eyes shut. Damien's breathing changed; it was as if he was holding it because anger was pooling inside him.

"He hit me again and again. I tried to block him. I tried to fight back; I tried to run. He was bigger and stronger than me, and he pinned me against the wall and slammed my skull so hard that I blacked out." I started to cry harder and slapped my hand over my mouth to stifle the sobs.

Damien was quiet. His jaw was clenched and his breathing grew shallow. I looked at him slowly, and his eyes darkened, his lips parted, and his heart was beating rapidly through his vest and dress shirt.

"Reese found me with blood everywhere. They took me to the hospital and did all the tests." I covered my face and cried harder.

"He tried to kill me." I flipped my wrist, sliding off the stack of beaded bracelets I wore in front of everyone besides Reese, Ezra, and Amira. Damien's gaze jolted downward, and his eyes slanted as I showed him the cut marks against my right arm near the veins. "He wanted to try to make it look like a suicide, I guess." I stared down at the scars—the ones I hated, the ones embedded in my flesh that no amount of scar cream or plastic surgery could remediate.

"Sophie..." Damien breathed out and lifted my wrist. He kissed every cut and goosebumps flew across my arms as the tears dribbled down my cheeks.

"My sweet, Sophie." He pressed his forehead against

mine and ran his hands through my hair, holding my head on both sides.

"Baby, I'm going to rip his spine out. I'm going to break every finger that touched you and then I'm going to kill him." Then, without any other words or questions, he pressed his lips to mine.

The kiss turned deep, hungry, and possessive. He was turning my pain into pleasure. He was rewriting my story—not for me, but *with* me. Climbing onto his lap, he gripped my hips as his lips locked with mine. His tongue pushed into my mouth as I groaned. Pausing, he pulled away. "Sophie, I don't want to do this if you're feeling vulnerable, and... I don't know how to be gentle." He stared into my eyes. He was scared that rough sex or being intimate would trigger me.

I didn't choose what my ex-boyfriend did to me, and I didn't want him to be a reason I changed what I wanted.

And now, I wanted more. I wanted to feel Damien inside me, deep and connected. I didn't want to think about the pain. I wanted to free myself.

"Damien, I want you to fuck me, and I don't want you to be gentle. I want to feel everything and feel alive."

Just like that, he peeled my shirt from my body and kept his gaze on my bare skin. The heat between my legs grew as my heartbeat quickened.

His mouth trailed down my neck while his teeth bit into my delicate skin, and I couldn't help but toss my head back and moan.

Popping up on my knees, he peeled my shorts down. This was really going to happen. I was going to have sex with Damien Moretti. I was going to have sex for the first time in over a year.

I crawled over to his lap and pushed him back onto the couch. He was still dressed in his vest, dress pants, and shirt. Grinding across his hardened crotch, he gripped my hips and rocked me over him, back and forth. The friction alone made me wet.

"Sophie..." he breathed out as I quickly unbuttoned his shirt, leaving his muscular abdomen on full display. His gray silk tie hung loosely around his neck. With my eyes on his, I undid his belt, and tugging in one swift motion, the *crack* of his belt being the only reason we both blinked.

He quickly unzipped his pants, and I sat up enough for him to slide them down. Our breathing was heavier, the desire to devour each other plunging within us. His cock sprung out and the thick, wide tip teased me. Pulling my face closer to his, Damien kissed me hungrily as his tongue swept against mine and our breathing stilled.

"Damien," I moaned as he rubbed his tip against my

folds. I was dripping wet for him. I couldn't wait any longer, I wanted him to fuck me. I *needed* him to.

"Sophie, wait. Wait..." He brushed his thumb across my bottom lip. He kissed my forehead before pressing his against mine.

"I can't do this right now." He mumbled against my lips.

I didn't know what emotion I was feeling. Anger? Sadness? Annoyance?

My body was tense and pulsing against his. "Please?" I pleaded.

"No, no...baby, don't beg. If anyone's begging for you it's me. I can't because what you just told me has my mind only fixated on how I'm going to kill the boy who touched you and hurt you. I can't do this right now because I'm terrified that this time, it'll be a man to disappoint you."

"Don't do this." I winced as he cupped my face in his palms.

"I'm protecting you, Soph, from another monster." His voice shook before his lips locked onto mine once more. He held me in his arms as I rested my head against his shoulder. An hour came and went as we sat there. His fingers raked against my back. I could tell he was writing something across my skin with his fingertips.

"What did you write?" I looked up at him through my lashes.

"I'm sorry." He sighed.

"Why are you sorry?" I closed my eyes.

Kissing my eyelids, he whispered, "because I wish I could be the man you deserved after that piece of shit. But please know, I'm going to burn the entire world down until I find him." Damien tucked a straggling piece of hair behind my ear.

"You wouldn't be scared to see the entire world burn over one man?"

"No I wouldn't be, as long as you're still standing. I don't care what I have to do to make sure the one who hurt you, hurts even more." He replied without hesitation.

My heart tightened at his words and then as I parted my lips, his phone rang.

No, no, no. Don't answer.

His head tilted in the direction of the ring, and I grabbed his face, bringing it back toward mine. "Don't you dare..." I whispered and kissed him.

It kept ringing, as if the cock-blocker on the other end of the line wouldn't let up.

"It's my personal phone, and very few people have it. I have to answer, Soph," he breathed out and slowly moved me off his lap.

What the hell? Sinking my teeth into my lower lip, I held my breath. My thighs clenched together as my arousal turned into anger, even though I had the perfect view of his ass, which was ridiculously toned.

"Carmen?" he answered.

Carmen?

Wasn't that a woman he worked with? Amira mentioned her to me when she thought I was crushing on Damien. Good grief, if she could see me now. I cringed and threw Damien's T-shirt back on my body. Meanwhile, Adonis was happily chatting away with his rock-hard cock and body on full display.

He hung up the phone and looked down at me. "Sophie... I'm so sorry, my friend needs me. It's an emergency."

Hot tears stung my eyes as embarrassment hung over my head like a storm cloud.

"Your *friend*? Does your friend happen to be a woman?" I stood and shook my head, irritated beyond belief.

"Sophie, don't be like that," he said casually as he picked his pants up from the floor.

"Be like what?" I fired back.

"Needy." His voice was arrogant and confident, which made me want to slap the flat look off his stupidly gorgeous face.

I angrily slid my pants back on. "Needy?" I mocked in shock, letting out a forced laugh and slapping my thigh to add the extra flair of dramatics.

"Yes. We aren't dating, and honestly, maybe the universe is telling us we shouldn't be doing this because obviously, you won't be able to handle the aftermath."

My jaw physically dropped, and I'm pretty sure like those cartoon characters, steam was coming out of my ears.

"I know we aren't dating, you ass-hat." I shoved his suit jacket to his chest and rolled my eyes as I walked past him.

"Point proven," he said calmly, which only burned more fury into my body.

Flinging around, I spewed out, "What?"

"You just called me an ass-hat because I need to leave, when five minutes ago, I was rubbing my cock against your dripping wet pussy." He tied his tie and looked at me, but I broke his gaze because my thighs clenched together as I grew wetter just from his damn dirty words.

"You are vile." I shook my head and opened my door. Waving my hand outside, I pouted as he stood still.

"Sophie."

"Damien, go see your girlfriend, Carmen." I knew how immature I sounded, but who wouldn't? The tip of his dick was literally about to penetrate me, and he picked up her call and left me to go to *her*.

"I'm so sorry about what happened, and I appreciate you telling me. I will go to the ends of the earth to make sure he pays. But...I'm not worthy of you." He shook his head and left, and I slammed the door behind him.

Piling onto the floor, I held my knees to my chest and buried my face in between. "Ass-hat," I whispered under my breath.

CHAPTER 22

Damien

Two weeks had come and gone, and it was brutal in ways I never thought it would be. After talking to Carmen the night I was at Sophie's, and later meeting up with her, I learned that someone from my past was hunting me and waiting to find my weak spot. He wanted to make sure I paid for ruining his life. I was being followed, meaning someone knew where I was. Worst of all, they knew *who* I was with. I couldn't afford to have a weak spot, and I sure wasn't going to drag Sophie to hell with me. I had to protect her.

So, I avoided the coffee stand and I avoided the direction of Jesson University. I avoided the invitations to Amira and Ezra's for dinner, knowing she'd probably be there. I avoided the box that was left with my doorman that had my leather jacket in it and pretended I didn't hold the damn thing to my nose, inhaling it because it now carried her scent instead of my own. I pretended to exist like I had before I met that fucking beautiful firecracker.

I defended my clients, I dealt with my side business, and just pretended I didn't think about her. Pretended I didn't think about her every fucking day.

I had a dinner meeting with Carmen again since she had more information I needed. She had inside men who could follow the man after me so it would never trace back to me. I didn't want to involve Ezra, especially because of Amira being an easy target. My dinner with Carmen wasn't sexual; it was strictly business. Not only did she have information for me that couldn't be sent through e-mail or phone calls, but she was also taking over a case for me because the client wanted a female attorney due to the nature of the case, and I wanted to brief her on everything before handing it over.

Pulling up, I fixed my leather jacket, which I almost considered throwing out because I couldn't stop smelling it like an idiot. But there I was, wearing it and her scent on me like a serial killer and his souvenir.

"Hey, handsome." Carmen smiled. "It's been a while... you know after you stood me up, half-naked," she purred. She was wearing a fitted red dress with her tits spilling out. Her hair pinned up, exposing most of her upper body.

"Well, something needed me more than your pussy." I shrugged and Carmen laughed.

When, in reality, it wasn't something that needed me... more so, *someone.*

"Anyway, tell me about the Jefferson case." She took a sip of her wine. I started discussing all the nitty-gritty details about the case and how I thought was best to handle it. Carmen listened carefully as we both cut into our meals.

Just as I went to take a sip of my drink, my eyes met a pair of magnetic, chocolate ones.

Sophie.

And she wasn't alone.

She was sitting across from some blond guy wearing a damn oxford button-down and khakis.

A bouquet of flowers laid neatly beside their plates. Wine was ordered, which was ridiculous, considering she couldn't even legally drink. Rage coursed through me, knowing he was getting her drunk.

Her eyes stayed on mine, then flicked to the back of Carmen's head. Rolling her lips and quickly shifting her eyes back to the man in front of her, she pretended to laugh at something he said.

She was wearing a flowy, yellow dress, with her long

dark hair straight down her back. She laughed again, this time leaning in with her chin resting in her palm and her tits squeezing together so the bastard could have a full access pass to them.

I clenched my fist so tightly that my knuckles turned white. "Damien? Did you hear what I said?" Carmen opened her hands, frustrated.

"Carmen, I'll be right back," I interrupted her and stood quickly, adjusting my jacket. Walking over to their table, I towered over them both. "Sophie."

Her eyes grew wide, and she immediately looked back at her date. Reaching her hand to his—and completely ignoring me—she said, "Sorry, Zach, what were you saying?"

Zach. All I need now is a last name so I know what to have engraved on his tombstone.

"Oh, do you know each other?" He pointed his finger between us as he looked up at me.

"Actually, yeah. Move," I demanded, tugging his chair out.

"What?" His eyebrows raised, and Sophie's jaw dropped.

"No, don't move, Zach. He's a psychopath." She shot daggers at me with her eyes.

"If you don't move, I'll have you chopped up like the

meat on your fucking plate." My voice dropped as I looked at *Zach*.

"What? No. I'm not going to leave her here with you..."

How *chivalrous*.

"Sophie, may I speak with you privately?" I feigned politeness.

"No." She threw her napkin onto the table and kept her eyes on the soon-to-be dead guy in front of her. Zach moved his chair closer to her and put his arm around her shoulder. He planted a kiss on her cheek, which clearly, took her by surprise.

"Do you want to get a to-go bag and head back to my place?" Zach asked her.

What he didn't realize was the only thing leaving in a bag was not his food, but him in a fucking body bag.

I exhaled a long breath and went back to Carmen. "Sorry, my friend's bratty sister is in trouble, and I have to take her home. See you soon." I winked at her and threw a stack of cash down before going back to Sophie.

"Damien!" she called out and shook her head. I made my way back to sort out the bigger issue in front of us.

"Sophie." I eyed her as my jaw twitched.

"Damien." She shook her head at me.

"Let's go." I swallowed and she crossed her arms

across her chest—and surprise, surprise, Zach's eyes went straight to her cleavage again.

He's going to die. Instead of committing murder over the cheesecake that Sophie most definitely didn't like, I scooped Sophie up and flung her over my shoulder.

"What the hell, man?" her date called as I carried Sophie out, who was kicking and punching my shoulder.

"Damien! Put me down," she squealed.

"She's fine, everyone. Just needs a spanking!" I waved to the guests who were eyeing us. Women flushed red and their dates smiled, admiring me.

Yes, I know. *Prince fucking Charming over here, folks.*

Once we got outside, the early September air hit our skin and I put her down. She immediately turned to go back to the door, but I pulled her into me and spun her around to the wall.

Planting one hand by her face and the other on her waist, I looked down at her.

"What are you doing?" she fumed.

"You let him touch you."

"He kissed my cheek! He's my friend! We weren't on a date; he's my study partner. Might I remind you of what you said earlier; we aren't dating, you psycho!" she cried out, shoving her palms against my chest without making an impact.

"The problem is, Soph, your body isn't to give to any

other man," I growled at her, moving my hand up from her waist. Her breathing grew faster, and I pushed my finger into her mouth.

"You're mine," I rasped as she sucked my finger with her eyes wide.

"You've always been mine, my beautiful, sweet little dandelion," I whispered in her ear, dropping my lips to her neck and biting her flesh.

She moaned and tossed her head back, giving me more access to her. I trailed my tongue down, then made my way right back up.

Aligning my mouth onto hers, I rasped, "All mine." She sucked in my air, and I pushed my tongue into her mouth, turning her head and kissing her with everything inside me. Pressing my hardening cock against her stomach, she moaned again.

I moved my hand under her short dress and peeled the thin material to the side. I swiped the finger she just sucked against her dripping pussy.

Taking my finger, I pushed it into my mouth and sucked. "So, fucking sweet." I licked my bottom lip.

Someone walked past us, and Sophie froze. "Damien..." she whispered.

"Let's go." I pushed her dress down and tugged her toward my bike.

"Sophie?" Zach called out as we got to my bike.

"Zach, I'm sorry. This is my..." She paused and looked up at me.

"Her man," I replied flatly. A light chill rippled through the evening air, and Sophie rubbed her arms. Zach quickly tore his jacket off to hand to her as I peeled mine off.

She flicked her eyes between us. "Whoever wears my jacket and rides my bike... rides me next," I whispered into her ear. Her cheeks warmed as she shyly glanced up at me, sinking her teeth into her bottom lip. I slid my jacket over her arms, soaking in the pleasure.

"I'll see you at school. I'm so sorry. I..." Sophie looked at the useless guy in front of her.

"No, it's fine. I knew we were just friends. I just wanted to make sure he wasn't trying to kill you, that's why I kissed your cheek." His cheeks reddened.

Poor fucker.

"The only person I'll kill is you, Zach. Keep your dirty, slimy lips and hands to yourself. If I see your eyes drop to any part of her that's only mine to look at, I'll gouge those baby blues that I'm sure all the ladies love out."

"Damien!" Sophie protested.

I revved my bike and took off as Sophie gripped me.

The world felt right. For once in my life, it didn't feel suffocating.

CHAPTER 23

Sophie

We sped through traffic as the wind brushed against my bare arms. The dark night sky was highlighted by the twinkling stars, and my heart was racing.

The adrenaline rush on the back of his bike was unreal.

What was I doing? What was happening? It had been two long weeks. Two weeks where I lagged behind and hoped I'd bump into him at the coffee stand. Two weeks of going to Ezra and Amira's, where they reassured me that Damien wasn't a killer, but that he had a very dark line of work and I needed to stay away.

Except, I didn't want to.

The more Ezra warned me and the more Amira coaxed me, the more I wanted him. I mean, he literally left me dripping wet and held me when I shared the worst details of my life with him. I knew he wasn't running from me; he was running from something else, I just didn't know who or what. I knew he cared. I knew he felt something because I felt, too.

We got back to his penthouse faster than humanly possible. Once in the elevator, he cornered me and lifted my dress, sliding his fingers inside me, pumping them in and out with his eyes staring straight into mine. He gripped both of my wrists in one hand and held them over my head. I felt so vulnerable and exposed, even with clothes on. His lips crashed into mine, but the kiss wasn't sweet, it wasn't delicate or innocent.

It was savage, possessive, and dominating.

The elevator doors opened and his hands dropped from mine, leaving me wet as I clenched my thighs together.

"Come." His cold and heavy voice matched his eyes.

"I intend to," I fired back and stalked behind him as we moved to his bedroom. The skyline was lit up, reflecting into his bedroom from the windows running across the wall.

Throwing his jacket off, he pulled his shirt off, revealing his perfect abs and chiseled body. The 'V' running down taunted me as I grew closer. I reached down and tugged his belt off, then unzipped his pants.

"There's two places a good girl belongs..." he started, and I looked up at him curiously. "On her back or on her knees. You're my good girl, right, Sophie?"

With a small obedient smirk, I dropped to my knees as I pulled his jeans and briefs down. His huge cock sprung out, and while I had taken a mental picture of it, I must have forgotten the enormity of it.

I'm talking Dasani water bottle huge. Girth, width, length...it was the entire package.

Grabbing a fistful of my hair, he positioned me in front of him, and I looked up at him.

"I'm sorry. I actually think I'm just too innocent and pure, Mr. Moretti..." I whispered and batted my eyelashes.

"Well, sweetheart, that's a good thing because I'm going to ruin you." He pushed his cock into my opened mouth, guiding me up and down his length until he hit the back of my throat, making me gag. I groped his heavy balls with my freehand as I licked every vein on his dick. "Fuck, you're such a good girl." He tossed his head back, which only made me pick up my pace.

"Baby... slow down," he breathed out, pulling me off. "I want to feel you. I want to feel every bit of you shake and come on my cock. Do you want that?" He lifted me from the floor.

"Yes." I bit into my bottom lip as he groaned and untied my dress, letting it pool on the floor.

He traced my body with his eyes, shamelessly and possessively. "Get on the bed and spread your legs for me, my sweet dandelion."

I laid back as he pulled himself between my legs. Gripping my knees, he spread me apart even more where my inner thighs ached.

"I want to feel you, Soph. Really feel you. Do you want to feel me? Will you suck me in with your throbbing pussy?"

"Yes." I nodded. I had never had sex without a condom, and while I was on birth control, I wouldn't have ever even thought about having unprotected sex with a man. But something tightened in my chest and I wanted to feel him. Really feel him.

"Wait. Have you done that before?" I paused. I wasn't some idiot, and there was nothing sexy about STIs.

"Not since I was in high school. It's been a long time..." His eyebrows dropped lower. "Have you?"

"No," I answered, "but I want to with you."

The moan that came from his mouth made me so wet, I was sure I was staining his sheets.

Rubbing the thick head of his dick along the crevice

of my folds made my thighs jerk together, but he pushed them right back down.

"So wet for me, baby... so damn wet." He licked his finger before he slowly rubbed my clit with his thumb. Closing my eyes, the anticipation and sensations of everything was overtaking me. "Open your eyes, sweetheart." He dipped the ridge of his cock inside me, teasing me. Then stretching me, he slid inside with ease, though it still hurt.

It had been over a year since I last had sex. It had been over a year since I last trusted anyone to see my body naked.

"You're so fucking tight, baby." He leaned in, plunging as deep as he could until the slapping of our bodies became synced.

I dug my fingers into the sheets, and I couldn't stop chanting his name with every thrust.

"Damien!" I shrieked out in pleasure as he thumbed my clit and picked up his pace.

"Fuck, Sophie...." He pulled out and picked me up off the bed, my body already sore.

Pressing me against the oversized windows, my palms fell against the cold glass. The entire skyline was lit up, with cars bustling and people walking by the river.

I felt so exposed, yet so protected.

"Do you see your reflection, gorgeous?" He pulled

my hair back into his hand. I nodded, the words caught in my throat.

"I want you to watch yourself come on my cock. I want you to see how you're only mine and memorize that look, because it'll never leave you. I've ruined you. You are mine and only mine," he growled and jerked my legs up higher, plunging back inside me.

"Ah!" I called out as my breasts bounced to the beat of our bodies smacking together. He grabbed my nipples and twisted them slightly. "Oh my god!" I screamed as my palms slid down the glass, slick with sweat.

"No, baby... God's not saving you from the devil." He moved my hips up and down his length so fast that the friction was too much to handle. I could feel every single vein on his pounding dick, and the way his pace was hard and fast made my body ache in pleasure.

"Damien, I'm going to come..." I moaned as my palms slid down the window in front of us. I could see our reflection. Him behind me, tall and muscular, and me crumbling in front of him as he owned my entire body. I had signed myself away without a second doubt or thought.

"I know, baby... and when you do, you won't be able to scream my name... you'll whisper it from being so fucking breathless." His jaw tightened and I clenched my eyes shut. He licked his finger and rubbed my clit in perfect rhythm to his deep thrusts.

"Don't you dare close your eyes. Watch yourself, Sophie. I want you to watch yourself come all over me and own me."

I opened my eyes and looked at myself in the window, then let go. Warmth washed all over me, and I swore my heart was going to burst out of my chest. My palms, slick from sweat, trailed down, causing me to almost collapse. Damien had to lace his arm under my stomach and hold me up. Right then, I felt him come inside me hard, filling me completely as I clenched down and sucked him out.

"Damien," I breathed out. He was right, I couldn't scream his name because he left me breathless.

"Fuck…" he yelled out and lifted me in his arms, placing me on his bed and collapsing next to me.

I closed my eyes, my entire body shaking and coated in sweat. "I think I'm dead…" I whispered.

Damien let out a laugh. "No, my beautiful dandelion. You are very much alive, and I think you made me come alive, too." He pulled my face toward his so the tips of our noses touched. Kissing me softly, I was overcome with emotion.

"Why do you keep calling me dandelion?" I asked as he brushed the strangling piece of hair from my face.

He pressed his lips against my forehead gently. "Dandelions are the only flower that represents the three celestial bodies during the phase of its life cycle—the sun, moon, and stars. The yellow flower itself represents the sun, the dispersing seeds are the stars, and the white ball represents the moon. You, my beautiful dandelion, are all three. You shine brightly in my life when all I am is darkness, just like the sun, moon, and stars do. You are my light. You are my dandelion."

Damien

Sophie looked at me with her thick, pink pout in a tight line, but her eyes sparkled.

"Damien..." she whispered, brushing her finger against my lips. I kissed her index finger and she sighed. "That's so beautiful."

"No, baby, you are." I ran my hand through her hair.

"When I was a little girl, I would lay in the grass surrounded by dandelions and make flower crowns. When they'd eventually turn into those white puff balls, I'd pluck them out, close my eyes, and blow it all at once with a wish. Except, all the seeds would never fly off all at once. So, I always assumed I wouldn't be loved... really loved." She looked at me carefully as her breathing steadied.

"I don't understand?" I lifted my head to my palm, letting my fingers trail in between her perfect breasts.

"There's a belief that if you blow the dandelion out in one breath and all the seeds come out, someone loves you truly, unconditionally, and without limits. But, if all the seeds don't blow out at the same time, then it means no one loves you on that deep of a level." She closed her eyes. "I hope one day all the little petals blow out at once and someone loves me like that." A small smile curled on her pink lips.

"Someone will. Someone who deserves you. All of you." I kissed her forehead.

I'm sorry, sweet dandelion, but it just can't be me.

She may be my light. She may be my moon, stars, and sun, but I'll never be that for her. I'll only draw her into the darkness. I knew what was running through that brilliant mind of hers, because as smart as she was when it came to everything else in her life, she wasn't smart with her heart. If she was, she'd never have signed her soul away to me.

She stayed silent as I drew her into my arms, but she quickly pulled away and turned, bringing the blanket around her.

"Soph..." I raked my fingers against her back.

"Have you ever been in love?" Her voice was muffled by the blanket as she tugged it up higher.

"No." I laid flat on my back and ran my hand through my hair. "And I never will," I added. I could hear the shift in her breath, and my chest tightened at the sound.

"Why?" She sounded unsure, as if she didn't want the answer.

"Everyone I love gets hurt—either by me or someone in my life. Between my line of work and having more enemies than friends, I can't afford to have anyone I care about enough in my life to love. Love will always break us. It's not *if*, it's *when* love breaks us," I said honestly. There was no need to beat around the bush with Sophie; she deserved to know.

She turned toward me, her forehead creased and the tip of her button nose reddened. "Then why did you call me your dandelion?"

"Just because I can't love someone doesn't mean I can't care about someone." I ran my finger across her arm.

"You care about me?" She looked up through her eyelashes.

"I usually don't go around beating guys to the ground for a girl..." I smirked at her.

"You do that because you said I was yours, but I'm

not yours, Damien. You and I want two different things. Care isn't enough for me; I want love. You'll never give that to me, so I'm not yours." She offered a small smile and leaned in to kiss me. Her lips brushing against mine ignited something deeper in my body.

"You're right." I exhaled at the icy tone of my voice. She pursed her lips with a small nod and turned back around. I don't know who fell asleep first, but I felt suffocated when she said she wasn't mine.

* * *

"Good morning..." Sophie was wearing my dress shirt. The sunlight streaming through the windows left nothing to my imagination, outlining every perfect curve of her body. Except, I no longer needed my imagination. I had memorized every freckle, every curve, every dimple, and every scar on her body. I replayed her words in my mind, knowing I'd be selfish if I kept doing this with her.

"How is it that you look more beautiful now?" I pushed a cup of coffee over to her as her eyes trickled down my exposed abdomen.

"Please don't do that," she whispered, lifting the steaming cup to her perfect lips.

"What?" I handed her a plate of eggs and avocado toast.

"Make me..." She eyed the plate and looked back at me. "You made this?" She lifted her fork.

"Soph, I'm a thirty-six-year-old grown ass man. If I can't provide you with some basic breakfast, then I'd hope you would have been out the door by now." I smirked at her, licking the knife off.

Really, my mind froze on her previous statement. What was I making her do?

"Fall for you." She filled in my thoughts without a hitch.

"If making you breakfast after having sex is setting the bar high, then I need you to do some major soul searching before you fall for any guy." I rested my elbows on the counter that separated us.

"Well, most college guys are assholes, so I guess my bar is low. Then, this, and I quote, thirty-six-year-old grown ass man I'm seeing basically told me not to expect anything from him... So, ya know, the bar isn't just low, it's basically non-existent." She pinched her lips to the side.

As soon as I parted my lips to speak, my phone rang. I flipped it over and was about to hit ignore, but couldn't.

It was my younger brother, who only called for two reasons.

He was in trouble or needed money.

"Eat." I pointed at Sophie's plate and turned to walk toward the balcony.

"So bossy..." Sophie huffed but picked her toast up.

I smiled as I answered, but my tone quickly shifted. "Ashton..."

"Look, I'm sorry. I know you said not to come here, but I'm here. I... I really fucked up, bro." His voice was scattered and he sounded paranoid.

He was high as a fucking kite.

"What the hell did you do now?" I hissed through clenched teeth.

"I owe money, bro... a lot of it. I got into too much shit with the wrong people."

"Text me where you are." I hung up the phone and clenched it in my fist. "Goddamn it!"

Turning around, Sophie stood there with my plate in her hands.

"I didn't hear anything. I just wanted to bring you your food because it was getting cold." She gave me a half-smile. "Everything okay?" Her voice dropped, and she looked at me with those big, magnetic eyes that drew me into her.

"My brother is tied up in something, so I have to get him. I don't want him to meet you, Soph. He's trouble." I took my plate from her and set it down, drawing her into me.

"Seems that runs in the family..." she teased.

"You have no idea, dandelion." I ran my hand through her hair. She tilted her chin up and looked at me. "Last night, Sophie... It was..." I trailed before crashing my lips to hers, my cock hardening as soon as her flesh touched mine.

Pushing the button-down draped on her body down, I lifted her into my arms, pressing her wet, bare pussy against my chest. The friction of my body against her soft spot made her moan as I plunged my tongue inside her mouth.

My phone buzzed, and I pulled my lips off of hers. "Wait, no..." she said as I placed her down.

Ashton had texted me. He was in the worst neighborhood in Chicago, meaning he was messing with Kane —and Kane wanted my blood. I had single-handedly locked up most of his gang members, and I had personally beat him to the ground. The thing was, Kane and I went back further than that. Rubbing my tattoo, I could still feel the sting all these years later.

Looking back at Sophie through the glass, my chest squeezed. She would only get hurt, and it wasn't just emotionally. I was compromising her physical well-being. She was officially my weak spot—the perfect target.

"No dessert with my breakfast, Mr. Moretti?" She smiled, but her forehead creased when my face dropped.

"Once is satisfying a craving, but twice is developing a habit. I can't afford a habit, dandelion." I pulled her face up toward mine as I gripped her hair, tightening my hold. "Goodbye, Soph." I kissed her forehead. "Don't be here when I get back. I really don't want my brother meeting you. He isn't worthy of that, and truthfully, I never was, either." I pulled away, too much of a coward to look into her eyes.

The way she sucked in the air I had left between us let me know my words had cut deep. But that was the only way she'd stay away.

I'm so sorry, Soph.

CHAPTER 25

Sophie

I watched him leave his penthouse, leaving me behind as if I were nothing. Ezra was right; Damien Moretti was a heartless man. How could someone be so seemingly complex, while so hollow inside. Why was he doing whatever he could to make sure no one got close to him? My stomach twisted as I looked over Chicago from Damien's balcony. I wrapped my arms around my chest, feeling emptier than ever. Last night had been the best and worst night. I knew what I was getting into with him, but then why did he get so jealous and possessive when I was out with Zach for dinner?

'Don't be here when I get back.' Ouch. The words felt like daggers after spending last night together. I couldn't stop seeing the intimate moments flicker in front of my

eyes. It was insane, toe-curling, back arching, sweat-inducing sex. But the small moments, when he'd lace his fingers with mine or brush away the straggling hair from my face, were the moments that made me flutter in a way I knew was forcing me on a dangerous path.

Why did he care so much if he didn't want more than just last night? Sure, he admitted caring about someone and loving someone were two different things, but the latter stems from the former. Without care there is no love, and without some form of love there is no care. After last year, the last thing I needed was a broken man in my life.

Unfortunately, Damien was just that, and I so desperately wanted to be the one to piece him back together.

But, fortunately, I had self-respect. I wasn't about to wait on any man, even if he could make me come with a flick of his tongue or how his dick was the fucking Zeus of cocks.

Shaking myself out of my sex trance, I realized I was done. I was done drooling over my brother's best friend. After all, that's all he was.

Right?

. . .

I walked back into the penthouse and went to look for my clothes. Instead of finding what I wore last night, there was a large bag sitting on the end of his bed.

Curiously, I pulled it open and tugged out the contents. A small smile curved on my lips.

You possessive son of a bitch.

Replacing my low-cut dress, he had bought jeans and crew neck T-shirts that clearly would cover up any sign of my ass or cleavage. Shaking my head, I pulled it on and took one last look around.

"Goodbye, Damien..." I grabbed my phone and purse, then headed down the elevator to the lobby.

"Miss Shah?"

I flung around. "Yes?" I replied to the doorman.

"I'm Nathaniel. Mr. Moretti wanted me to walk you to your car." He smiled with his wrinkles deepening around his eyes.

"Oh no, I didn't bring a car... I actually don't even have one." I let out an embarrassed laugh.

"Mr. Moretti has a car waiting for you. His driver, Tavin, is waiting for you." Nathaniel guided me toward the golden revolving doors. A man in a three-piece suit and head piece nodded at me.

"Hello, Miss Shah, I'm Tavin. Where are we headed?" He opened the door for me.

This was crazy. But more than that, what really made

my heart flutter was the fact that Damien had a driver, yet he always came to pick me up whenever I needed him to. He didn't just send his driver to do that... until now.

Climbing in, I asked Tavin to take me to Ezra and Amira's apartment. I didn't want to be alone, and I really needed to use their printer for class tomorrow.

Priorities.

Once we got there, I went straight up and walked in. The best thing about my brother and Amira was that they always made sure I knew their home was mine. I didn't feel the formality that many siblings did once a partner was in the picture.

"Hey, sis." Ezra was coming out of his office and wrapped me in a hug. Things had been slightly strange ever since Ezra lost it when he thought Damien and I had slept together two weeks ago. I knew he had so much going on already, and he didn't need more to panic over. Luckily, he dropped it. Guilt panged through me. I didn't keep secrets with Ezra, especially after last year when I had let things spiral so badly that he didn't even know what was happening until it was too late.

"Are you doing good?" He let me go as I walked to their kitchen, pulling their fridge opened.

"Mm-hmm... why wouldn't I be?" I couldn't even look him in the eye.

"Well, for starters, you're wearing clothes you didn't

pick out." Amira's voice echoed behind me. I turned with a cake in my hands and looked at them both. Ezra was now scanning my outfit, and Amira bit her bottom lip and suppressed a growing smile.

I widened my eyes at her and shook my head, and Ezra quickly looked between us.

"Okay, what the hell is going on?" Ezra crossed his arms across his chest.

"So... how was your date with Zach?" Amira smiled mischievously.

Ezra's forehead creased as he looked at me. "Who the hell is Zach?"

I squinted at Amira, who laughed loudly. Really, Zach was the perfect cover up. "Ezra, will you give us girls a minute?" Amira looked at my brother, who nodded.

"Fine. But once you both have your little pow-wow, you better believe I need answers about this Zach guy." He waved his finger at me.

Once my brother left and we heard his office door shut, I went to Amira. Grabbing her elbows, I pulled her in close. "What was that?" I hissed.

"You know you can't hide a guy from us!" She wiggled her shoulders with excitement. "So... did you both visit coochie town?" She winked obnoxiously.

"Coochie town? I have no idea what that is, and I am disturbed if that's what you and Ezra refer to as sex."

Amira giggled and pulled me onto the stool next to her. "Give me the tea... That's what all the cool kids say, right?" She smiled and held my hands in hers. "But seriously, Soph you haven't been alone with a guy since..."

"Well, I spent the night at Damien's," I replied.

Her eyes widened and the smile on her face faded. "W-what?" she stammered.

"No, I mean two weeks ago, when he slept on the couch." I chickened out and exhaled.

She flung her hand over her chest. "Shit, Soph...you almost gave me a heart attack."

"I didn't sleep with Zach. I just... spent the night with him and he got me some clothes because my dress got dirty." I hated lying to Amira and Ezra, yet here I was.

It was true. Damien and I couldn't work. He was over a decade older than me, he was doing something shady as hell, and regardless if my brother said he wasn't out there killing people like some sexy hitman, he obviously had issues. Besides, Ezra would definitely kill us both if he ever found out.

"Do you know anything about Damien's younger

brother?" Just as the words left my mouth, Ezra walked in.

"Why are you talking about Damien? Did you see him last night?" Ezra's voice rose. "No, I brought him up about wedding stuff." Amira quickly filled in for me.

"Oh…" He went around to get a water bottle.

"I was asking if Amira knew anything about his brother? He mentioned him that night I stayed over weeks ago," I started.

"We've never met him. Apparently, he's a giant mess and basically uses Damien for his money. I think he lives in California or something. Who knows? Why the sudden interest?" Ezra glanced at me.

"I don't know, just curious. Damien seemed like he had only-child syndrome, so I was surprised he had a sibling." I shrugged and dug my fork into the fluffy cake.

Scooping up the piece of mango cake, I couldn't help but want to know more. I wanted to know everything about the man who would never be mine.

The man who *couldn't* be mine.

* * *

The next day, I headed to class and Zach spotted me from a distance. "Hey Sophie." His smile was forced and somewhat sad. I felt terrible about how things ended for our dinner. I wouldn't even have called it a date as much as it was a dinner with a friend, but I don't think Zach felt that way.

"Zach, I am so sorry for leaving dinner and... Well, I'm embarrassed." I sank into the seat next to him as the lecture hall filled with students.

"No, you don't have to apologize. I was just worried about you after... well, after your boyfriend carried you out of the restaurant?" His eyebrow arched as he waited for my response.

I swallowed and looked ahead. "He's not my boyfriend."

"He said he was your man." Zach cringed as he said the words.

"It's complicated... but no, I'm not dating him." Saying that out loud hurt more than I thought possible. Zach's eyes grew hopeful, and just as he opened his mouth to speak, I quickly fired out, "But, I want you to know that I really can't date anyone right now. I got out of a really toxic relationship last year, and as you can see, I think I'm a magnet for nutcases." I tried to lighten the mood.

Zach's grin grew wider. "Sophie, I'm cool with being just friends. Seriously, I think you're great. Besides, I'm not looking for a relationship, either. Honestly, medical school is my priority."

Breathing out a sigh of relief, I smiled. "That sounds great, Zach." I pulled out my laptop as Professor Ko began the lecture.

While Professor Ko rambled on and on about everything and anything, I dazed out and picked up my phone. I had an unread email on my personal account. Furrowing my brows together, I opened it.

My breathing quickened as soon as I saw it was from Damien. It was in the format of a letter. Looking up at Professor Ko and glancing around the room full of students, I felt like I couldn't breathe.

I quietly packed away my laptop and textbooks, and Zach looked up at me. "You okay, Sophie?" he whispered.

"Yeah, something came up. Text you later." I ducked down the crowded aisles and jogged down the auditorium stairs, thankful for the dark room.

Once opening the door, the sunlight felt blinding and it took a moment for my eyes to adjust.

I headed toward the quad with my heart beating against my chest. Sinking onto the bench, the early Fall breeze rippled through, providing solace from the sun's direct heat.

Opening the email once again, I started to read.

. . .

Soph,

Last night was amazing. You are amazing. I also have been meaning to thank you for opening up to me and telling me your story. I know it wasn't easy to do so. I don't want you to think of me as the guy who added you as another notch on his belt, because my sweet dandelion, you could never be that. You are perfection. You make me feel in a way I have never felt before. But Ezra is my best friend, and if he ever found out about any of this, he'd never speak to me again. But that's not it. I'd be willing to give up every last person in my life to be with you, Sophie. The only thing is, I'm not willing to give you up. Because if the wrong person found out about how I feel about you… that's exactly what would happen. They'd do anything and everything in their power to take you away from me. Forever. I'm not the man you think I am, nor am I the man who deserves you. But I'm also not the man who will sit there, allowing you to think something is wrong with you and that you're not deserving of love and respect. I don't want you to spend the rest of your time thinking about me and wondering what went wrong. I need you to forget every touch, every word, and everything that you think you feel about me. Go find your happi-

ness. You are all things perfect, and I just so badly wish I wasn't imperfect. In another life, I hope you choose me, and when you do, I'll make sure to be everything and anything for you, my dandelion. Thank you for being my sun, my moon, and all of my stars in my otherwise darkened life.

Love,

D.M.

My heart slowed so much, I was scared I'd faint. What in the world? Chills grew along my arms and tears stung my eyes, but I didn't know why or what had triggered them. Perhaps the fact that, in a million years, I would have never in my wildest dreams pictured Damien Moretti sending me a love letter like this. I would have never thought he'd admit to having feelings for me. But most of all, I knew this wasn't a normal love letter... this was a goodbye letter. One that ensured I knew there was no way he'd ever be mine.

A single tear dripped onto my phone, and I wiped it away. Looking up, I saw students happily walking by with laughter written across their faces and some laying under the large oak trees, studying. The birds were chirping and sunlight dripped through the canopy of trees, providing warmth and light.

He was right. Amira had warned me privately. She could see it in my eyes when I asked about Damien's younger brother. She could tell I cared about him more than I should have. She also made sure to tell me that, under no circumstance, could I ever be with him. When you play with fire the only thing that happens is that you end up burned.

I couldn't do that to Ezra. We had lost our parents, and he had sacrificed so much to make sure I was always safe. After the traumatic experience with my ex-boyfriend, it broke my brother. I hadn't seen him that depressed or worried since my parents died, and I couldn't do that to him now that he was finally getting his beautiful fresh start with Amira. I knew they had planned to try for a baby right away, and I couldn't be more excited for them. Attempting to be with Damien was selfish, and now I realized more than ever, dangerous.

I didn't know what Damien really meant by, 'if the wrong people knew about us he'd lose me forever,' but I knew after overhearing his conversation...

Damien Moretti was the one playing with fire and most of all, life and death.

CHAPTER 26

Damien

I had become an expert at disappearing, and making disappear was one of my fortes.

But I couldn't just leave my life over a girl, especially since I had many pressing matters to deal with.

For instance, having to meet and negotiate with Chicago's drug cartel lord, Kane, who had my idiotic brother dangling by a noose in an abandoned warehouse until I wired him four hundred thousand dollars.

"Just like old times, Damien," Kane scoffed as he spit tobacco onto the dirty floor and cut my brother down with a blood-stained knife.

Ashton came stumbling toward me with limited remorse in his eyes, but a hell of a lot of fear.

"The deal included that you'd never contact my brother or anyone in my life," I fired back at Kane.

He stood there, his head shaved, tattoos scattered all over his body and piercings lining his ears, and smiled a toothless grin at me. "I didn't contact him; he contacted me. You know, I almost had him come work with me… but there came big brother to pay his debt. Little bitch." Kane roared with laughter as Ashton cowered behind me.

"Leave him alone, Kane, or I'll fucking wipe Chicago clean of you and the rest of the scum you bring here."

"You know, I don't like when someone threatens me, Moretti. Watch your fucking back," Kane yelled behind me. I turned and grabbed Ashton by his collar, dragging his ass out.

Tossing my brother into the car, I slammed his door shut and got in. Gripping the steering wheel tightly, I started to drive. "What the hell are you doing back here?" I boomed.

Ashton sank into the passenger seat. His clothes were dirty, and he smelled like shit, liquor, and drugs. His eyes were bright red from being strung out.

"I missed you." He sighed.

"No, you ran out of fucking money and drugs." I shook my head and made a sharp right turn.

"Where are we going?" Ashton whined.

"You are twenty-two years old, Ashton. You're a grown fucking man, and I'm sick of watching you act like you're ten. I'm sick of feeling a damn pit in my stom-ach, waiting to get that call to find out you overdosed and I need to come identify your body in an alley." I made another sharp turn and finally, we had arrived. Pushing my door open, I grabbed a duffel bag from my trunk and walked toward the entrance.

Ashton begrudgingly got out of the car. "No fucking way! No way in hell, man! Rehab? I'm outta here!" He started walking in the opposite direction.

"Walk away and you'll never, and I mean *never*, hear from me or get a dime from me again, Ashton." My voice was low but impactful. He knew better than to think I'd ever bluff.

Freezing in his place, his chest heaved once before he spun around. Storming back, he pushed past me and went through the opened doors.

I left Ashton at Chicago's most expensive and best rehabilitation center. We had tried this before, but he'd keep running away, and then finally, he was in too much trouble and I made him disappear. I set him up with an entirely new life far away, yet here we were again. My chest felt tight from the stress between work, Ashton, and my past seemingly never staying where it needed to be... in the past.

Exhaustion pooled in my body, but the one thing I wanted more than anything in this moment was her.

I wanted her touch.

I wanted her smile.

I wanted her completely.

But more than anything, I needed her.

I had sent her the e-mail this morning, wiping my hands clean and hoping she'd understand. Between Kane, Ashton, and all the weight of the world collapsing in on me, I knew it was the right thing. But if it was the right thing, then why does it feel so damn wrong?

I collapsed into my bed and closed my eyes, but as soon as I did my phone buzzed. "Fucking hell," I mumbled and grabbed it off my nightstand. Very few people had my personal number, but keeping it that way let me know it was actually worth my time to check.

It was an email. I held my breath as I opened it. It was from her.

Dear Damien, aka "D.M" (Super weird that you sign things with your initials by the way),

Who e-mails love letters these days? I mean come on? You could have handwritten it and had it delivered with some chocolate to make more of an impact. Instead, I missed a good amount of class to read it out in the quad. After I read it, I started to walk around campus to process it all. I stopped and saw a dandelion—the puffball version... the moon. I lifted it up and guess what? When I blew it, all the little petals came off at the same time.

That means someone, right now, in this very moment, loves me. Can you believe that?

I wonder who it is?

I wonder if he drives a motorcycle and got a second helmet? I wonder if he wears a leather jacket and drapes it over me? I wonder if he carries my backpack so I don't have to carry the weight? I wonder if he paid the old coffee stand owner an entire year's worth so all my coffee is always 'on the house?' I wonder if he watches me sleep next to him in bed after years of sneaking out? I wonder if he clenches his fists and swings when he sees any other man look my way? I wonder if he kisses me the way he fucked me? Hard. Possessive. Loving.

I really wonder who he is?

Sophie, aka S.S.

. . .

My chest rose and fell rapidly as I re-read her words, each one searing into me.

Dear Sophie,
I'm coming over.
D.M.

I tossed the blankets off, threw a fresh V-neck on, and grabbed my leather jacket. Fuck it. I needed to see her. *Now.*

Getting on my bike, I sped and weaved through the Chicago night traffic. The lights and buildings lit up the sky, and while the air had grown cooler, my body was fiery hot.

I pulled up to her building and paged her apartment. The buzzer sounded and before it ended, I was halfway up the stairs, making my way to her place.

The door swung open before I could knock, and I stopped. My heart pulsed as her beautiful lips curved upward. She was wearing nothing but a thin silk robe, and her long hair draped over her shoulders in waves.

"Sophie," I breathed out, letting my eyes shamelessly drift over her body.

"Damien." She pinched her lips to the side with mischief dancing in those gorgeous brown eyes.

Reaching in, I put my palms on each side of her face and drew her toward me, crashing my lips to the softness of hers.

My cock twitched and jerked in appreciation. I rubbed my bulge against her stomach as she kissed me hungrily. She began walking backward, not letting go of our touch.

Kicking my shoes off, I peeled my jacket off and let everything fall behind me. Our tongues swirled together, taking every ounce of the other in.

"Baby." I ripped my jeans off, and as she tugged down my briefs, her eyes fell to my cock as it dripped, completely hard at the mere touch of her.

Her eyes shot back up to mine, and she moved a step away from me. I stood in front of her completely naked. Slowly, she untied the strap of her robe and let the silk fall open, exposing just a sliver of her flat, toned abdomen. The shiny material covered her nipples that poked through, begging for my mouth, and she lifted an eyebrow with a playful smile.

Biting her bottom lip, my cock pulsed as she kept walking backward into her bedroom. Following her like a fucking lost puppy, I stood in front of her and dropped my hands to her hips.

"I thought you said goodbye..." she whispered.

"I'm starting to think I'll have to be dead before I spend a day without you, Soph." I leaned in and kissed her. She stood on her tiptoes, and I quickly lifted her into my arms, peeling the robe off her perfect body.

"Fuck, you're gorgeous, baby." Laying her down on the bed, I kissed her neck, her collarbone, and then sucked her pink nipples. Squeezing them gently, I bit and licked as she moaned out.

Hovering over her, I pushed my fingers into her dripping wet pussy. "So fucking wet for me... Only mine," I breathed out as I spread her wetness through her folds and rubbed it around her clit. She was panting, her face flushed.

"Don't you dare come yet. I want you to either come on my mouth or on my cock. Do you understand?" I growled as her back arched and she slammed her eyes shut. I knew she was on the brink, so I tugged my fingers out. "Open your eyes, Sophie." She did as she was told immediately.

"That's my good girl. Now open your mouth. I want you to taste how fucking sweet you are, baby." I shoved my fingers into her mouth, and she groaned as she licked herself off my wet fingers.

"You aren't so innocent, are you?" She smiled shyly at me. "Answer me!"

"No, I'm not." Her lips parted as her breathing picked up.

"Who do you belong to?" I brushed the tip of my cock against her wet folds, rubbing myself over and over and barely pushing the tip inside her.

"You," she cried out, biting her lip. "Only you."

"Damien, please!" she pleaded with me. My eyes slanted as I kissed her belly button and kissed my way down until I pushed my tongue inside her. Licking her and sucking her perfect clit until her hands shot down and grabbed my hair desperately.

"Damien!" Her thighs clenched around my face as I pushed my tongue inside her faster, devouring her. My fingers stretched her out as my tongue moved in rhythm.

Her grip in my hair grew tighter and she chanted my name, and it only made me grow harder.

Her body shook as she shattered with her orgasm. Once she stilled, I swiped my tongue once more across her pussy and licked her up.

"Absolutely fucking delicious." I kissed her pussy once more before I trailed my lips upward.

Opening her eyes, she smiled. "That was... incredible." Her voice was low, and she sounded self-conscious.

"Yeah? Well, spread your fucking legs wide for me. I'll show just how incredible my cock feels when I fill you with my come."

She whimpered with excitement as I pressed her legs apart so quickly, she let out a small cry.

Her eyes widened as I dipped my cock inside her, rubbing the tip against her clit before stretching her around me. As soon as I pushed inside of her, she tightened.

"You're so damn tight, baby. You want to come again, sweetheart? All over my cock?" I plunged deeper inside her as her fingers dug into my back.

"Damien! Yes!" she cried out as my balls slapped against her pussy over and over again. I knew she could feel every vein, every bit of my cock inside her.

I pulled out of her and commanded, "Straddle me." I got onto the bed and she crawled over my lap, sinking onto my cock with ease. Her pussy was slick with come and heat as she swallowed me.

Facing one another, her tits bounced and slapped against her skin as I pumped into her with long, fast strokes.

Her warm breath brushed my mouth as she moaned into it. "I'm going to fill you up with every last drop of myself, and you're going to suck me in." She nodded with sweat dripping between her perfect tits and I sank my teeth into her neck. Piling her hair into my hand, I jerked her head back, giving myself more flesh to kiss.

"Damien! Please, I'm begging you! I need to...

Damien! I'm going to...." she moaned again, chanting my name over and over again.

"I know baby. I know." I thrusted into her hard and rough until she clenched around me so tight that I exploded inside of her. I groaned then fell backward into the bed with my cock still inside her. She collapsed onto my chest, pressing her face against my pecs.

"That was perfect," she whispered, the word shaking from her lips. Her body trembled from the two orgasms that rippled through her.

She looked up at me with her chin digging into my chest, her big, brown eyes twinkling. I leaned in and kissed her forehead gently, brushing her hair out of her face. "No baby, you are perfect," I whispered. She closed her eyes as I kissed her forehead once again. "You never have to beg me to let you come, it's a fucking privilege for me." I ran my fingertips across her arm as goose-bumps followed.

"Damien..." she said so low that my chest tightened with the way my name rolled off her lips.

"I know, baby. I know." We both felt it. This wasn't just sex—it never was, and it never will be. I just didn't know how the hell I was going to ensure the one person I couldn't lose wouldn't be ripped away from me.

CHAPTER 27

Sophie

I was making breakfast, swaying to *Lost Stars* by Adam Levine with nothing on but Damien's button-down. The sunlight was trickling in through the windows and everything felt strangely normal.

Strong hands gripped me from behind, tugging me against him. His erection pressed into me as he dropped his head into the groove between my cheek and neck, kissing me softly. Reaching my hand up, I held his face closer to mine as I looked up at him.

"Good morning." I grinned as he grinded into me. "Damien…" I giggled as his fingers went down and he immediately let out a groan when he ran his fingers across me, knowing I didn't have any panties on. He rubbed his fingers along my clit, making me clutch the kitchen counter. "Damien." I sighed as he drew my wetness across my pussy.

Right as he pushed his fingers inside, my phone rang.

"No," he said into my ear.

Letting out a laugh, I pulled away from him. "I have to answer that. It's probably Amira about tonight."

"Hey Amira," I answered trying to suppress the giddiness in my voice.

"Hey Sophie, where are you? We're in the front of your building with breakfast," Amira said.

Anxiety pooled inside me. I looked over at Damien, who glanced down at the outline of his dick in the fitted gray joggers. Widening my eyes, I shook my head.

"I'm over at Reese's for breakfast." I cleared my throat.

"Really? Ezra texted Reese when you didn't pick up, and she said she didn't know where you were." Amira sounded suspicious.

My heart raced as I was caught in a lie. "I... I'm with Zach," I stammered. Glancing over at Damien, his brows dropped lower and his jaw ticked.

Shit.

"Oh, now I see why you're being shady." Amira giggled, and I could hear Ezra grumble in the background. "Well, bring him over to dinner tonight. Damien's coming, too; he's bringing Carmen." Amira sounded excited, and of course, she was. She thought she was going to have a triple date with some of her favorite people—because that's what normal couples did. Suddenly my heart sank. Damien had already planned to bring Carmen, the stunning, leggy, smart attorney. We didn't belong. We didn't fit.

"That sounds good," I replied and quickly said goodbye before hanging up.

"Zach?" Damien didn't wait a second.

"They showed up with food and knew I wasn't with Reese." I shrugged but the pit in my stomach was still there.

"Why didn't you tell me you were bringing Carmen to dinner tonight?" I hated how moist my eyes felt with the hot tears teasing my waterline.

"Are you seeing Zach?" He didn't even care about what I had just said. Walking closer to me, he pinned me against the wall and his hand dropping to my waist. "Have you let him touch you? Has he touched what's mine?"

My thighs clenched and I moaned when he pinned my hands above my head with one hand. "Answer me now. Did you let him touch what's mine?" He pushed his fingers inside me.

"No," I breathed out.

"Who does this pussy belong to?" His voice dropped low.

"You," I moaned as his fingers rubbed me faster. Pulling his fingers out, he shoved them into his mouth, licking me off him and then kissed me hard.

"Whose mouth is this?"

"Yours," I panted as my body begged for his. But then, what he did next made the world shatter.

"Who own's this heart?" His voice dropped low, though the possessiveness lined every syllable.

"Damien..." I looked up in his eyes and found his gaze searing into mine.

"That's right, dandelion. It's Damien's." My breathing stopped for a moment as every fiber in my body froze.

His lips crashed into mine as he lifted me in his arms. Sliding his pants down quickly, he pushed inside me.

Tossing my head back, my mouth dropped open as his strokes grew longer and slower. "Baby," he moaned as the sensation overcame us both. Pulling his cock out, he suddenly plunged right back in, causing me to scream. He pumped into me quickly, possessively, over and over again.

"Damien!" My hips jerked back and forth across his length as he held me in place. I bit his bottom lip, tugging it between my teeth as I let myself go. An orgasm rippled through my body as sweat trickled down my neck.

Pulling out of me, his eyes grew darker.

"Get on your knees and take my cock in that sweet mouth of yours." How was it possible to feel so damn aroused after coming just three seconds ago? I happily dropped to my knees, his throbbing cock dripping in front of me.

"Suck my cock, now," he growled. Slowly, I licked his length, looking up at him through my eyelashes as he piled my hair between his fingers.

He pulled my head down as I took him into my mouth, hitting the back of my throat. I gagged a moment before I got positioned to accommodate the massive cock inside my mouth.

I played with his taut balls as I sucked him, and he let out a long moan, which fueled the fire inside me to take him as deep as I could. Suctioning harder, he jerked his hips until I swirled my tongue around his tip and sucked with my teeth lightly grazing his flesh. Gripping my hair, he thrusted inside and exploded down the back of my throat, filling my mouth with his salty, thick come. Swallowing it all, he pulled out of me, lifting me off the floor, and shuddered.

I loved that I did that to him. I wasn't just some lonely, destroyed girl. Someone wanted me and more than that, the look in his eyes made me realize that he *needed* me.

"I never want to hear Zach's name on your lips, or any other man's for that matter. You belong to me and no one else. Do you understand?" Damien tilted my face up to his.

Chewing my bottom lip, I smiled. "I so badly want to say no so you'll spank me, but yes... I understand. For the record, I better not hear any other woman's name on your lips, either. Especially not Carmen's. Understood, Moretti?" I poked his perfectly carved chest.

"Yes ma'am." He leaned down and kissed me softly. Everything felt so perfect, and I didn't want this moment to end.

"Baby, one more thing... do you..." he paused.

I looked at him with slanted eyes. "What?"

"Do you think I'm too rough with you? Do you think I say things..." His eyes dropped to the ground.

He was worried about me, given my past with my ex-boyfriend. My breathing hitched as I wrapped my arms around his waist. "Damien, I love that you don't treat me like a glass doll, and I love that you're teaching me about my body and helping me figure out what I love."

"Okay, dandelion." He nodded slowly. For a moment, we just stood there, wrapped in each other, feeling something words couldn't describe. Or maybe I knew exactly what the words were, but I was still terrified of it.

We both got dressed and sank into my couch, my feet resting over his lap as he massaged them.

"Damien, what do you really do for work?" The question had hung over my head for a while now.

"You know what I do, Soph. I'm an attorney. I run my own law firm." His brow raised as he studied my face carefully.

"I mean, what do you really do besides that? The phone call, Ezra and Amira warning me that you were too dangerous to even consider being with. Please, just be honest with me," I pleaded with him. If we were doing this—whatever this was—then I needed to know him. I needed to feel safe with the man I knew I was starting to truly feel things for.

Letting out a long exhale, he stopped rubbing my feet. "You'll never look at me the same, Soph. You won't want to be alone with me." He tilted his head, and I could see the pain flickering in his beautiful eyes.

"If there was one man standing on this Earth with me, I'd without a doubt hope it would be you. I've never felt safer than when I'm with you, Damien. How can we be an *us* if you choose to keep yourself locked away from me?"

"I was in a gang, Sophie. I did really, really bad shit. My dad was an abusive piece of shit, and he finally left after I beat his face in for hurting my mom. After that, I felt powerful. Maybe it was the violence he always put us through, or maybe it was the fact that we had no money and I had to take care of my mom, brother, and myself from the time I was sixteen because my mom spiraled out of control and into severe depression. I met the wrong guy at the wrong time, and he took me under his wing. Kane Stewart, Chicago's drug cartel king. The one who has more blood on his hands than imaginable. He provided my family an easy out. I worked for him, and he paid well. Eventually, I wanted out, but that came with a hefty price tag. Becoming an attorney was a double-ended sword. I promised I'd keep him out of prison and protect the gang... until they started killing and taking lives for the hell of it. Now, he's got a mark on my head and anyone I will ever care or... possibly love."

Damien paused, his beautiful eyes growing lost. As if

he had endless regrets and not enough hope left inside him.

My heart constricted as I swallowed the lump in my throat. "Damien, I didn't know any of this. I didn't know about your parents, or..." I paused and crawled toward him. I traced the large tattoos all over his arm. Suddenly, for the first time, I realized the tattoos weren't there just for design or meaning. They covered up large scars... and not just scars, but burns and cuts.

"Did Kane... Did he do this to you?" Tears stung my eyes and Damien looked down at his tattoo.

"If we didn't carry out a deal correctly or to his liking, he'd burn or stab us. He'd have our gang members hold one another down and dig dirty blades into our flesh. It was a warning, a preview of what would happen if we ever disobeyed. I was young and desperate, basically clay he could mold into whoever he needed me to be." His voice was low and pain stricken.

"Your brother helped me out. I met him one day when he was studying at a coffee shop and he spotted me." Damien laughed lightly as he looked up at the ceiling with a small smile on his face.

"I had just left the gym and he saw my tattoo. This one." He pointed to the largest of them that covered his entire shoulder and dripped down. "He said, and I quote in Ezra's most proper way, 'Wow, man, that's bad ass." Damien grinned and my heart fluttered at the happiness he found in the friendship with my big brother.

Speaking of my brother... Shit. I had been in such a bubble with Damien and everything between us—this new level of trust and vulnerability—that I had hardly thought about what we were planning to do once we were forced out of our safe haven.

"How'd a college student who was around your age help you out?" I asked curiously. My brother never told me about how he and Damien met, but I had always assumed they met as classmates in law school.

"I had been secretly taking online college classes at Jesson, so Ezra and I were both seniors. He started telling me all about his dreams of getting into their law school, and we got into politics, crime... talked about everything and anything. He was in awe about my take on the justice and criminal system and the influx of crime amongst gangs and drug cartels that were very much an issue in Chicago." Damien paused.

"I guess he was surprised I knew what I did, but I think deep down, he always knew, especially by my appearance—the tattoos, the bike, and the way I spoke. I wasn't just a normal college student. He saw my cuts that were fresher at the time; he saw the burns..."

Damien blinked and shifted slightly. "He knew, and he convinced me to go to law school with him."

My heart was racing with the knowledge that my brother had saved Damien. He saved him from possibly never seeing this age. He saved him from a life of crime and blood on his hands.

"Wow. Ezra never told me anything about you beyond how you both were best friends and lawyers. Then when we had our meet-cute, I honestly kinda hated you." I pinched my lips to the side.

"Meet-cute?" Damien raised his brows, his beautiful, mossy-green eyes lightened with intrigue.

"You know, when the two main characters in a book or movie meet for the first time. The girl slips and falls and the guy catches her, or something romantic. My dream meet-cute is on the Navy Pier Ferris wheel. You know, like I'm sitting alone and right before it takes off, someone slides in and fireworks explode between us and above us. Ours was at Le Petit Bistro when you decided to almost kill a guy for looking at me." I winced, recalling our so-called meet-cute.

"It's like a proposal?" Damien questioned.

"Kind of, but the first meeting. I sure hope the proposal would be better than that first meeting." Suddenly my cheeks heated at my insinuation. *Why did I just say that?*

"I mean, you know… like one day when I get married or whatever. I know that's not your scene," I stammered nervously as Damien raked his fingers across my bare legs. He didn't say anything for what felt like eternity.

"Since, apparently marriage isn't my scene, are you implying you're going to eventually marry some other man?" Damien licked his bottom lip, and my face was on fire.

"Do I need to remind you who you belong to?" His eyes dropped to my lips.

My phone rang, startling me but allowing for there to be a reason for me to break his gaze.

"Hey Reese!" I squeaked when I answered. "Yeah, I'm heading over now. Mm-hmm. I'll text you the number. Great. See you soon, girl." I swiped my phone off and looked at Damien, who looked irritated.

"I have to go study with Reese, so I'll see you tonight at dinner?" I slid off the couch.

"Who else is going to be studying with you?" Damien walked closer behind me.

I hated lying; I wasn't good at it and it showed. "Just another classmate." I tugged my Jesson hoodie on over my T-shirt and slid into some jeans.

"I'm a lawyer, Sophie. I can smell bullshit three miles away."

"Zach is coming, too," I answered as confidently as I could.

"You're not going."

"Yes, I am." I grabbed my backpack off the floor and shoved some scattered textbooks into it. Glancing around, I quickly ran into my room and grabbed a dress out of my closet. I'd have to change for dinner at Ezra's.

"Then I'll come, too." Damien grabbed his keys off my coffee table and slid his suit back on.

Within moments, he was standing in front of me, wearing his three-piece suit, looking like a damn Armani ad.

"No, you can't come. What would you do with some college students." I shook my head at him.

Growing closer and cornering me, he ran his hand against my cheek. "I know what I would do with this one," he purred in his velvety smooth voice, sending heat straight between my legs.

"Look at you being all jealous..." A smile crept on my face as I looked up at him. "Damien, go home. I'll see you tonight." I bit into my lower lip.

"Do I have a reason to be jealous?" He sounded annoyed.

"Damien Moretti, we are not exclusive. I don't even know what we are, therefore, I have no clue if you have the right to be jealous." I was being a brat, I knew it, but he was being overly possessive and bossy.

"Fine. I need to go study some cases with Carmen, anyway. I'll see you tonight." He pulled away from me and grabbed his leather wallet, sliding it into his pants.

My mouth parted, and I angrily spat out, "No, you will not."

Turning over his shoulder, he mocked me, "We are not exclusive. I don't even know what we are; therefore, I have no clue if you have the right to be jealous, Sophie Shah."

"Ha! So cute, charming, actually. Asshat." I rolled my eyes and pushed past him, but strong hands gripped me from behind and spun me around.

My hands landed on his chest and he looked down at me. "You are mine, and only mine. We are exclusive. You are exclusively mine, and I'm exclusively yours. If any, and I mean, *any* man looks at you or shares the same air as you, I'll fucking end him," he said, his minty breath brushing against my face.

I couldn't say anything. I just stood there with my backpack on, wearing a worn-down hoodie, smiling goofily at the sexiest man I'd ever laid eyes on, wearing a suit that probably could pay rent for a month.

Yet, here he was, telling me we were exclusive and looking at me like I was walking down the red carpet.

I suppressed the immense satisfaction I felt. "Fine."

"I'll drop you off to your friend's place. I've got to check in on someone, and then I'll pick you up for dinner?" Damien's face softened and his voice was so low, it shot chills up my spine.

He brought my face between his palms, planting the sweetest kiss across my lips. Just as he pulled his mouth from mine, I bit his bottom lip between my teeth.

"Keep that up, dandelion, and I'll spread you wide and fuck you until you see stars," he groaned as I scrunched my nose.

"I'd much rather do you than homework, but I also really don't want to fail. Come on, Casanova." I giggled as he tickled my sides and followed behind me. I felt his hands tug my backpack straps off me and he took it. Glancing over my shoulder, he smirked back at me.

There, Damien Moretti stood, wearing my pale pink backpack over his designer suit.

"I really wish I knew you when you were in college." I walked down the stairs.

"You'd have been a kid." He cringed and I laughed loudly.

"You're right, such a cradle robber, old man." I winked at him and jogged down as he raced behind me, my laughter echoing into the stairwell.

"Oh, you're getting spanked now." His voice

boomed behind as I laughed even harder until we got outside.

My heart was happy. My entire being was happy. The sun was beaming, and I looked behind and saw him frozen in his spot, and for the first time, Damien Moretti was smiling big.

Because of me.

CHAPTER 28
Damien

We got to Reese's apartment—which was right down the block from Sophie's—and Reese was waiting for us outside.

Physically, she was the exact opposite of Sophie. Her shorter blonde hair and blue eyes were a stark contrast to Sophie's raven, long hair and deep brown eyes that I was crazy about.

"Hi, I'm Damien." I stuck my hand out just after giving Sophie her backpack, which Reese most definitely blushed at the small gesture.

Fuck, these girls needed to set the damn bar higher. I'm sure the Jesson pretty boys couldn't carry a simple backpack—probably too busy jerking off because of their lack of ability to get laid.

"I'm Reese." Her face turned red as she shook my hand, darting her eyes between me and Sophie. Sophie looked at her feet and shook her head.

A shameless grin grew on my face. "Nice to meet you, Reese. I've heard nothing but amazing things about you from Sophie." I pulled my hand back. "Are you guys—"

"Oh my gosh. Sophie!" Reese looked between us.

Sophie's eyes widened as she warned her friend without words, shaking her head and covering her face.

"We're dating. Right, Soph?" I raised an eyebrow and smirked, causing her to grow even more embarrassed.

"Yeah. It's really new. I'll tell you inside," she said in a hushed tone to her friend, who was overly excited, clutching her fists and jumping up and down.

"I'll pick you up at six for dinner, baby." I leaned down and kissed Sophie, though I pulled away far quicker than I would have liked because I didn't want to impose on her study time, which I knew was going to turn into gossiping about her new relationship.

Reese laced her arm in Sophie's and they galloped away. I could hear their hushed giggles and turned away with the dumbest, but biggest, smile on my face.

The door shut behind Sophie and Reese, but right

before it did, Sophie turned over her shoulder and smiled at me. That fucking beautiful, sexy smile could melt a damn rock.

As soon as she left, the happiness I felt dissipated. My phone rang and I answered without looking at the screen.

"Looks like you do have a heart after all, Moretti. Now we know where it lies." Kane's wicked laugh radiated through the phone as I jerked around and looked everywhere. The bustling street in front of Reese's apartment was crowded with food vendors and normal pedestrians roaming.

"I don't know what you think you know, Kane, but I can assure you the only heart here will be yours when I fucking rip it out of your chest if you go near her," I grit into the phone.

His laughter grew louder. "What's the saying, Damien? Snitches land in ditches? How about snitches and *their bitches* land in ditches. Poetic, right?" he added before ending the call.

My chest pounded as I closed my eyes and slid my phone back into my suit jacket pocket.

My chest tightened. Why did I ever think I could do this? Why did I ever think I could be with someone without dragging them down to my hell?

Not only had I put Sophie at risk, but I had put Ezra's last remaining blood relative and my best friend's younger sister at risk. *I'm a selfish asshole.*

Kane wouldn't let me live in peace. Once you left a gang, you were never truly free. I tried with my legal power to protect myself, and for the most part, I had done well. I kept Kane out of prison to keep my end of the deal up, but secretly, I was tearing down the gang, locking up the assholes who dragged down young teenagers who had no other options than drug dealing and worse. Like he did with me.

Now he knew my weak spot.

Now he wasn't just after my blood; he was after hers, too.

I glanced back at the building where Sophie was completely oblivious to what was happening on the outside. She didn't deserve this, especially after every-thing her asshole ex-boyfriend had put her through, and not to mention losing her parents when she was younger. She had always been dealt a bad stack of cards, and here I was, trying to flush her out.

I had tried to dig up her ex-boyfriend, but it was just like Ezra had said. He disappeared into thin air. How some college kid was able to do that and not be found by my guys, who usually could find a goddamn needle in the Pacific Ocean, I wasn't sure. Maybe the son of a bitch died, which would be good luck for him.

I needed to check on Ashton, too. Kane had always wanted to swap me out for Ashton, which was another reason he was intent on ruining me. Ashton was younger, impressionable, and desperate for the things I once was. I pushed him into college and multiple rehab programs, keeping him out of gangs and the shit path I originally went down. Yet saving someone isn't simple, especially when they don't want to be saved.

I drove over to the rehab center to check in on him. When I got to the receptionist, she looked like her eyes were going to pop out of her head. "Mr. Moretti," she stammered and glanced around.

I hadn't showered yet, I was wearing my suit from yesterday, and I really needed to get home to take care of some work before picking Sophie up for dinner at Ezra and Amira's.

"What is going on?" I knew something was clearly off by the way the receptionist's pale face turned bright red.

"He… Well, you know what… Oh, there's Mr. Carson, now. He'll see you in his office, sir." She waved toward an older man with small glasses and fear embedded in his face.

Storming over, I turned into his office and sat in his chair, allowing him to sit across from me in the 'guest' chair.

"Speak," I growled as he stared at his hands.

"Mr. Moretti, we have always been so appreciative of your kindness and significant donations... but it seems Ashton has run away." His words were shaky and the man was lucky I was out of my old ways... *somewhat.*

I slammed my fist against the wooden desk that cut between us.

He jolted upright and trembled.

"Fuck!" I yelled out.

"I'm so, so sorry, Mr. Moretti. Please..."

I tightened my fist and eyed him with fury raging through me.

Suddenly, just as I thought about how I wanted to paint the room red with this incompetent fool's blood, my phone vibrated. Dropping my gaze to it, I saw Sophie's text.

I miss you, already.

All the rage that was pooling in my body, all the concern and anger I felt toward Ashton, had evaporated into thin air.

I had someone who missed me. I had someone who

wanted me, even with my endless flaws, and I sure as hell didn't make it easy for her to like me.

Standing, I shook my head at Bill Carson, then pushed out of his office, hearing him exhale loudly as soon as I crossed the archway.

I miss you, too, baby.

I texted her back and took in the fresh air when I walked outside. I needed to find Ashton. I called his phone over and over until I started calling his friends. The problem with a junkie is that you don't really have real friends, just ones you use for drugs, money, and a sofa to crash on until they get sick of your shit and throw you out.

Hitting my phone against my forehead, I yelled out. This was a disaster. He was probably out there somewhere, either going to get killed or kill himself.

I was sick of worrying about him. I hated how, for my entire life, I've had to protect him, baby him, and not only be his older brother, but also his parent. I hated how my dad was an abusive piece of shit, and that my mom was too weak to leave him. I hated that I had to be the one to make him bleed in order for him to leave.

Hate. That's what I was made of. I looked up to the bright blue sky and let the warmth of the sun glaze across my skin. Ashton would have to wait. I was no longer going to be controlled—by Kane, the gang, and now my idiotic brother. I headed back to my place to get some work done, and then to get ready to go get the one person in this world who made all the hate in my body feel less suffocating. I just didn't know what the hell we were going to tell her older brother tonight.

Sophie

"I can't believe you didn't tell me you were dating Mr. Sexy Biker Gang Man!" Reese squealed as we sat with our legs crisscrossed and textbooks scattered all around us. So far, we've accomplished zero studying and infinite gushing.

"Mr. Sexy Biker Gang Man?" I cringed. "He's not in a biker gang." My breathing hitched as I said the words.

"You know the last name Moretti is totally Italian mobster material, but he also rides that sexy motorcycle, so biker gang is a close second. I mean, the guy can shed blood in two seconds flat, especially if anyone looks your way. And let's not mention if anyone shares the same air as you; he'll suck the life out of them. But I bet you're enjoying sucking..."

"Oh my gosh, Reese!" I shrieked and shoved her arm as she erupted into laughter.

"He has to have a huge dick. Admit it! I know he has BDE... You know, big dick energy?" Reese was lying on the carpet with her chin on her palm, eyeing me with intrigue.

I sighed. "It's enormous. I'm talking, Dasani water bottle width, length... crazy." I clenched my eyes shut as Reese gasped.

"What the hell are you doing here studying with me, then? How did you even leave his sexy ass?" She popped another Cheeto into her mouth.

"Ezra's going to freak out. We're going to dinner at their place tonight, and we never talked about what we should say, or more so... not say." I rubbed my head as the thoughts and anxiety spiraled inside.

"I mean, big bro is going to have to get over it." Reese shrugged. "Besides, after everything you've been through, he can't tell you what to do. You deserve happiness, girl," she added with a small smile.

"It's not that, Reese. Amira and Ezra basically warned me about him. He's got some enemies, and his line of work can be dangerous."

"As a lawyer?" Reese squinted at me. "No, he's totally in a biker gang."

"He was, Reese. *Was*," I whispered as if the walls could hear our words.

Her eyes grew larger and she slapped her hands over her mouth. "Are you insane, Sophie! I was *kidding*! You're dating someone from a biker gang! This is not hot like *Sons of Anarchy*. No wonder Ezra and Amira were concerned. No, this is not good." Reese sat up and grabbed my elbows. "Sophie..."

"He was caught up in it when he was younger, but he isn't anymore. He's a well-respected attorney, Reese. Ezra trusts him."

"Ezra trusts him, but not with you, Sophie. There's a huge difference." Suddenly, the look of excitement and fun faded into concern and questions on her face.

"I'm going to tell Ezra and Amira tonight at dinner... Well, we are going to tell them." I rubbed lips and glanced down at a random page in my textbook.

"Does Damien know that?" Reese asked with hesitation.

"I'll tell him on the drive over. Now, can we please get some actual studying done? I really don't want to fail my quiz tomorrow." I flipped through and turned my laptop on to hopefully divert Reese from the questions that were clearly racing through her mind.

I couldn't blame her. She was worried about me. She helped piece me back together after what had happened with my ex-boyfriend. She saw the wounds, and she blamed herself for leaving me alone with him. She saw the pain that went deeper than my physical ones, but I hope she knew I wasn't going to make the same mistake twice. I wasn't going to give someone my heart who would only break it.

Hours flew by, and we were both consumed by the mounting stacks of homework and studying. My phone buzzed.

"Hey, Amira!" I held my phone in between my chin and ear while finishing the last paragraph on an essay.

"Hey sweetie, so change of plans. I got caught up at a design gig and thought it would be fun to go out at Club Fourizo tonight. I know you have a late start to classes tomorrow, so I figured we could all use some fun. Ezra lost a big case, and he's really just beating himself up over it."

"Oh wow, he didn't tell me. Is he okay?" I envisioned Damien and me walking into my brother's home, arm-in-arm, dropping a bombshell on him when he was already in a bad mood.

"Eh, you know Ezra... He blames himself if he doesn't win the impossible-to-win cases. Let's have fun tonight. You in?" Amira asked. "Oh, and bring Reese and Zach, too."

"Oh... uh, yea, I'm sure Reese would be down." I glanced up at my best friend, who was eyeing me curiously. I held my pointer finger up at her.

"What about Zach?" Amira questioned.

"Um... I'll have to see. I'm going to let Reese know the plan and start getting ready over here. I'll just ride with her." I swallowed as my stomach twisted. Did Damien know the plan?

"Okay sweetie, let us know if you girls need us to pick you up. I'm going to call Damien now and let him know, too." My heart pounded against my chest. Maybe we needed to just keep whatever we were doing under wraps until we thought things through.

After getting off the phone with Amira, I filled Reese, who was more than excited to ditch studying to hit the nicest restaurant and club in Chicago. Hidden away from tourists, it was an exclusive club. The only reason we'd even be allowed in—and since we weren't even twenty-one yet—is because Ezra knew the owner. I had only been once and it was an experience of its own. The food and drinks were exquisite, and the center was a glass lit dance floor with globally acclaimed DJs and musicians performing.

The simple dress I had brought from my apartment wouldn't cut it, so I started perusing through Reese's closet as she showered.

Tugging out a silky, emerald-green dress, I tied my hair up in a messy bun before taking my clothes off and sliding into it.

I spun around and glanced into the mirror. It fit perfectly.

"Well damn, that dress was made for you. My boobs are too big for it." Reese came out wrapped in a towel.

"You know I'm keeping it." I laughed and pulled out a dress from her closet. "Like you kept this one of mine, and I still can't find my favorite denim cut-offs." I gave Reese a side-eye, and she tossed her head back with a loud laugh that made me smile.

"I'm going to do my makeup and then call Damien," I said nervously.

"I don't think he should pick us up, and I definitely don't think tonight's the night to tell Ezra and Amira. Ezra lost a major case, and I just... I don't know. I'm starting to think telling them before their wedding is plain selfish." I was telling Reese but really, I was rationalizing with myself.

Reese looked at me as she puffed out a long sigh. "I think you're right. I don't think you should tell Ezra, especially until after their wedding. Truthfully, the guy has been there for you through it all, and I know he's your older brother and all, but he really was there as a dad, too. I think you've got to let him have this wedding be his time to be happy. But, I also think it'll give you and Damien time to make sure you really know what this is… if it's anything at all." She looked at me carefully as she brushed through her hair, and I paused at my eyes with a makeup brush.

"It's amazing how insightful you can be, Reesie Cup." I paused and chewed my bottom lip. "But I also hate how you're right." I sighed while adding dark shadow to my lids and feeling even more confused than I already did.

After Reese and I got ready, I walked out to the balcony to call Damien. The phone ringing had my heartbeat grow faster.

"Hey, baby." He sounded different, almost defeated, yet the way he called me baby had my stomach flutter.

"Hey. Is everything okay?" I asked slowly.

"Yeah… something personal came up. I'm going to head out to pick you and Reese up. Amira told me about the change of plans," he said, keeping his voice low.

Something about the way he said 'something personal' bothered me. Why couldn't he tell me what it was? Did it have to do with Carmen? Exhaling, I shook my head. I wasn't going to be *that* girl—the girl who badgered her boyfriend... Wait, was Damien my boyfriend? I mean, he technically said we were together, but I didn't know if we were actually labeling this. Filing those things aside, I quickly said, "Damien, I think we should hold off on telling Ezra and Amira. Reese and I are going to just grab an Uber and ride over there. Ezra lost a big case, and with their wedding coming up... I just..." I bit my bottom lip, hating the way this whole conversation sounded.

"Okay," he replied flatly.

"Okay, then," I said back, my chest tightening.

What was that? Is he mad?

Rubbing my face, I went back inside. Reese looked beautiful with her blonde hair curled, wearing a short but flowy skirt with a fitted lace camisole. Her long legs dipped into black heels, completing her look.

My face had more makeup on it then I ever wore. My brown eyes stood out against the black smoky shadow. My lips were lined and filled in with a sultry nude, and my tan skin was glowing with some fancy body oil Reese insisted I plaster all over.

I felt sexy wearing the slinky, emerald-green dress,

gold heels, and hoops. My long black hair silky straight, and of course I wore the colorful stack of bracelets around my wrist.

"Uber's here, babe," Reese called out as I grabbed my purse. Walking down, we slid outside and headed over. For some reason I was nervous, yet excited to see Damien. We had just seen each other this morning, but I didn't think he'd ever seen me so dressed up and made up before. This morning he saw me in my glasses, bare-faced, and in my worn-out college hoodie.

We walked outside, and Reese looked to match the Uber with what was on her phone.

"Wait, this isn't our car." Her brows furrowed. A man in a suit and ear piece came out and held the door opened for us.

I pulled Reese back with me.

"Aw, hell no. We aren't going into this kidnapping trap, motherfucker." I tugged my pepper spray from my bag and pointed.

The man threw his hands up and shook his head. "Ms. Shah, Mr. Moretti asked me to pick you both up. I'm Donovan, his security detail and driver."

I eyed him carefully and quickly pulled my phone out to call Damien.

"Hey baby, did Donovan get you?" Damien

answered immediately, but I could hear tiredness still lingering in his words.

"Oh wow, I didn't know you had another driver and security. We could have taken an Uber." I slid into the car after Reese, and Donovan carefully closed the door behind us.

"Sophie, do you actually understand that you are mine. That means the sheer thought of a man I don't know and trust breathing the same air as you infuriates me," Damien rasped into the phone, making chills rise on my arms.

"Thank you," I whispered, unsure what more to say.

"For what?" he asked.

"I don't know... caring?" I answered.

"I'd move every star in the sky if you asked me to, Sophie. All you have to do is ask me. I'll do anything for you." He paused as if he could sense how his words had consumed my mind and body, even though we weren't even in the same car. "I'll see you soon, my dandelion." The call ended, and my breathing hitched.

"Woah." Reese studied my face and her eyes widened. "You are utterly fucked, my friend."

Oh, you have no idea.

CHAPTER 30

Damien

I sat at a corner table with Ezra and Amira. Ezra was bitching about the case he lost, while I aimlessly spun the cocktail straw in my drink.

Amira looked at me curiously. "I don't think I've seen you drink before, Damien."

"He only does when he's about to implode, but leave it to Damien to not tell us what's really going on," Ezra said dryly.

I didn't take it personally. The man just lost a massive case that would have garnered him a huge boost in his reputation. I didn't say it out loud, but it was because Ezra wasn't like me—he wasn't a shark. For an attorney to be the best of the best, it meant you go head-on at the first sign of blood.

"You'll be fine. I probably have a case I can hand over

to you." I slapped him on his shoulder and took a long sip. The alcohol burned my throat, and I cringed at the fact I had let Kane and Ashton get into my fucking head.

Amira looked over my shoulder. "There's the girls!"

I spun around so quickly, I gave myself whiplash. Sucking in a breath of air, I watched her walk in, looking so beautiful that I hated knowing other eyes had the luxury of seeing her. Her gaze finally found mine, and a small but beautiful smile curved her perfect full lips that I wanted to taste.

I couldn't believe I was the reason for her smile; I didn't know I was capable of that. I felt like the most powerful fucking man in the world, and I would do anything and everything to make sure that smile stayed there.

I stood and Amira cleared her throat.

"What are you doing?" Ezra asked, waving down the waiter for another round of whatever he was nursing his bruised ego with.

"I'm going to grab another drink at the bar." I realized I didn't know how to hide the fact that my entire body reacted to Sophie's, but I had to respect her wishes to wait to tell her brother, who would most definitely attempt to bury me alive.

The most dangerous people in the world to piss off would be attorneys, because they would be the most likely to talk their way out of murder charges. Hell, he'd probably plea insanity or self-defense. Ezra was the golden boy, and I was... well more of the devil's advocate.

Walking toward Sophie and Reese, I brushed my hand against Sophie's, and she instantly dropped those stunning eyes to our hands touching.

She looked up at me. "Hey."

Fuck, she was gorgeous. I'd never seen her this dressed up or with that much makeup before. Although, I preferred her bare. *Everywhere.* But she looked sexy as hell.

"You look good, Soph... really good." I paused, and dropped my mouth close to her ear. "I can't wait to eat that perfect pussy of yours for dessert." Squeezing her arm, she parted her lips in shock. "You'll need to open it more to fit my cock..." I winked at her and continued my way toward the bar.

I hated this. I hated hiding the fact that she was mine. Mine to touch, mine to kiss, mine to hold. In public, in private. Everywhere and anytime.

I headed to the bar, even though I didn't care for another drink. I was just looking for any excuse to touch her before we sat down with everyone and had to pretend that my cock wasn't inside her this morning... or how she came so hard by the flick of my tongue.

Grinning as my lips pressed against the glass, I leaned

into the bar and turned to see her. She was sitting with her brother, Amira, and Reese, and while they were all chatting, her eyes scoured around.

She's looking for me.

Club Fourizo was dimly lit and crowded. The music blared, the waiters shimmied around with silver plates full of food and drinks as guests talked nonstop. It was a multi-million-dollar-making business. Everyone who was a somebody came here when in Chicago.

Grabbing a drink, I watched as Reese tugged Sophie to the dance floor. The DJ revved up the songs, and both Sophie and Reese started to scream, throwing their hands up in the air as they mouthed the words to some catchy hip-hop song I'd never heard of. Sophie's body swayed to the beat as she rolled her perfect ass to the rhythm.

Fuck. All the things I was thinking of doing to her right now... Thinking of her gorgeous bare body rocking and grinding against my cock until she screamed my name.

Ezra walked up beside me. "Hey. You good, man?" He slapped my shoulder and I quickly looked away from Sophie.

"Yeah, long day." I raised my brow at him as he took the shot the bartender slid over to him.

"You're telling me." He sank into the stool, and I

glanced back to where Amira was sitting. Another woman was seated next to her, which wasn't surprising since Amira always knew someone everywhere. She was the person who collected friends and never met a stranger.

"I ordered some food, so once it comes we can head back. I don't want to hear Amira and her friend Leighton churn out wedding details again." Ezra yawned and tapped the bar for another shot.

"Slow your pace, maybe?" I eyed him carefully. Unlike me, Ezra was clean-shaven, but today his five o'clock shadow was coming in. The bags under his eyes looked deeper, and when I really looked at him, he seemed defeated.

"Are you going to seriously whine like a little bitch over one case?" I sank into the stool next to him.

"It's not just that, man. I'm fucking exhausted. It's been a lot. The wedding, Sophie, and now shit luck with my cases." He was about to grab another drink, but I shook my head at the bartender.

"What's going on with Sophie?" I quickly turned and checked on her. She was still happily dancing with Reese on the dance floor, and I could see Amira in clear view of her.

Turning back to Ezra, I waited.

"She skipped her therapy sessions, and then she's

been a little... off lately. I don't know. I swear it's this fucking kid from school she won't let us meet. I'm just worried. I was so caught up with my own shit, and then her fucking ex-boyfriend almost killed her." He rubbed his hands across his face.

"Why didn't you get the police involved? Why didn't you go beat his ass yourself?" I could feel my fists tightening.

"I don't know. I tried hunting him down, and then I got the cops involved, but you know how this shit goes. According to them, Chicago PD apparently has more rigorous crimes to manage than a domestic dispute between college kids. Assholes."

"His name was Matthew Carson, right?" I took another sip of my drink.

"Yeah." Ezra nodded without a second thought.

"I'll try to find him. You know my guys are the best. We'll get that bastard." I patted his back and turned back to look at the dance floor.

Knowing in my mind *we* weren't going to do anything. *I was.*

I was going to find that motherfucker and break every finger on both of his hands for touching her. That was a promise I intended on keeping.

· · ·

Watching Sophie get lost in the music and the smile on her face made me happy. Until some guy decided to slide in behind her and drop his dirty hands on her hips. She flinched and looked at him, but he grinned and said something to which she shook her head. She tried to move but he gripped her tighter. I could see his fingers dig into the thin, silky material that covered her body.

He tugged her into his crotch, grinding on her. The glass I had clutched in my hand shattered against my palm and crumbled to the floor.

"Fuck, man!" Ezra shouted as the caramel liquid seeped out, and I tossed the rest of the glass shards to the side.

"What's wrong?" Ezra's voice trailed behind me as I stormed over to the dance floor. Grabbing the asshole behind Sophie, who was swatting at him, I gripped his collar and flung him to the ground.

His face dropped with shock as his eyes widened when I planted my feet by his face. He started to get up, but I slid one foot on his chest, slamming him down to the floor. I stepped harder as people gasped around and his pale, bitch face reddened. I continued to crush his chest until his weasel ass started to cry.

He's crying.

"If you ever touch what doesn't belong to you, I'll rip your fucking spine out and make sure you can't move. Never show your face in here again." I pressed harder until I swore his eyes would pop out of his head before I let go.

He scrambled to get up and once he did, he was about to run, but I grabbed his arm and jerked him back toward Sophie. Bending one of his fingers back as hard as I could, I knew I had broken it when he cried out, "Just let me go, man!"

"Apologize to the lady," I growled at him as Sophie flicked her eyes between us with her mouth parted.

"I'm... I'm so sorry, miss," he said almost inaudibly.

"What was that, little bitch?" I yelled, cupping my ear.

"I'm sorry... I'm so sorry!" he cried out.

Sophie nodded and looked at me with pursed lips.

"Get the fuck out of *my* club. If you step foot in here again, I'll make sure you never dance, walk, or move again." I flung him away like the trash he was. My security team came and carried him out before tossing him outside.

CHAPTER 31

Sophie

I stood there, staring up at Damien, who looked like he was going to murder someone a minute ago but his gorgeous face softened as soon as his eyes met mine. He was wearing a perfectly fitted gray suit, with a white button-down and cognac brown shoes that matched his belt. His dark hair was slightly messy from tossing another grown man around like a rag doll.

"This is *your* club?" I tilted my head as Ezra came up behind Damien.

"Yeah, I own it." He grew closer and let his hand drop to my elbow. "Are you okay, Sophie?" I nodded as my eyes met my older brother, who stood completely confused.

"What the hell just happened? Sophie, are you good?" Ezra's eyes were tinged red, and I knew he was a little too tipsy to process anything more than Damien being protective.

"Yes, I'm fine." I wiggled my elbow out of Damien's grasp when Ezra's gaze dropped to it. Luckily, my older brother was two drinks over his limit and waddled away to Amira, while Reese quickly pretended to need to use the bathroom, leaving us alone.

"Why didn't you tell us you own the damn club? I'd have definitely ordered more food." I crossed my arms and smirked at Damien.

Damien grew closer, filling the gap between us. "Baby, you can have anything, and I mean anything, you ever want. Nothing has a price tag on it for you." His eyes darkened as they stayed fixed on my lips.

"Well, what about you, Mr. Moretti? What is your favorite meal here?" I licked my bottom lip as his minty breath grazed my ear.

"You. And all I want to do is spread you out on the bar and bury my cock deep inside you until you scream my name." His words were smooth, deep, and so damn hot, I could feel myself grow slick as I followed his eyes to the crowded bar, and I knew he was picturing everything he just drew out for me.

Because I was.

"Hey, guys. Amira and Ezra said the food has arrived and wanted me to summon you back." Reese appeared with her cheeks flushed. I couldn't help but let out a small laugh. My best friend was clearly taking Damien in and no doubt, she realized why I was possessed by him.

Following her, I felt a quick grab of my ass and looked over my shoulder at Damien, who winked at me with mischief dancing in his eyes.

I couldn't believe he owned Club Fourizo. No wonder Ezra said Damien was listed as one of the richest men under forty.

Looking behind me once again, I saw his eyes were still on my ass. "Perv," I whispered under my breath as we slid into the booth.

"Mine," he whispered back with his dark brows lowered.

I couldn't help but grin at the simple word.

"So, how's wedding stuff going?" Reese looked at Amira after spooning food into her mouth.

"It's going good. I know I'm ready. Are you ready, sweetheart?" Amira nudged my brother, who quickly smiled at his fiancée.

"I've been ready to call you my wife from the moment I met you, my love," he replied.

My heart felt so full. Looking at Damien, his eyes met mine, and I don't know what that look was, but it made something inside of me do a somersault.

Would Damien and I ever have a real future? Did he

want to get married? Did he want kids? Did he want what I wanted?

The questions danced through my mind. I was only nineteen, and I had so much time to think of these things, but sitting with Ezra, Amira, and Damien, who were all in their thirties, made me realize these were the chapters of their stories they were already working on.

I still had to graduate from college, then go to dental school. I had so much time dedicated to my career and education—easily another ten years. That would make Damien in his forties before I was even ready to think about kids. And maybe five years before I was ready to think about marriage.

Breaking our gaze, I busied myself with the food in front of me. "I can't believe you guys are crazy enough to get married," Damien said with ease and every word stung.

Amira wasn't even fazed by him, and Ezra let out a laugh. It's as if they were used to him being this way. *Anti-marriage. Anti-love?*

"Why would getting married to the person you love be crazy?" I fired back, putting my fork down.

"Marriage is just a legal document, Soph. There's nothing romantic or loving about it. It's an idea of control. Controlling the person you think you want to spend the rest of your days with. But monogamy has an expiration date."

My heart raced as I looked at the man I thought I had a connection with—something, anything more than just a physical bond. He said we were exclusive; he said I was his.

But I suppose that didn't make him mine.

"People who think that about love and marriage are cowards," I spat out before turning away and looking at Amira. "I'm so ready for your wedding day and cannot wait to officially have a sister." I smiled at her.

Her eyes darted between Damien's and mine, as if she were desperately trying to figure out what had changed.

Everything had changed.

Damien didn't even try to fight back; instead, he started talking to my brother, who was oblivious to the tension that was hovering over us like a storm cloud.

Shoveling food into my mouth angrily, I waved down the waitress. "Can we add one of each dessert, too, please?"

Amira scooted closer to me, and brushed her hand against mine. "Is everything okay, Sophie?"

"Yeah, he just gets under my skin…" I huffed.

"He sure does," Reese said under her breath, which made me elbow her as she laughed.

"When are we meeting Zach?" Ezra asked across the table, breaking through the moment.

I didn't even have to look at Damien to know his eyes were searing into me.

"Maybe at your wedding." I shrugged. I knew that was a low blow, but the fact that Damien just said monogamy had an expiration date had my entire body fueled with anger.

Afterward, we spent the rest of the meal in mostly silence, and shortly after, Ezra called it an early night. I considered dancing with Reese, but she had an eight a.m. class tomorrow and needed to get back, too.

Reese lived closer to Amira and Ezra, while I lived closer to Damien, so my oblivious older brother decided to put me on the back of Damien's bike while Reese rode back home with them.

"When did you get a second helmet?" Ezra asked as Damien handed me the feminine helmet.

He glanced at me before sliding his helmet to cover his beautiful but very angry face. "Recently."

"Oh shit, Miss Carmen is finally getting to you..." Ezra taunted.

"Can we go?" I snapped. "I have homework still to do, and I have class in the morning." I rolled my eyes.

I could have sworn the cocky gorgeous man on the bike in front of me smirked before sliding on his bike.

Damien started driving, cutting through cars and traffic as the wind picked up my hair and covered my arms in the cool breeze. The lights were beaming brightly, a stark contrast against the darkened night sky. The sounds of the cars flying by us, the scent of the rubber burning against the gravel with intense speed was exhilarating.

Yet, even with all of the noise and motion around me, it didn't cover the way my heart was beating outside my body with the words, "Monogamy has an expiration date," on repeat.

Clutching Damien's abdomen tighter, I pressed my head against his back.

I really hope he'd change his mind, because for me, I couldn't imagine anything about us expiring.

CHAPTER 32

Damien

I parked my bike in the private garage that led to my penthouse. Sophie didn't protest or ask to be taken home, so I was hoping that the agitating conversation about marriage—that I knew bothered her —would quickly be forgotten. I wasn't a man who would pretend that I wanted something I knew I never would do.

Marriage was useless. It made two people far more comfortable with one another to the point of destruction. It made you weaker and vulnerable to being taken advantage of and ripped apart.

Marriage and even a long-term relationship meant changing yourself into a person you wouldn't be able to recognize. And I wasn't about to go down a path I never envisioned for myself. Thankfully, my parents and their shitty marriage set me up nicely, with zero expectations for the infamous happily ever after bullshit.

Sliding off my bike, I removed my helmet and reached to help Sophie down. She took her helmet off and revealed her gorgeous face that made everything inside of me shatter.

I was treading on very thin ice, and I knew I needed to set the expiration date for this. For us. And sooner, rather than later.

But tonight... *tonight* wasn't that night.

"What did I tell you about putting another man's name on your lips?" I growled as her eyes widened.

"I don't know what you're talking about." She rolled her eyes and turned to the elevator. Inhaling deeply, I nodded. She was going to play with me, but she didn't know how hard I was about to play with her.

Getting into the elevator, we stood on opposite sides, the heat and tension between our bodies palpable.

The doors opened, and we both slid out into my penthouse. I threw my suit jacket off as Sophie sat down to slide her heels off.

"Don't," I demanded.

Her big brown eyes flicked up to mine as I slowly began to unbutton my dress shirt. "Don't what?"

"Take those heels off," I answered. Her lips parted as she looked up at me curiously. I knew she was pissed off, but so was I. Saying she was going to bring that idiotic college guy to Ezra's wedding as her date was ridiculous.

"I warned you, Sophie. No man's name should ever be on your lips besides mine." I watched her swallow as she stood and straightened her back. Sliding my finger under her dress strap, I pulled it down on both sides. The silky material took no effort for me to peel off her perfect, tanned body.

I shamelessly took her in as the material pooled under her heels and she stepped out, wearing no bra and just a thin lace black thong.

"You've been a bad girl." I sank into the sofa and unhooked my belt, then tossed it to the side as she turned toward me.

Biting her bottom lip, she lifted her eyebrow. "And what are you going to do about it?"

"Get over here." I tugged her into my lap and laid her on her abdomen, leaving her perky ass on full display as I slapped it hard with my palm.

She cried out my name and gasped.

"Don't you dare ever think about, or talk about, another man again." I slapped her ass once more, harder. Grabbing her thong, I ripped it off as she cried out in excitement.

"Damien!" she shouted, looking at me with lust in

her eyes. Sliding off my lap, she dropped to her knees in front of me.

"That's my good girl." I unzipped my pants and tugged them off as her tits squeezed together when she leaned in. My cock sprung free, oozing at the sight of her lips ready to wrap around my length.

The slickness of her mouth and suction had my entire body shake as she took my cock into her throat. Gagging slightly, her eyes watered as she looked up at me under those thick lashes.

"Fuck, Soph..." I moaned as I piled her long, raven hair into my hands and pumped my cock in and out of her.

"That's it, baby. Just like that..." I groaned as she swirled her tongue around my tip.

Taking my shirt off, I threw it to the side and stopped her. "Come sit on my face so I can feel you drip down my neck." I rasped and leaned back into the couch. Hesitating for a moment, she climbed over my face and let me eat the most delicious meal I'd ever have. Lapping her up as she moaned in pleasure had me biting down on her clit and sucking her pussy harder.

"Now get on my cock so I can remind you of the only name that will ever leave those pretty lips."

Sliding off my face and onto my hardened cock, Sophie's mouth dropped as I stretched her over my width. "Ah," she moaned, closing her eyes as she dropped on me. Jerking my hips up and down, while rocking her over my length, had her tossing her head back in sheer ecstasy. Flinging her over on to the couch, I clasped my hands around her throat as she panted. Plunging inside her, I let my tongue intertwine with hers. I could feel her pussy suck me in as she let go and screamed loudly.

My fucking name. Mine. Pulling out of her, I slid my hand over my cock and came all over her perky, thick tits. She sucked in a breath of air as I smeared my come all over her nipples.

"Damien..." She sighed with a satisfied smile curving her lips.

Pressing my lips against hers, I whispered into her parted mouth, "That's right, baby. Only my name."

A few minutes later, I got a wet cloth and wiped Sophie clean—a gesture that had her cheeks turning red. Afterward, we climbed into bed; the bed I had never allowed any woman to spend the night in or even feel completely comfortable in. Now, here I was, with her in my arms, and Sophie was trailing her fingers against my tattoos. Tracing the old scars, she pressed her chin against my bicep and looked up at me.

"Did you mean that?" she whispered.

"Mean what?" I asked, running my fingertips against her smooth back.

"Monogamy has an expiration date," she repeated my earlier words.

"I did. But I am starting to realize that you make me want to defy that." I brushed my lips against her forehead, and the small gasp that came from her had my cock jerk in appreciation.

My phone rang, breaking me out of the moment where something within me felt shifted with the way Sophie looked at me.

Fuck. Ezra...

Clearing my throat, I answered as Sophie's forehead creased and I put my finger against my lips. "Hey, man."

"I'm at your door. Let me in. We need to talk," Ezra replied hastily. My eyes widened as I looked at Sophie, naked, in my arms and wrapped around my body in my bed.

"You're at my place?" I repeated.

"Yeah? Listen..." he lowered his voice, "it's urgent."

"I'm coming." I quickly slid out of the bed and hung up.

"Your brother is here." I looked at Sophie, who immediately shot up and tugged the sheets around her breasts.

"What?" she gasped. "Don't you dare let him in, Damien!"

I tugged on my pants and shirt and said, "Baby, this must be really important. He knows I'm home."

Sophie's face softened, and she looked significantly more relaxed.

I shook my head at her, confused.

Her lips ticked up in a small, shy smile. "I like when you call me baby."

"I like you, dandelion." I winked at her.

"Don't let him in this room, or we'll both be dead," she warned as I nodded and quickly locked the door behind me.

Ezra tumbled in as soon as I opened the main penthouse door. It was late at night, his tie was loose and his eyes were red. "Carmen's dead," he poured out without even a breath.

I jerked back with almost a dry laugh seeping through the shock of my mouth.

"You clearly had too much to drink tonight. I hope you didn't drive here." I looked at my best friend, who was heading toward the sofa.

"She's dead, Damien. Frank called me. We've been

calling you for the past fucking hour. It's goddamn Kane." He rubbed his face and kept his eyes down.

My fists clenched as I processed everything. *Carmen, dead?* Kane didn't even know her; she had nothing to do with him or my past. We met through work as two attorneys who often landed in the same courtrooms. Two lonely souls looking for something physical but not emotional. That was the extent of us.

I cared about her, sure. She wasn't just someone to fuck; she was a friend, a colleague, and a companion. My breathing grew unsteady as I sat in the lone chair across from Ezra.

"Aren't you going to say something? I mean, you have been together for years," he spewed at me angrily.

"How do you know it was Kane?" My voice dropped lower as my mind raced.

"Because I just got this fucking message couriered to my house where my soon-to-be wife is sleeping." He shoved a manila envelope across the coffee table that divided us.

I tugged the papers out and found an image of Ezra, Amira, me, and Sophie sitting at the table at Club Fourizo with a sticky note on it.

One by one, they all go boom.

"Amira and Sophie are next, Damien. He's going to fucking kill my girls—" Ezra's voice broke.

My eyes stayed on Sophie's smiling face in the image. He wasn't after Amira, he wasn't after Ezra... He was after *me.*

And that meant he was now after Sophie. He was after *my girl.*

You never left the gang. No matter how many deals I cut with Kane to buy my freedom, he knew I had sold my soul to the damn devil, and now he was finally going to make me pay. His way.

But why? Why now? Oh, no...

Ashton. My idiot brother must have done something, and put us all at risk.

"I have to make a call." I stood and went to the balcony, shutting the door behind me.

My chest tightened as the cool breeze rippled through, and a howl of wind taunted me. Carmen was murdered. She was collateral damage because of me. Grief and anger tugged inside me.

"Kane. What do you want?" I immediately said when he answered. A wicked laugh erupted on the other end. I fought back the emotion I felt about innocent Carmen being terrorized because of me.

"I hated watching the life leave those beautiful, exotic eyes... it took all my strength to not fuck her before I killed the bitch," he said, laughing louder.

All I wanted to do was kill him, end him for good.

"What. Do. You. Want?" I hissed, as my hand threatened to shatter the phone in my hand.

He clicked his tongue and sighed. "Oh, not much... just the love of your life."

"I don't know who the fuck you're talking about or what you think you know." My heart pounded against my chest rapidly.

"Sophie Shah. Sweet, Sophie. She's beautiful and smart... I'll give you that. I just can't believe she is *also* Ezra's baby sister." Cruel laughter left him again.

"Tell your asshole brother Ashton, that no one, and I mean no one, steals from us. He will have all your blood on his hands and then some. If he wants this to stop, then he has to come and pay his dues himself." My mouth was dry, my ribs ached, and my body twisted.

"If you touch her, I'll gut you like the fucking animal you are." Hanging up, sweat danced across my forehead as I gripped the glass balcony rail and screamed out into the Chicago skyline.

Regret pooled inside me as Kane's words rang deep into me.

The love of your life...

The bastard was finally right about one thing.

I was in love with Sophie Shah, and now, I had to make her hate me.

Because that was the only way to protect her.

CHAPTER 33

Sophie

I had my ear pressed against the thick black door as tears strummed down my cheeks. My older brother was talking to Damien about Carmen being found dead. Fear coursed through his words as he worried about Amira and me. Worried about our lives being in danger? Who was Kane? What was happening? Here I was, standing behind the door wearing Damien's T-shirt with panic racing through every bit of my body.

I wanted to run out and into the arms of my older brother and tell him everything. Tell him to take me home, away from the questions I didn't know the answers to, and probably wouldn't want them, either.

But instead I stood there, wiping the straggling tears away until I heard Damien's voice again. "Go home, Ezra. Get some sleep," he said without emotion.

"Damien... don't shut down," my older brother quickly replied.

"I'm not. I need fucking time to think before he starts playing dominoes with everyone in my life." Damien sounded angry, and I could feel it in each word.

"Stay away from Sophie. I know you both have some weird shit between you, but if you ever lay a finger on her and try anything with her, then that's the end of our friendship. I saved you, Damien. Don't ever forget that. This life you're living is because I took your word, and now I need you to promise me you'll stay the fuck away from my only living family member."

My heart shattered to the floor at Ezra words. Tears ran rampant and my nose began to run as I covered my mouth to stifle the sobs.

Damien and I should have never gotten involved with one another. It was the most selfish thing to do. Not only that, but I'm realizing now more than ever that it was also the most dangerous thing I could have ever done.

I crawled into his bed, drawing the covers over my body, hoping it would swallow me whole. I didn't know what I was supposed to do. Where I was supposed to go? I was terrified to go back to my apartment alone. I just wanted to go back to classes, eat lunch with my friends in the quad on the grass, complaining about professors and boys. Now, here I was, not sure what I was doing anymore with anything or anyone.

"Soph..." his voice trailed in as he climbed into bed next to me. The soft yet masculine scent of sandalwood grazed my nose.

"Baby..." He brought the blanket off my face. Opening my eyes, I was met with his stunning green ones, the flecks of gold shimmering. For the first time, I saw Damien Moretti look *sad*.

"I'm sorry about Carmen." I pinched my lips to the side, hoping I wouldn't burst into tears again.

"Me, too." He nodded slowly, letting his index finger pad against my abdomen, leaving goosebumps behind.

"Sophie, I need you to listen to me. You're going to leave Chicago and stay somewhere safe until I can figure some stuff out." He wrapped his arm around my waist as I stared at the ceiling.

"I'm not leaving. I have school." My voice cracked with uncertainty swooping in.

"You can do classes online. Sophie, this is not the time to fight me. Please, I am begging you, baby. You don't realize how dangerous everything is right now." Damien looked at me carefully.

"Then tell me. Stop treating me like I'm some fragile

doll who can't take anything. I'm tired of all the secrets, Damien. First, our relationship... if that's even what this is? Then, your line of work, the fact that you were in a biker gang... *A fucking biker gang*!" I paused and covered my face, shaking my head in my palms.

"Sophie, when I got out, I thought it was a clean cut. I thought I was free to live my life. The blood on my hands, the darkest memories, and the things I've done will live inside me forever, but I thought I could at least just live on my own terms. They wanted my younger brother to fill my spot, and I protected him as much as I could.

"I tried to stop him, but he went to them, anyway. He's a drug addict with no job or money, and they know his weak spot. Now, he's stolen from them, and Kane doesn't let anything go. I could pay the debt, but it still wouldn't be enough. Nothing will be enough until he takes everything away from me." The lines in Damien's forehead deepened as if what he had just said was physically painful.

"I'm not scared of some guy named Kane. I mean seriously, what the hell kind of gang name is that? Isn't it supposed to be like Bloodshed or something?" I started pacing the room, not able to wrap my head around the fact that I was having this discussion with my boyfriend.

"I'm not leaving Jesson. I'm finishing the year. Too

much of my future depends on this, and no one, especially no man, is going to make me destroy that." I wiggled my finger at Damien. I let out a long breath. "Either be with me or don't, but I'm done with the secrets, Damien."

He grew closer to me, filling the space between us before tilting my head up. "I'd rather die than be without you, dandelion." He smashed his lips to mine and reached down to lift me into his arms. My legs snaked around his waist as my ass rested on his forearms. Kissing me hard, our breathing grew heavier. The world was crumbling around us moment by moment, yet right here, right now, all that mattered was us.

Two hearts beating into one.

Tossing me onto his bed, he peeled his shirt off my body, planting his lips where the fabric had covered. My hands flung into his hair, pulling him up toward me. Our eyes locked and as if the world tilted on its axis, Damien brushed my hair from my face and whispered into my ear, "I'm not going to fuck you, Soph." He bit my earlobe. "I'm going to make love to you."

His lips moved over mine and as he spread my legs apart, then pushed inside me with long, steady strides.

I closed my eyes, parting my lips and suddenly, tears

teased my eyes as Damien's breathing picked up. "Baby, look at me," he said softly.

I was scared. I was scared he'd see it clear as day in my eyes.

I am in love with him.

He kissed me again, softly and whispered again, "Please, don't deprive me of those gorgeous brown eyes, baby."

I slowly opened my eyes and looked into the deep green ones in front of me. He was buried deep inside me, and not just physically, but I realized in that moment that he had reached my soul. I didn't know who I was anymore without him. And I didn't want to.

His hips moved over and over as he slowly rubbed my clit with his thumb. The way he was being gentle with me only made the intimacy soar through every limb in my body.

"I'm scared I'm falling in love with you," I murmured vulnerably.

Smirking, he brushed his hands through my hair. "You don't have to be scared baby, because I'm here. I've already fallen and it's the best place to be."

"I love you, dandelion," he whispered into my mouth before kissing my neck softly. Lacing his fingers with mine, he pushed his tongue inside my mouth, swirling it with mine. My entire body shook as my toes curled and an orgasm rippled through me. Spreading my legs wider, he kept his eyes locked on mine.

He could feel how I clenched around him, and his movements picked up. Long, strong thrusts inside me until his jaw clenched and he filled me.

Collapsing next to me, I turned toward him. "I love you, Damien." The tips of our noses grazed.

He loves me.

"I'm not leaving Chicago, and I'm not leaving you," I whispered to him. "Because for the first time in my life, I'm not holding my breath. With you, I can just breathe." I paused. "After all, Chicago is my home. Where is home for you?"

"You're so damn stubborn, Miss Shah." He sighed and kissed my forehead, wrapping me in his arms. "My home is you..." he whispered into my ear and dug his teeth into my earlobe, "and inside you..."

"I feel like loving you is going to hurt." I said softly.

"It's not love if it doesn't hurt." His eyes dropped between my legs with a small smirk curving across his lips.

My heart pounded against my chest as my thighs clenched together. "Think you'll be able to keep up with me?" I arched my brow and looked at him carefully.

"I hope so... I just hope your brother doesn't kill me first." He tightened his hold around me and closed his eyes.

I hope he doesn't, either.

CHAPTER 34

Damien

One month had come and gone. Sophie still wasn't ready to tell Ezra about us, and I wasn't in any rush considering everything seemed to be spiraling around us with Kane, my brother, and Ezra's upcoming wedding. Sophie was busy with school, but we spent most of our evenings together. In our own twisted way, we found a new normal. She accompanied me to Carmen's funeral, which I knew was terrifying for her.

She saw a woman who was once in bed with me, laying in a coffin. But I swore to Sophie there would be no way on earth I'd let something happen to her. I slept with a gun under my pillow, and I had security interwoven in our lives. I did whatever I needed to in order to protect the love of my life.

Sophie had been staying with Ezra and Amira, but was in my bed every night, though they assumed she was with Reese. I was still looking for Ashton with no luck. I suppose when you teach someone how to disappear from the world, they keep those skills close.

"Can you believe the wedding is this weekend?" Sophie was lying on her stomach, completely naked in my bed. I was tracing my finger against her wrist when I saw the scar on her beautiful, smooth skin. It was where that asshole cut her. It was the reason she always kept the stacks of beaded bracelets on her wrists.

"I'm going to kill him," I said as my blood curled at the thought of someone doing something like that to my girl.

Touching and hurting what's mine.

"Damien... he's long gone. You even said it, you can't find anything on Matt." Sophie closed her textbook.

She sat up and looked at me, and I nodded slowly. I had my best men on the job looking for Matt, but, much to my displeasure, Sophie's ex-boyfriend had fallen off the face of earth. My greatest life goal was to make sure he never took a breath of air again.

"I'll find him. I always do." My jaw ticked as frustration built inside me.

"Amira asked me who I was bringing as my date to the wedding." Sophie stroked my cheek. With everything going on, Amira and Ezra moved their wedding date up, and they were planning to leave for an extended honeymoon while I cleaned up the enormous mess pooling around me. Ezra's plan was to send Sophie to her grandmother's house in Texas while she finished the semester virtually. I let him believe that, but there was no way I was letting Sophie out of my sight.

"What did you tell her?" I asked curiously.

"I just said I was flying solo." She shrugged, but chewed her bottom lip.

"We can tell them, Sophie," I offered.

"Ezra's going to hate you, Damien, now more than ever. I want them to enjoy their wedding. It's been chaos, and I don't want our relationship to become a debate. I just... I just wish we could have at least shared a dance. But even doing that will make Ezra mad. He's worried sick about Amira and me after Carmen's death." She looked away.

"Baby, you know I'd never let anyone hurt you. I promise you." I lifted her hands into mine and kissed them both.

Sophie rolled her lips together and nodded at me. "I know."

"The man who pulled the trigger is locked away." I ran my hands through my hair. It wasn't hard figuring out which one of Kane's little bitches was cowardly enough to kill an innocent woman, and once I did, I made sure to get my revenge by beating him to near death before calling the cops.

He was locked away for life, but there would be no peace until I put Kane away. Pulling the trigger was one thing, but the one who orders the hit is the devil himself.

"I hate hiding." Sophie looked toward the windows.

"Hiding?"

"Us." Her lips were pinched to the side and sadness was clear over her face. We weren't just laying low because of Ezra, but also because of Kane. The last thing I needed was him to know Sophie and I were really together.

Once I found Ashton and dragged his ass out of the mess he pulled me into, I was hoping Kane would let go of his vendetta that I left the gang, and that I wasn't going to watch my younger brother sink the way I had.

"I'm going to head out and meet with Reese and Zach to study, then stay over at Ezra's. Amira has a list of wedding things she needs my help with." Sophie climbed out of my bed and quickly put her clothes back on.

"I don't mind coming to study with you." I sat up and climbed into my joggers, then followed Sophie into the living room.

She let out a small laugh and looked up at me. "We

are studying biochem, Mr. Moretti. Aren't you a lawyer?"

"I'm good at other stuff, too." I filled the gap between us and held her face between my palms as we got into the elevator.

"Oh, I know that." She giggled, pressing her face into my hand.

"Let me drive you." I snaked my arm around her waist as we walked to my garage.

Once there, Sophie slid her helmet on and smiled at me.

"I want to drive." She opened the visor on the helmet and looked at me with naughtiness in her eyes.

"No," I answered without a second doubt.

"Yes," she fired back and slid to the front of my bike.

"Sophie, hell would have to freeze over before I let you drive. Slide back," I demanded.

"No. I'm driving."

I leaned in and whispered to her, "You know what happens when you don't listen, Sophie. You get into trouble."

Her eyes crinkled with excitement. "You say it like that's a bad thing. Now, get on and let me ride, Moretti."

I tossed my head back and groaned. Climbing on the back, I put my helmet on. "For the record, there is only one thing I like you riding." I wrapped my arms around her waist.

"And what would that be?" she asked deviously.

"Me," I answered as she revved the bike and the tires screeched against the pavement.

"Fuck!" I held on and started firing out instructions, but Sophie wasn't listening; she was laughing and speeding out before I could even take a breath.

I didn't believe in God, but in that moment, I prayed for our fucking lives.

Miraculously, we made it to Reese's apartment, and my badass girlfriend climbed off the bike, took her helmet off, and shook her long dark hair in this sexy way that had my cock hardening at the mere thought of taking her on my bike.

"Fuck. Dandelion, you are perfect." I gripped her waist as she scrunched her nose at me.

"Thanks, baby." She stood on her tiptoes and planted a kiss against my lips. "But I do hope you'll still spank me later, daddy." She winked and turned.

I followed after her and slapped her ass as she jumped and laughed loudly. "I'll walk you up." I slid my hand into hers and grabbed her backpack, carrying it upstairs to Reese's apartment.

The door opened and Zach appeared.

Fucking, Zach.

"Hey, Sophie!" he said cheerily and leaned in for a hug. Before he could wrap his dirty hands around her, I slid in between.

Jerking back, he looked at me. "Hey man." He nodded and took a step back.

Sophie cleared her throat and gave me a side-eye.

"What?" I mouthed.

"Behave," she hissed at me as Zach turned and walked in.

Winking at her, I whispered, "Never."

Reese was hunched over her laptop, typing away rapidly as Zach sank into the sofa next to her.

Reese lit up and smiled big. "Hey, Damien."

"Hey, Reese." As soon as I spoke, her cheeks filled with red.

"I'll be at home, baby. Call me and I'll pick you up." I bent down and kissed Sophie's soft lips, feeling Zach's eyes on us.

"Reese is going to drop me off at Ezra's. Remember, wedding stuff?"

"Oh, right. Okay. Well, be safe. I love you." I kissed her forehead before turning away, and Reese gasped after I said those three little words. Biting back a smile, I walked to the door.

"I love you, too," Sophie called out sweetly behind me.

Nodding, I opened the door and shut it behind me.

I had to make my way to the tux shop to do my final fitting with Ezra today before their wedding over the weekend. It would also be a good time for us to discuss everything we both knew needed to be talked about. Ezra had been on edge since Carmen died, and I didn't blame him. I was, too; I just knew I couldn't show it.

Ezra was my best friend, yet he'd never met Ashton. I didn't want Ashton to meet the people most important in my life because I knew my brother. He'd weasel his way into anyone's life to take advantage of them, just like he did with me.

Once I found him, this would all be over. We'd be okay. I'd tell Ezra the truth about Sophie and me, and we'd all move forward.

Pulling up to the tuxedo shop, I walked in and saw Ezra being fitted.

"Hey, bro!" he called out to me. I let my hand out and he took it, drawing me into him.

Ezra Shah was not just my best friend; he was the one who showed me I could be more than the guy who would have eventually either been dead or behind bars.

Part of me hated myself for falling for his little sister when he'd done nothing but trust me and believe in me.

"You ready to be pussy whipped for the rest of your days, my man?" I swatted his hands away and tied his bowtie for him.

"I miss my parents," he said, looking down.

I didn't say anything until I finished tying the bow and stepped back. "You're lucky to have had parents that you actually miss." I slapped his shoulder.

"You look good. Not as good as I will, but good enough," I said to him, which made him laugh. "They'd be proud of you."

Ezra immediately tightened his lips and closed his eyes. "Thanks, brother." He exhaled as I quickly turned away and went to go find my tux for the fitting. Guilt started to creep inside me; I hated lying to my best friend, and I hated that I seemingly only brought pain and problems to the table. After this weekend, I'd tell him everything. They'd go to their honeymoon, I'd be there for Sophie, and we'd all be okay. Life was too short to live the way we were.

CHAPTER 35

Sophie

"I don't understand, Sophie. He's really in a biker gang?" Reese had her mouth dropped, and Zach was staring between us in complete shock.

"He *was*. Then some lunatic killed the woman he used to hook up with. Apparently, his little brother stole money from them or didn't keep his word, and then ran away, so now they are adamant about hurting Damien." I couldn't believe the words that were coming out of my mouth, but here we were. I knew I shouldn't have told Zach and Reese, but truthfully, I had been terrified. I hadn't been back to my apartment without someone coming with me, and I hated this sense of fear and terror that lurked all around me.

"Okay, this is actually outrageous. You need to tell your brother. I mean, he's an attorney; he can protect you. You need to end things with this guy, Sophie," Zach poured out and I knew he wasn't doing it to be cruel. Concern was splattered all across his face.

Leaning back into the couch, I shook my head, running my hands through my hair. "I can't end things with him. We haven't really had our chance to even begin things yet." I blinked repeatedly because, for some reason, tears started to sting my eyes.

Reese came closer and brushed my hand gently. "After the wedding, you have to tell Amira and Ezra."

"Yeah, I will. Well, *we* will. It's going to be okay." I knew I wasn't trying to convince Zach or Reese; I was trying to convince myself.

The next few days flew by in a whirlwind of classes, studying, and helping Amira with all the last few bits and pieces for their wedding day.

Saturday morning came quickly, and Chicago decided to bless us all with a gorgeous fall day. Tinges of orange and red were starting to make its way through the lush green trees and everything seemed to have a blanket of peace wrapped around it.

Ezra stayed over at Damien's, and I stayed with Amira. It didn't go past me seeing the two hulk-sized body guards inside their home, making sure we were safe.

Amira's family was swarming around the apartment, and I tried to stay out of everyone's way. Sliding into my bridesmaid dress, I did a quick spin. It really was beautiful. Long and silky, it hugged me perfectly with a deep cut in the front. It was also ivory, which I thought was strange, but Amira was going to be wearing a red, traditional Indian wedding outfit and wanted me to wear ivory. They didn't have a big bridal party, just Damien and me, and Ezra's other friend was going to be their officiant. Their original wedding was planned to be this enormous, big, fat Indian wedding, but they were eager to marry early and leave for the honeymoon.

More so, Ezra was. He was constantly worried something was going to spiral and happen to me and Amira after the ominous letter he got from Kane.

A light knock on the door sounded, and I opened it slowly. "Wow. Amira." I slapped my hands across my mouth. She looked like a princess. She was mesmerizing in her gorgeous Indian wedding outfit and adorned in stunning gold jewelry. Tears built in both of our eyes as I wrapped my arms around her.

"You are the most beautiful bride I've ever seen. Are you sure you want to marry my crazy brother?" I laughed as she sniffled into my shoulder.

"I love you, Sophie." She planted a small kiss on my cheek and looked at me with her hands on my arms. "You are gorgeous." She smiled.

I wiggled my shoulders and scrunched my nose. "I guess I clean up a little nice."

Laughing through our tears, we knew it was wedding time. They were getting married at a local garden in a small, intimate ceremony.

"Ready?" Amira nodded toward the door.

"I'm so ready to have you officially become my sister. Are you ready?" I jumped excitedly, clutching my hands together.

"So ready." We laced our hands together and made our way down to the venue.

We drank champagne during the limo ride over to the venue and the excitement hung over us like sunshine. Nothing else mattered. All of the pain, uncertainties, all the fears... it all dissipated into thin air. The driver opened our door and security quickly lined up as we slid out. My heart pounded against my chest as I looked around. I peeked my head back into the limo. "See you inside, sis." I smiled at Amira, who was hiding out with her dad until everyone got seated.

I walked to the gate by the ceremony and watched as

everyone trickled in and took their seats. Rose petals lined the aisle leading to a gorgeous arch filled with blush and ivory flowers. Fairy lights twinkled all around, and I couldn't help the goofy smile on my face. Something about weddings made all the bad in the world disappear.

The security guards stood close to me as I waited for my cue to walk in. We hadn't done any form of a rehearsal or discussed the way things were going to happen since the wedding was moved so quickly.

Suddenly, a strong hand slid into mine and I turned around. My eyes met with the sparkling green eyes that penetrated into mine.

"Soph, you are beautiful." Damien exhaled as his eyes traced every part of me. The way he looked at me with possession and admiration set a fire inside my body.

"Thank you..." I looked away for a moment before looking back at him.

I could feel his gaze still on me.

"What is it?" I asked.

"If only you could see what I do. You... standing in front of me wearing that white dress..." As soon as he said those words, my heart fluttered and a twist in my stomach made my nerves go wild.

Is he picturing me as his bride?

He was wearing a perfectly fitted tuxedo, his dark

hair styled and his eyes standing out against his beautiful natural tan.

"You don't look so bad yourself, Mr. Moretti." I bit my bottom lip as his hand squeezed mine tighter.

"I love you, Soph." He started to lean in, but then Ezra cleared his throat and appeared right behind us.

I jerked my hand out of Damien's. "Hey, big brother," I squeaked. When I looked at my brother, who wore a similar tuxedo as Damien and looked handsome as ever. "Ezra." I paused and moved closer to him. He smiled as soon as my arms wrapped around him.

"Mom and Dad would definitely think I was the prettier child today, but you look amazing and they'd be so proud." I scrunched my nose as he let out a laugh.

"Thanks, kid." He kissed the top of my head and rubbed my back. "I love you, and even though I'm getting married, nothing changes. I'm here for you always, and I hope you know that." Something about the way he was looking at me with concern made me feel sad.

I hated that he had carried this weight on his shoulders, constantly having to worry about me. I wish I could just tell him that I was fine, that I was more than capable of taking care of myself. School was going great, and I'd be financially independent one day. I also wished in this moment I could tell him about Damien.

"Mr. Shah, it is time to take your place." The wedding planner's voice cut through the palpable thoughts and emotions between us.

"Damien. Sophie." Ezra nodded at us and smiled. He walked down the aisle as a pianist played, and Damien bent his arm out. Looking down at it, I smiled and looped mine in it.

"What's on your mind?" Damien whispered.

Pausing, I tilted my head up. "I was just thinking about how hot the best man is."

Damien tossed his head back and laughed, but quickly quieted himself as soon as the wedding planner shot us daggers with her eyes.

The music shifted and we were directed to walk out. Clutching his arm, my heart pounded against my chest as we walked down the aisle.

There we were, two people in love, walking arm in arm down an aisle in a tuxedo and white gown.

Glancing at Damien, his jaw tightened and he kept his face straight. But then, just as we got to the end, he lifted my hand in his and my breath stopped for a moment as he looked at me in a way that made the world stop spinning.

He didn't have to kiss me, he didn't have to say a thing. I knew he was thinking, wishing, and hoping that maybe one day... one day it would be in the cards for us to stand here and promise forever to each other.

I just didn't think it would be so hard to get to that day. I just didn't realize how foolish it was for both of us to ever think we'd even get a chance at that one day.

CHAPTER 36

Damien

I stood behind Ezra as Sophie stood on the other side. She was absolutely breathtaking, and I couldn't take my eyes off her.

My angel. My world. My heart.

I wasn't deserving of her love. I had ruined her for any other man, and now I didn't know how we would be able to stay together when her future was set to be beautiful and mine would always be scarred with ugly memories and people who would always threaten any form of a future.

Carmen's death had been painful. Sophie had asked me countless times if I wanted to talk about it, or talk about her. I didn't.

I never loved Carmen, but she and I had a relationship that wasn't just sexual. We both had this drive to success that overtook us and that general understanding connected us. Because of me, she was dead. All the sacrifices and hard work she did in her life was over in the snap of Kane's fingers.

I couldn't prove it was Kane yet, but I was able to lock up the man who pulled the trigger. Kane was untouchable. My mind was spinning with what I should do versus what I wanted to do.

As my mind clouded with unease, I looked at Sophie and her lips curved into a small smile when our eyes met.

I did that to her. I made her smile. I made her happy. And now, I'd do anything in this world, even if I had to burn it to ashes, to keep it that way.

The music picked up, and the guests stood. We all turned and watched as Amira walked down the aisle with her dad holding her arm. Looking back at Sophie, she was wiping under her eyes as tears fell. I wished more than anything that I could go wrap my arms around her.

Suddenly, I realized Sophie wasn't just crying because of the beauty of a wedding, but she was crying because her father would never walk her down the aisle.

Ezra would.

My best friend who trusted me when he didn't have many people to trust would be crushed to know I had taken his most beloved possession and put her in harm's way. After all, that is what I was.

Harm.

But there would be no man in this world who'd ever love her the way I do. There would be no man in this universe who'd move all the stars in the sky for her.

For that, I would fight. I'd fight for Sophie; I'd fight for us.

Ezra and Amira exchanged vows, and with their words, I kept my eyes on Sophie. She kept looking down and back at me, with her heart clearly beating fast as her chest rose and fell quickly. The guests cheered when Ezra kissed Amira and they raced down the aisle covered in rose petals.

I knew I couldn't give a fairytale life to Sophie. I wasn't the prince charming like her older brother was; I was always the villain.

But suddenly, I really fucking badly wanted to be everything she needed me to be.

Walking closer, I bent my arm for her again, and she laced hers in mine. Everyone was bustling around us and I kept Sophie close. I had spent one hundred thousand dollars on security but ultimately, I knew she was mine to protect. No one would get to her without killing me first. No one would touch her without them burning to the ground.

No one.

After taking countless photos with the excited bride

and groom, the photographer went off to take pictures of the venue. "Sophie, come with me," I whispered into her ear as Amira and Ezra busied themselves with others.

"Where are we going?" She smiled up at me, looking over her shoulder before picking up her pace.

"Hey, Martin. We're here." I nodded at the photographer, who grinned as soon as he saw us. The sun was setting and I pulled Sophie closer. "We don't have any pictures together." I brushed her hair from her face and kissed her.

Opening her eyes slowly, she batted her lashes. "I didn't know you were a romantic, Mr. Moretti." She wrapped her arms around my waist and the photographer clicked a few pictures.

"Will you take one of just her for me?" I moved out of the frame and Sophie grew bashful.

She started to laugh as I stood next to Martin and I just knew. I knew that would be the picture I'd engrain into my heart and soul for the rest of my days.

Martin went back to the reception since the first dance was about to start, along with all the other wedding frills I had no interest in.

Sophie started to walk away, but I grabbed her hand.

Turning her into me, I held her face between my palms, leaned in, and kissed her.

She smiled under the touch of our lips, and I kissed

her again. Pulling her into me even more, she opened her eyes, able to feel how hard my cock was for her.

"Damien..." she started, but stopped when Amira called out for her.

"Shoot. I have to get back. We have to get back. You need to do something about..." Her eyes flicked back down to my crotch.

"How about we do something about it after the reception?" I dropped my gaze.

Laughing, she started to jog away as we quickly made our way back to the reception. Ezra had his arms on Amira's waist as a song played. Sophie stood on the other side, watching me intently with her arms crossed. I knew how badly she wanted to dance, but there was no way we could without Ezra suspecting something. I didn't dance and he knew that. If I was dancing with his little sister, then he'd look at me like a bull and a red flag. I didn't want to upset him on his wedding day.

Instead, like a coward, I'd disappoint him while he was across the Atlantic on his honeymoon in my Italian villa I had set up for Amira and him to stay in.

The first dance, cake cutting, and endless small talk took up the rest of the evening. Besides continually making sure I could see Sophie for her own safety, we were separated. Friends and family all flocked around her to catch up on lost time while I hovered around like a lone wolf.

Ezra came up beside me and slapped my shoulder. "Not looking for your next conquest?"

Scanning the room forcefully, I shook my head and looked over at him. "Nah. I'm good."

"Congratulations, brother." I raised my glass and he clinked his against mine.

"I hope you let yourself experience this one day, Damien. You deserve to." He sighed.

I guess now would definitely not be the time to tell him I had experienced it, but the only problem was, it was with his little sister.

I nodded. "Yeah, maybe." Looking back at the dance floor, I saw some guy dancing with Sophie.

Fuck, no. My girl. My dance.

"Who the fuck is that?" I pointed, quickly handing my glass to a wandering waiter.

"Oh, that's my friend, Brent, from high school," Ezra answered without a second thought.

"Why is he dancing with Sophie?" I asked through clenched teeth.

"He's harmless, man. She didn't bring a date, and she loves to dance. Better Brent than some guy she brought who I don't know." Ezra shrugged and quickly got distracted by someone congratulating him.

Cutting through the crowded dance floor, I grabbed the foolish man who had his hands on someone that didn't belong to him and jerked him back, trying my best to not make a scene. The music was blaring, people were laughing and yelling out the words to the song.

"What the hell!" Brent shouted.

"Do you like breathing?" I asked him with his shitty Men's Warehouse suit clutched in my hand.

"What?" His forehead creased in confusion, and Sophie started to hiss at me.

"Do. You. Like. Breathing?" I repeated slightly louder.

"Yeah?" he answered while swatting at my hand.

"Then keep your fucking hands off her. I'll break each and every finger if you even think about touching her again." Shoving him as hard as I could, he wobbled backward into the crowd with terror in his eyes.

"Damien!" Sophie shrieked and smacked me on the back.

"What was that?" I lowered my voice and grew closer to her as she took a step back.

"It was a dance!" She shook her head and spun around. Grabbing her arm from behind, I pulled her into my chest.

"Damien, someone might see us..."

"Let them see. Baby, you don't deserve to be hidden;

you deserve to shine." I gripped her hand in mine and wrapped my other arm around the small of her waist.

Just on cue, the DJ played *Dandelions* by Ruth B.

Sophie's head jerked up and she looked at me with so much damn love.

"This song..." She smiled.

"I know, dandelion. I love you." She pressed into me as we swayed to the song she was singing and dancing to the first morning she was in my penthouse. The morning I didn't know, but I had become consumed by her. By every piece of her.

"My sun, my moon, my stars..." I whispered into her hair as she clutched my hand tighter.

"I love you, Damien. Don't ever let me go." Sophie closed her eyes and a small tear made its way down her cheek.

"You light up the darkest of skies for me, baby. I could never." I spun her around.

For the first time in my life, I loved dancing.

Sophie

The reception was over, and by God's grace, Ezra and Amira didn't see Damien and me dancing. They sped off after asking me countless times if I'd be okay. Ultimately, there was no way anyone could convince me to leave college and hide away.

"Where are we going?" I asked as we got onto Damien's bike and sped down the bustling Chicago streets. My gown flew behind us and I couldn't suppress the smile of how sexy Damien looked riding his motorcycle in a full tuxedo.

He didn't answer me until we parked and he helped slide me off. The night sky was full of stars dancing along the sky and we walked along the sidewalk hand in hand.

"Is Damien Moretti seriously about to walk the

Magnificent Mile with me?" I cocked my head and looked at him with shock. We were dressed to the nines, and walking through the crowded pathway down to Navy Pier.

"I guess everywhere feels like paradise with you, baby." He held my hand tightly and we made our way until we were standing at the Ferris wheel.

"Are we going to ride it?" I asked excitedly, jumping up and down with my gown held up in one hand.

The attendant opened the safety gate and I slid onto the seat. He locked and pushed me upward alone. "Wait!" I shook my head but the man didn't bring me back down; instead, Damien just stood there watching me as the Ferris wheel kept going.

"Damien!" I shouted down. Sinking back into my seat, I looked at the water and the lights brightening up the evening. What the hell was he doing?

Once the Ferris wheel made a complete circle and got back down, I was about to get off but Damien quickly slid in next to me.

"Hey, is this seat taken?" He smirked at me as I scooted back in.

Slanting my eyes at him, I chewed my bottom lip. "No..." I answered as he placed his hands in his lap.

"Oh, by the way... I'm Damien." He stuck his hand out for me.

Suddenly, it all flooded back to me. He was giving me a meet-cute. The meet-cute I always wanted... the one I told him about when I first met him.

Holding my hand and shaking his, I couldn't help the goofy, enormous smile that made its way on my face. "Hi, I'm Sophie." As soon as our hands met, my heart fluttered.

"Thank you, Sophie."

"Thank you for what?" I asked.

"For giving my eyes the most beautiful sight they've ever seen." He drew his hand against my face and brought my lips toward his.

Slowly pulling away and exhaling, I murmured, "I don't think my boyfriend would be pleased to know some random stranger was kissing me."

"Oh yeah? Then he definitely won't like what I have planned for you once we get off this Ferris wheel," he rasped against my face.

The heat between my legs grew, and my muscles clenched as the Ferris wheel froze at the top. Damien slid my gown up until his hand had full access to my leg and slid further up until his fingers met between my legs.

"Damien, someone will see us!" I looked around, seeing hundreds of people below flocking the strip and pier.

"Well let's give them something good to watch." His fingers pushed inside me and my head flung back.

"I need you stretched out for when my cock buries inside you tonight, baby girl." He blew into my ear as he slid another finger inside me and pumped them in and out. I was slick, and my clit was throbbing as his thumb put pressure on it.

"Damien..." I chanted his name with my breath hitching.

"You're so tight baby, so damn tight." He fingered me harder until I clenched down and tightened around him. My release came so fast, and just as the wheel started to move again, I let out a long, satisfied moan. Pulling out of me, he drew his fingers covered in my come and licked them clean.

"So, fucking sweet," he groaned.

Once we got off of the Ferris wheel, he picked up his speed and we both jogged to get back to his bike and get back home.

I didn't think we could cut through traffic and make it back to the penthouse as fast as we did, but Damien made it happen. We hadn't even gotten halfway out of the elevator before our clothes were pooled at our feet.

Damien lifted me in his arms and pressed me against the windows, where the skyline was lit up and the world watching us.

"As much as the Ferris wheel was a fun ride... I would much rather be riding your cock," I said as I locked my lips with his. He let out a satisfied grunt and took me to his room.

"You are a very naughty girl, Miss Shah. Do you know what happens to naughty girls?" Heat flooded my body as he flung me onto his bed.

"Get on all fours," he demanded. Once I was, he got behind me and slapped my ass so hard, my back arched.

The pain stung but pleasure quickly took over as he slapped my ass again. Letting out a small cry, I held myself up as the bed creaked and I felt Damien's mouth on my pussy. Looking down, he was on his back and licking me as I was on my knees and palms, fully exposed to him.

Holy hell.

His tongue crept inside me, and he swiped it along my folds. "You're drenched for me, baby. I love how you're dripping down my fucking neck," he rasped as I gripped the sheets, praying my screams wouldn't come out.

"Damien, I need you," I begged.

"Tell me what you want from me," he demanded with arrogance lining his words.

"I want your cock." I exhaled as he pulled out from under me and came around to face me. But it wasn't his face that matched mine; his hardened and huge cock was aligned at my mouth.

"Open that dirty little mouth of yours. I want you to suck my cock so hard, you choke on it and tears line that gorgeous face." He squeezed my jaw with his thumb and index finger. I was wrecked. I wanted to taste every bit of him and feel him inside me. Opening my mouth obediently, he plunged his dick inside so deep that I gagged hard.

"Fuck, Soph." I grabbed his balls and massaged them as I rocked my mouth over his length until tears stung my eyes and he jerked out.

"I'm not coming in your mouth. I'm going to fill your pussy with every last drop of myself. Spread your legs, baby. Spread your legs for me." Damien didn't miss a beat. His attention was locked into me completely. It was as if the entire world had iced over and I was the last woman standing. His eyes were hungry, his lips were thirsty... and all he wanted was me.

Falling backward, my head hit the pillows as I splayed my legs apart, and he moaned as he looked at me, completely open to him.

For him.

Taking the tip of his cock, he rubbed it along my folds. Every time we had sex, I had to brace myself. Damien was huge, and the way he fucked me made me now know I didn't just need a physical preparation, I needed a mental one, too. The sensations were all too intense when this gorgeous, sexy man was deep inside me, saying the filthiest of things that made every ounce of my body burst into flames.

"Damien, now." I tilted my head up as a dark smile crept over his face.

"So needy." He pushed inside me, gripping my hips and rocking me over his length. My arm flung over my mouth as I cried out from the intensity of his thrusts.

Pulling my legs up, he rested my ankles on top of his shoulders and plunged inside.

"You're so deep, Damien," I panted as he kissed my ankle and foot. He smiled seductively as his breathing picked up and he repeated his motions. Licking his finger, he began playing with my clit, making my body go into overdrive. My hips lifted as my back arched and an intense tremor rippled through my entire body. Damien and I rode our orgasms out together, my breathing hitched as my nails dug into his biceps.

Falling next to me, his body glistened with sweat as he planted a soft kiss against my forehead.

"That was amazing..." I breathed out.

"Obviously, it was baby." He smiled sheepishly.

"Wow... cocky much?" I play slapped his arm.

"Anything that involves you is amazing, my love." He

trailed his fingers against my abdomen.

"I have something for you." He leaned away and opened his nightstand drawer, bringing out a small box and an envelope.

"Damien, what is this?" I sat up and cracked the black box opened, gasping at the silver inside.

A dandelion was engraved into the smooth metal. It was stunning. Not flashy, not over the top, but simple and completely us. Damien took the ring from my hand and slid it on my right-hand ring finger.

Lifting it up to his lips, he kissed it and then my hand.

"Forever my moon, my stars, my sun... my dandelion." Letting my hand fall on my heart, I held the envelope as Damien rested his face in his palm.

"This is the most beautiful ring, thank you so much. I love it. I love you, Damien."

"I love you, too. Now, open your next gift." He pointed at the envelope. I opened it quickly and tugged the paper out.

"Damien, this is too much." I unfolded the paper and dropped my jaw. It was two tickets to Paris.

"What?" I paused, tears stinging my eyes.

"You said one day you dreamed of your meet cute on the Ferris wheel so I wanted to give that to you. Then I thought you'd maybe want to go to the City of Lights with me since that's exactly what you are in my life, my light. Baby, I want to make every single dream of yours come alive. Today, tomorrow, and always. With you, one day is today."

I started to cry, and Damien wrapped his strong arms around me, holding me close into his bare chest.

"I love you so much." I sniffled into him.

"I love you, my queen." He kissed the top of my head. Smiling, I closed my eyes. Today was the most perfect day. He was right... one day is today.

The sun streamed through the windows, and I let my hand graze Damien's side of the bed.

Empty.

Opening my eyes, I looked over at the time. It was Sunday morning, so he probably ran out to get breakfast. Pushing the comforter off me, I slid out of bed and walked to the closet. I had a few things here, but I needed to go back to my apartment and pick up more of my clothes.

Checking my phone, I saw Damien's text.

Hey baby, I didn't want to wake you. Had to run into the office to pick up some files and then grabbing breakfast for us. I love you, dandelion.

With a grin on my face I texted back.

Good morning handsome. I'm off to my apartment to grab a few of my things for classes tomorrow. I'll be back soon. Love you.

I grabbed my purse and keys and headed out.

Taking a deep breath in, the scent of autumn was hanging through the crisp air. I couldn't help but smile with the stunning shades of red, orange, and yellow taking over the trees that lined the streets.

Grabbing a cup of coffee from a small stand, I skipped cheerily down, replaying every single moment of yesterday. Ezra and Amira were already in Italy and sent some pictures of Damien's villa. I couldn't believe how many places Damien owned around the world and here in Chicago. To me, he was just Damien. I was a nineteen-year-old college girl with a boyfriend who had millions of dollars. I literally couldn't wrap my brain around it.

Holding my hand up, I admired the ring on my finger and took in the fresh breeze that rippled around me. We were going to Paris for fall break and life had never felt sweeter. For the first time in a very long time, the gaping hole in my heart from the loss of my parents and the trauma by my ex-boyfriend started to feel less noticeable.

I walked up the stairs and went to my apartment. Unlocking the door, still consumed by everything beautiful that was happening, I didn't even think twice as I walked into my bedroom.

Until I wish I had.

A loud crashing sounded and then he appeared.

It was a moment where you're stuck between seeing your happiness and heartbreak fighting for the spotlight.

"Matt?" My voice trembled as my ex-boyfriend appeared. His eyes were stained red, with dark circles lining the once beautiful eyes I would get lost in. Glancing at his arm, I saw track marks lining his flesh and my heart stopped.

He was holding a gun.

"Matt..." I started to walk backward but he was quicker. Slamming my bedroom door shut, he jammed the gun into my abdomen, causing me to cry out.

"Please. Please, don't do this. What do you want?" My words were weak, and I hated that was the effect he had on me.

"Sophie, my beautiful girlfriend." His hands brushed against my cheek, instantly making me flinch and move my head away from his. I didn't want to even share the same air as the man who destroyed me.

Beat me.

Hurt me.

Left me to die.

"Please just go, Matt," I whispered, wishing I could

find the strength to scream or yell, but I couldn't. I was shaking and trembling, replaying my trauma and fear in my mind. My hand slid to my shorts pocket and I tugged my phone out carefully, but Matt saw and grabbed it from me, slamming it so hard into the hardwood floors beneath us.

"What do you want? I'll do anything." I choked on my words.

Jerking my head up with his hands in my hair, he slammed it back into the door. The pain was both shocking and stinging, but my body grew numb as I froze in fear.

"I love you, Sophie. You just could never see that," he spewed so close to my face I could feel his spit splatter against my skin.

"You are incapable of loving anyone but yourself. Get. Off. Me." I cleared my throat and smacked his hand from me, but Matt was significantly bigger and stronger.

He let out a sinister laugh and with the hand holding the gun, he slapped me. I screamed so loudly as soon as the crack of the metal and his fist hit my face that my teeth dug into my cheek.

Tears poured out against my raw face. My nose began to run into my lips as fear coursed through every part of my body.

"I missed you, babe." Matt grew closer, running his

lips against the side of my neck as I dug my nails into his arm, trying to pry him off me.

Laughing at my feeble attempt, he flung me to the floor and pinned me down with his knees planted on either side of me. My arms were swinging all around as I screamed, praying and hoping my neighbors or anyone would hear me. Help me. Save me.

But then, he unzipped and dragged my denim shorts down and my screams grew louder as I begged.

Begged him to stop.

Begged him to not do what he had in mind. Licking his bottom lip, darkness grew over his features as he unzipped his pants. My legs and body were pinned, but my arms were my one last hope, and I slapped him across his face with all my might..

"No!" I screeched. The slap only made him angrier and then, just before I could try to fight anymore, he punched me.

My head dropped hard to the ground beneath my body. I didn't stand a chance. He was going to rape me, and then he'd probably kill me.

Crying harder, I closed my eyes as he ripped my panties from my body.

But then, the door slammed opened.

I didn't open my eyes. I was scared that if I did, I'd see I was hallucinating.

"Sophie!" Damien's voice sliced through every ounce of terror and then... silence.

My body no longer felt heavy.

"Ashton..." Damien said, and I opened my eyes.

Ashton?

My eyes were blurry as I cried harder and tugged my shorts back on as Ashton and Damien stood staring at each other. It was as if Damien was in a state of shock.

Damien's eyes dropped to me and then shot back to him. His fists clenched and, in a flash, he had Matt pinned to the wall. His fist pumped with such force and speed blood began to drip all over.

"Ashton! You motherfucker! You're going to die! How dare you? How dare you fucking touch her?" Damien screamed so loudly that my heart shattered at each word.

Crawling on my hands and knees, I sank into the corner of my bedroom, crying hysterically.

"Damien, that's not Ashton, that's my ex, Matt!" I said through thick sobs. But Damien wasn't listening; he was possessed, kneeing Matt in the gut before throwing him to the ground and stepping over him. His knuckles were covered in blood, his T-shirt was streaked and stained. I heard cracking, and realized Damien was doing exactly what he said he'd do if he ever found my ex-boyfriend.

He was breaking every finger that hurt me.

Sinking my head into my knees, I wept harder, not able to process anything. "You're my brother!" Damien yelled and I looked up. *His brother?* If Matt was really his brother, then I didn't want Damien to live with this forever.

"Damien, stop!" I yelled as Matt laid there, unconscious and covered in blood.

Damien's fist froze mid-air as he slowly turned and looked at me. My tank top was ripped, my shorts barely on.

"I don't understand." I shook my head with tears falling.

"I didn't know... Sophie, I didn't know." Damien's words were pain stricken.

"Matt Carson doesn't exist, but Ashton Moretti does." Damien came to me and sank down, dropping his head, defeated.

"Ashton's always been in trouble, Sophie. While I was traveling out of Chicago, I sent him to someone I knew could get him an entire new identity. I didn't want to know it; I didn't want to know anything about the name he chose. I thought if I knew anything about him, then Kane would find it out, too. He came to me and told me he had done something horrible." Damien covered his face with his bloodied hands. "I just didn't know that something horrible was attacking you, Sophie." He paused.

"I helped him disappear. That's why when I tried to find Matt Carson, I couldn't. That's why when I tried to find your ex-boyfriend, I couldn't. I didn't even know, but I was looking for someone *I had hidden away.*" Damien kept his face in his palms and the tears in my eyes stung.

It hurt too much. Damien was his older brother; he was the reason he got away without any repercussions. He was the reason the man who wrecked me was able to come back and hurt me again.

"You helped save an abuser." I sniffled and stood on trembling legs. Damien looked up at me from the floor, and for the first time in the entire time I knew Damien Moretti, he looked weak and destroyed.

"I didn't know... Baby, I didn't know. I would have killed him if you didn't stop me. Love is thicker than blood. I love you, Sophie. I love you. I'm so sorry, my love." His forehead creased as his eyes pleaded with mine.

I scoffed at the word love coming from Damien's mouth. "First Kane, and now Ashton... You bring nothing but bad men into my life, and I'm starting to realize that men keep the same company. You're a bad man, Damien, and I think I always knew that you can't wipe a slate clean. You're always going to bring bad men into my life... men who want to hurt me. When I look into your eyes, I'm just going to see him now." I shook my head.

"Baby, I didn't know what he had done. I swear to you." Damien stood and I stepped over Ashton's body.

"But you knew he did something bad... bad enough to need to disappear. And you helped him do that, never caring about the destruction he left behind. Not caring that he ruined someone's life. My brother was right about you; you are darkness, Damien." I bit my lower lip hoping to stop it from quivering as tears and heartbreak radiated throughout my body.

"Baby... you're right. I am darkness, but that's why I need you. You are my moon, my stars, and my sun. You are my light. You've always been my light. Without you, I can't see clearly, I can't breathe freely. Without you, I can't go on." His words cut through my heart in a way physical pain couldn't even compare.

"But that's the thing... I can't let you take the light from me anymore, because then all I'm left with is darkness." I wiped the tears from under my eyes and turned away, realizing that sometimes you have to be the one to leave the destruction behind, because otherwise, it'll consume you for life.

CHAPTER 38

Damien

I had my brother locked away. I had him dragged out of Sophie's apartment, covered in blood and dropped him off at the police station with broken fingers. Sophie stopped me from killing him... she stopped me even though she shouldn't have. She told me if I killed him, she'd hate me even more for taking a life.

He wouldn't get to disappear anymore. It was time he paid for his sins.

People talk about heartbreak all the time.

Broken hearts.

Heartache.

But I didn't feel that when Sophie left me. Instead, I felt cold, empty. I felt my soul leave my body and go with her. Because that's what Sophie was for me. She wasn't just my heart, she was my soul.

She warmed me with her light, but she knew I couldn't return it. Without light, a dandelion would die.

* * *

Two months had come and gone. Two agonizing months of begging Reese to tell me how she was. Two months of my best friend hating every part of me.

I had to call Ezra and Amira after everything that happened—Sophie did, too. They were on my private jet back within the hour, and the next day, they had Sophie with them.

No one would tell me anything; no one would look at me.

Sitting at the Le Petit Bistro in the back booth, memories flooded me. This is where I had met Sophie. This was our meet-cute. But there wasn't anything cute about it.

What she didn't know was while we bickered and fought from the moment we met, the only true thoughts that were running through my mind was how she was the most gorgeous woman I'd ever laid my eyes on. How all I wanted was to know her.

. . .

"Damien." I looked up from the hot coffee mug that was warming my hands.

"Amira." I sighed. She had finally agreed to meet with me. "How is she?" I fired out before she even sat down.

Tilting her head, she studied me. I knew I looked like hell, but that's what happens when you walk through the flames and let it scorch you.

I lost her. I had lost her forever, and now nothing mattered. I didn't care if the world stripped me of every belonging in my life. The only thing I cared and loved in my life was gone.

"Damien, Kane sent us another threatening note." Amira tapped the table in front of her.

I had spent the past two months hunting him down, but he had disappeared once I threatened to expose everything I knew if he didn't stand down.

"We're moving." Amira kept her eyes on the table as she began tracing the grooves.

"I'm going to kill him. You know I will," I breathed out as my chest walls began to cave in around me. The thought of Sophie no longer being in the same city as me made the air deplete quicker than anything.

"No, you're not. Because if you do, you'll end up in prison with men who work for him, and they'll kill you.

So, we're going to move. We're going to start fresh, and we're taking Sophie with us. Ezra already spoke with the dean at Jesson and they are going to set her up with virtual classes." Amira finally met my eyes.

"Please don't do this. I need to see her. I can protect her," I pleaded.

"Damien, she can't even look at you without seeing him. You protected the man who hurt her, who almost killed her." Amira reached her hand out.

"Damien, sometimes the best thing to do in love is to let it go…" She held my hands in hers. "You should have never pursued her. Now you've lost her, Ezra, and yourself." She shook her head with tears trickling down her face.

"Can I see her?" I asked again.

"I'll ask her. We leave tomorrow. But if she doesn't want to see you, please respect her enough to leave her alone." Amira slid out of the booth and started to walk away.

"Amira?" I called out, and she looked over her shoulder, raising a brow.

"I texted and called him. I showed up to your place, but he didn't hear me. Tell Ezra… I'm sorry for hurting him, but I'm not sorry for loving her. He'll hear you." I turned back and stared into the black coffee that had turned cool. Snow flurries began to fall from the gray sky as the clouds hung low.

I'd never be sorry for loving her. Because loving her was the only thing I did right in my life.

✱ ✱ ✱

Two Years Later

Time is such a peculiar concept. As humans, it dictates every ounce of our lives. Time to wake up, time to shower, time to go to work, time to eat, time to sleep. *Time.* Twenty-four months had come and gone. The seasons shifted, the sun rose and set. Life went on for the world. But when was it truly time to live?

I did live. I got to live when Sophie was in my life. Her laughter fueled my heart. Her touch saved my soul. She made me want to live. *Without her, I was merely living to die. With her, I was dying to live.*

Sophie wouldn't talk to me. I called, I texted. I begged and pleaded. But she didn't accept. She had Amira tell me to leave her alone.

Alone.

The state of my life I had always lived in and craved, but now, I was hating every second of being alone.

Maybe one day Sophie would understand. Maybe one day Sophie would realize I didn't know her connection to my brother, and if I had, I would have burned the world down with him in it. Maybe one day Sophie would see that Kane was a dangerous man from my past —a past I didn't want and was punished with a future I couldn't change. Maybe one day Sophie would see that I love her more than anything in the world. Maybe one day Sophie would see that without her, my world is dark and cold. Maybe one day Sophie would know the only reason I'm still breathing today is because I'm clinging to the sliver of hope that my one day with her would still come.

I had sold my law firm. I had packed away my things and sold my penthouse. I moved into a small house in the outskirts of Chicago and started to take pro-bono cases. But more than anything, I had found Kane.

He was hiding away in the Bahamas, so naturally, I set his house on fire in the middle of the night with him in it. Bending over, I lit my cigar up with the flames before leaving and never looking back.

That meant I had a red target plastered against my heart even more than ever. But I didn't care. My life no longer had meaning. I had taken my brother and Kane off the streets and knew the world was slightly better without them.

My phone rang, and I answered it without even looking at the screen.

"Hey," he said flatly.

Pulling my phone from my ear, I looked down at the contact name to make sure I wasn't delirious. "Ezra." I had so much to say, yet the words didn't form together to make sense. "How are you? How's—" I stopped as he cleared his throat.

"I don't know... I don't know how I'm supposed to be, Damien. I uprooted my entire life, along with my wife and younger sister. I lost my best friend, and we lived in fear up until recently when I found out Kane was dead and Ashton was locked up." I didn't know what I was supposed to say. The guilt, the depression, the anxiety all collided into one.

"Do you know what it's like to worry that someone you love more than anything is in harm's way?" Ezra asked dryly.

"Yeah, I do... I really do," I answered without any hesitation in my voice.

Ezra scoffed, and I could feel his frustration through the phone. "You were my best friend... I considered you a brother. You wrecked her. You hurt her more than ever, because you made her believe you were a good guy, Damien. But you're nothing but a selfish coward who can't own up to the fact that you'll always have blood on your hands. You'll always be the guy I had to piece together and push to make something of himself."

I thought the words would sting, but they didn't. I didn't feel anything anymore.

"You're right, Ezra. I'm not the good guy. I've hurt people, I've stolen, I've killed. I've done it all. But I changed the moment Sophie came into my life."

"Don't say her fucking name," Ezra roared with anger. If we were having this conversation in person, I was positive he'd have met his fist with my face.

"What do you want, man? I have nothing to give you, tell you... I have nothing more to say. I've apologized to you and Soph in every goddamn way possible, and at this rate, an owl should be showing up with my apology letter any day now." I rubbed my face, exhaustion creeping in.

"I wanted to make sure you were still alive," Ezra said.

"What?"

"Sophie, for some reason, wanted to make sure you were okay. She also sent you a letter. I got your address from Tony."

"Can I talk to her?" I asked quietly.

"No. She doesn't want to speak to you."

"Where are you guys? Please, Ezra, just tell me that," I begged the man who knew where the love of my life was. I had searched, I had hired the best, but the thing was, Ezra knew all of my tricks. He had managed to make sure I would never find them. Truthfully, even if I knew where they were, I wouldn't go to Sophie.

I wouldn't go to her unless she wanted me to, and all signs indicated she was safer and better off without me. Safer without me.

"You are so much older than her. You should have known better. You really should have." Ezra ended the call abruptly.

My chest tightened as I replayed his words. Standing, I walked to my mailbox. It was overflowing with mostly junk mail, which I threw to the side, but froze when the small pale pink letter in her writing appeared.

It was dated a week ago.

Fuck.

Ripping it open, I tugged out the cream paper and emotion crashed through me as I studied her handwriting. I thought about all the nights she was studying and taking notes by my side, lost in her books and eager to make sure her future was bright.

Dear Damien,

I've written this letter over and over and ripped it apart again and again. Here I am,

knowing I need to do this. Maybe, selfishly more for me and less for you, because I need closure. I need closure, but don't think that's possible. You've engrained yourself into my life in a magnitude that no matter how hard I try, I can't erase. Maybe I don't want to erase you from it. It's ironic, isn't it? You, Damien, are the creator of my most beautiful memories but also my most painful ones. It's been almost two years since I last saw you. Two years. A lot can happen in two years.

I'm about to graduate from college. I don't know how I managed to push through, but I did. I did it for me. I did it for Ezra and Amira. I did it for my parents. I did it for the ones I love.

I did it for you.

Because I still love you. I'll always love you. Part of me hates you because you've ruined me, and I don't think I'll ever find love again.

Not our kind of love.

Messy and wild. Hard and easy. Most of all, true.

I want you to know that I don't blame you for why someone from my past hurt me and almost killed me. I don't blame you for your connection to horrible men. I know you didn't choose to be related to him. I know you got involved with the wrong people because you thought you had no other options.

But life is safer and calmer without you, Damien. And I need that right now. I can't afford to watch someone I love get hurt. I can't take the risk that loving you is more valuable than loving my family.

I hope you know we didn't grow apart like most couples who end things do. We grew. That's it.

I grew.

And truthfully, growth isn't a bad thing. Growth is what makes the dandelions turn into what gives us our wishes.

Maybe one day the stars won't be lost. Maybe one day they'll find each other and align to bring light to the darkness, and they won't be so scared to shine brightly. Because together, they can break the darkness easier than alone. Maybe one day things will be different. But today, I'm still hurting. Today, I blew out a dandelion puff and all the petals scattered, and that hurt even more.

Because I know you're out there loving me, too. There couldn't be a more painful punishment for either of us. But we always knew, didn't we? That it wasn't if, but when love breaks us.

Love,

Sophie

Tears stung my eyes. In my entire life, I couldn't recall the last time I cried. Collapsing to the pavement, I clutched the letter against my face knowing her fingers and hands touched it. I also knew, without a doubt, her lips did, too.

CHAPTER 39

Sophie

"I cannot believe my baby sister is starting dental school." Ezra sat across from me with Amira next to him.

"It's kind of crazy, right? I can't believe it's finally happening." I let out a soft laugh, tearing a piece of bread off and dipping it into the olive oil.

"But out of all the dental schools in the country that would have been thrilled to have you... you really think Chicago is where you need to be?" Ezra asked warily.

"Ezra, it's been over two years. It's one of the best programs in the country. I'm not letting anyone hold me back from what I want." I offered a small smile.

"She's going to be fine, and I'm going to visit all the time. Right?" Amira added and rubbed Ezra's arm. She was five months pregnant with their baby boy, and it felt like the perfect time to leave the secluded coastal town in Florida. As much as I loved living with them and having the safe space to heal myself, I knew it was time to give one another space. Ezra and Amira deserved a chance to be a happy family together. That didn't mean I wasn't a part of their family, it just meant I respected their need to learn and grow together as husband and wife and mother and father.

"I love you both so much." I reached over and squeezed my brother's hand.

"What if you see him?" Ezra asked with his brow raised and concern embedded in the creases by his eyes.

"He never wrote me back. He never came looking for me. He's moved on. We were a fling." The words tasted bitter on my tongue but felt factual.

It was true. Damien never tried to contact me. He had to have received my letter. I made sure Ezra told him about it. I wasn't sure I wanted him to find me though, especially with a certain new person in my life.

I was scared he'd react in some insane way and lash out.

Reese, Zach, and I had stayed in touch. Zach was going to be a student at Chicago medical school. Reese got an amazing job in the finance world. We'd all be reuniting. It felt right.

I didn't want to run from the city I loved and considered home. Chicago was an overpopulated, bustling city. Damien worked in law, and I knew for a fact he had moved to the suburbs—thanks to Amira for filling in small details she had learned from mutual friends back home.

The chances of us bumping into one another would be rare. With Damien, I knew there could never be a middle ground—it was all in or nothing. Once I found out my life was changing in a huge way with that one test, I knew I had to make that choice not just for myself, but for her, too.

For our daughter.

"Estelle! Sweetheart, it's time to leave." I bent down and lifted my beautiful, green-eyed daughter into my arms.

Estelle turned two years old and was absolute perfection. She had dark, beautiful ringlets with eyes that shined like emeralds. The night Ashton attacked me, I had to be taken to the hospital. What I assumed was to be checked just to put my brother and Amira's minds at ease turned into the most pivotal moment of my entire life.

I was pregnant with Damien's baby.

The blueberry-sized life growing inside me was the

reason we chose to leave Chicago and stay hidden from Damien.

Kane was still at large when I found out about the pregnancy, and his one goal was hurting everyone Damien loved and cared about.

Estelle would have made that list. As much as my heart thought it couldn't handle being away from him, I knew I had someone who needed my love more.

Our daughter.

Kane was dead and Ashton was locked up. They were gone, but that didn't mean their men weren't still holding a target over Damien's head.

Moving back to Chicago was a decision I didn't take lightly, but I didn't want to keep running anymore. I wanted to bring my daughter home to the city I loved. To the city my parents loved, and most of all, to the city that gave me her.

We'd been in Chicago for four months, and we didn't see him. He didn't know we were here, but I knew he was, and for some reason, I looked for him at every corner I turned.

Ezra and Amira didn't think it was a good idea for him to know about Estelle. They were scared that his past and enemies would catch up to her, too. I agreed to keep away from him, but this Chicago dental school scholarship was one I couldn't afford to pass up. I needed to set my future for the both of us.

The crisp autumn air hung over us as we made our way to Navy Pier. The sun was setting and I pushed the stroller down the walkway. Today was Ezra and Amira's wedding anniversary, and also the day Damien and I came here when he recreated the meet-cute I had always dreamt of.

It was silly but, in some way, I thought taking our daughter to the Ferris wheel where I knew I wanted to spend the rest of my life with her dad was symbolic.

"You ready, baby girl?" I parked the stroller to the side and tugged my leather jacket tighter.

Another part of Damien.

So much of me was carrying him.

When I looked at her, he was all I saw.

Estelle squealed as we slid into the seat on the Ferris wheel. The sky was streaked with pinks, oranges, and midnight blue as the sun hid away. Holding her tightly, I took a deep breath and we got to the top. Looking around, my heart beat rapidly as I looked at the straggling people below. Some children were waving, some couples were holding one another, kissing, and some friends were laughing.

But then, I saw *him. No. This couldn't be real.*

Blinking over and over again, my body trembled as I took a deep breath in.

His forehead creased as his head tilted. I swore I stopped breathing in that moment when his eyes moved from mine to hers.

The time that lapsed between where we were high in the sky, to getting down to the ground felt fast and slow all at the same time.

Taking Estelle's hand, she wobbled next to me as we moved away from the Ferris wheel.

He was right there, standing in front of me.

Standing in front of *us*.

"Sophie..." he breathed out and sucked the breath out of my lungs.

Tears stung my eyes as I looked up at him. Gorgeous as ever and eyes that matched the little ones next to me. His chest was rising and falling rapidly as the lines in his forehead deepened.

"Sophie..." he repeated my name, but this time, he was looking at her.

Looking at *his* daughter.

Our daughter.

Swallowing, I clutched her little hand tighter. The bustling crowds around us faded into the night sky and a chill from the wind hovered all around.

Damien dropped to his knees and got eye level with

Estelle. The way he was studying her with his lips parted had my stomach twist.

There was no doubt who she was. She was looking into her reflection, and he was looking into his.

Shaking his head slowly, his hands lifted but froze beside her face in the air as if he were terrified to touch her and realize she was real.

Estelle giggled and stuck her tongue out at Damien as speckles of her spit touched his face.

"Hi, baby girl." His voice was shaky as his eyes began to glisten, looking into the matching green ones before him. Glancing back at me, the lines between his eyes deepened. "Soph." He sank his teeth into his bottom lip and reached his hand out to mine.

Sinking down beside Estelle, I placed mine in his. Wrapping his arms around me and Estelle, he drew us in closer. The words I wanted to say were lodged in my throat as I stared in shock.

"Damien..." I whispered. "How did you know I'd be here?"

"Ezra." He exhaled. "I don't feel lost, anymore," he whispered into my hair as tears streamed down my cheeks. He pressed his head against mine. "How could you do this all alone? How could you have not told me? I...I can't believe you've had to do this...alone?" He sighed as he pressed his lips against Estelle's cheek. He was breathless as he spoke with his words blurring together.

"We have a daughter." He shook his head and exhaled as if, for the first time in a really long time, he could breathe.

Slowly standing, we made our way to a bench with our eyes locked onto one another. Sitting down, I swallowed as I handed Estelle her sippy cup and snack to buy us time to talk.

"I don't understand…" Damien brushed his hand over his face.

"Are you upset?" I said with hushed words, a light sniffle breaking the three words I feared to verbalize.

"Yeah, Soph. I'm upset. I'm upset that I'm the kind of man you had to hide my daughter from. I'm upset that I'm the kind of man that couldn't take care of you while you carried our baby. I'm upset at myself for being who I am." Damien closed his eyes as if it physically pained him to say what he was knowing in his mind it was the truth.

"Oh, Damien…" I breathed out. "I didn't hide her from you because of you. I hid her because I didn't want someone from your past to use her as…" I paused.

"I know, I know, Sophie. And, I can't thank you enough for doing that for not just her, but me. Thank you for protecting someone I didn't know I'd miss loving so much." He opened his palm and looked at me. I hated that I hesitated even though I didn't want to, but as soon as I lifted my hand up I saw Estelle toss her cup to the ground.

She tugged away from us and shrieked excitedly, waving her little, stubby hands at the small stand nearby. "Ice cweam!" Sprinting away, Damien and I jolted up and chased after her.

Swooping her into his arms, he held her. I stopped in my spot, watching them. He'd only just met her, yet he looked at her like he'd known her from the moment she was born.

I closed my eyes, thinking back to the day I was in that hospital room, holding Amira's hand, crying because I wanted him there. I wanted to hear his voice, I wanted to feel his touch.

"Soph, can she have ice cream?" Damien's words broke me out of my thoughts. The simple sentence made the last two years feel like two minutes.

"I don't know... You're her dad, you decide." I rolled my lips together because the look Damien gave me could have melted the entire continent of Antarctica.

I couldn't help but smile as I walked up to them, Damien ordered a strawberry ice cream with sprinkles. We had so much to talk about. A world of words needed to be exchanged but, in this moment, it could wait.

I was watching a father meet his little girl for the first time, and that didn't need any words.

He kept stealing glances at me and back to Estelle with a smile growing on his face as she happily licked the ice cream.

He was wearing his leather jacket, fitted dark denim jeans, and sprinkles of silver lined the sides of his dark hair.

Estelle was giggling as drips of her pink ice cream trickled onto Damien's jacket. Instinctually, I nervously wiped it off, apologizing.

Damien grabbed my hand and stopped me, letting his lips touch my hand. "Like mother, like daughter. Both my girls really have it out for my jackets."

My girls.

"Damien... we should talk." I exhaled and realized it was getting too late. Estelle's eyes grew sleepier as the crowds completely cleared and only a few stragglers were left.

"Come home, please. Come home." Damien's eyes darkened as his brows lowered.

Nodding, I laced my hand into his and we walked back to my car.

"Bike?" I asked.

He smiled. "Yeah..."

"I have my car. Do you want to come back to my

place?" I directed my attention to Estelle, who had placed her head full of curls on Damien's shoulder. In his arms, she looked even smaller, even safer.

"Yes," Damien said softly as he rubbed Estelle's back with care.

Opening the car door, Damien carefully put her in her car seat, as if he'd done it a million times or maybe I just never realized that he may have actually wanted to do this.

We stayed silent the drive back, as if we were terrified that if we spoke, we may say the wrong thing and ruin the moment. A moment that I knew was sacred for us. For Estelle.

"I'm sorry. I know you wanted to go home, but she's going to need to get into bed," I said while clutching the steering wheel tightly. The silence felt too heavy. It felt wrong. With Damien, I never could stop talking or wanting to listen to him.

"I haven't had a home in two years. Home has always been where you are, dandelion." Damien reached over and touched my ring—the same ring he gave me what felt like a lifetime ago, carved with a dandelion on it.

What he didn't realize was that he was home to me, too.

CHAPTER 40
Damien

Bending down, I lifted Estelle out of the car seat. She was deep asleep, and the way her dark lashes fluttered without a single fear in her small body made my heart tighten. Sophie had been doing this all alone. She held the door open as I carried her inside.

"You're living here?" I whispered as she waved me down a tight hallway and into Estelle's room. I laid her in her small bed, then I looked around and saw dandelions painted along the wall.

Turning back, Sophie flipped the lights off and led me back out.

Sinking into a stained and worn-down couch, I took it all in. This wasn't the best area of Chicago, and it most definitely was an old condo. How could Ezra let her live like this?

As if she could read my mind, she followed my eyes.

"Ezra hasn't visited. I'm paying for this with student loans, and I know it's not much, but I also have to pay for daycare and I'm a full-time dental student, so it didn't really leave much..." she stammered out nervously.

"Why didn't you tell me?" I cut in. "Why didn't you tell me you were pregnant, Sophie?" I tried to keep my voice calm and steady, but resentment was pooling inside me.

She looked at her fingers and began to spin the ring I gave her. "It wasn't safe, Damien. Between your brother and Kane."

"Don't call him my brother, because he's not. He died to me the moment I knew he laid a hand on you," I rasped.

Sophie's shoulders dropped as she looked at me carefully, studying my face and then dropped her gaze.

"I have spent every single day missing you. Every single waking hour wishing I could see you, find you, hold you, and touch you. Now I feel cheated, knowing I should have been missing someone else, too." I picked her hand up into mine.

"I'm not a good man, Sophie. I'm not. I've done horrible things, but I'm good for you." I grew closer to her. She sucked in a breath as I pressed my forehead against hers.

"I know… I know you are. You always were. You forever will be, but I'm scared, Damien. So many people want to hurt you for leaving the gang. So many people want to hurt you for killing Kane. I can't risk Estelle's life. I can't do it. I still feel pain knowing it was you who helped the man who hurt me, beat me, and left me for dead… vanish." Tears started to drip down her beautiful face.

"I didn't know what I was helping him escape from, Sophie. You have to understand that. I thought it was drugs not… hurting a woman. Not hurting you. Baby…" I ran my hand through her hair, pulling her face closer where only a small sliver remained between our lips.

"I'm scared." She shook her head with the tips of our noses brushing as our breathing mingled into one.

"Baby girl, I wouldn't ask you to jump if I didn't think I could catch you." I smashed my lips into hers and electricity coursed through me as if, for the past two years, the light had been sucked out of me. It had. I was living in darkness without her.

Pushing my tongue into her mouth, she let out a soft moan as she kissed me back hungrily.

She was kissing me as if she'd been starving for two years.

Pulling back, I gripped her face between my palms. "We have a daughter." I sighed with the realization still feeling like a dream.

She smiled, tilting her head. "We do."

"I have so many questions, Sophie... I..." I paused, not even knowing where to begin. But Sophie stayed quiet, studying me carefully with tired eyes.

Running her fingers across the side of my hair, she let out a small laugh. When did this happen? I grabbed her hand. "Are you teasing me for the silver in my hair? I'm thirty-eight, Sophie." I slanted my eyes at her.

"I didn't think people in their thirties went gray, old man." She scrunched her nose and I lifted a brow.

"Do I need to remind you what happens when you are a bad girl?" I dropped my gaze to her cleavage shamelessly. I wasn't prince charming, and I never claimed to be a gentleman.

She knew that all along.

Nodding slowly, she chewed her bottom lip and stood, walking away to a bedroom.

Looking over her shoulder, she paused with a sexy, mischievous smile on her beautiful face. "Come on, daddy..."

Groaning, I stood as my cock twitched in excitement. Taking her hand, she led me into her bedroom.

Pausing at the end of her bed, she stood still and looked up at me with her gorgeous, big brown eyes I'd missed more than anything.

Brushing my thumb over her lips, I breathed out, "I've missed you. I've missed you so much, my love."

"It's been a long time... I don't look the same." She closed her eyes and wrapped her arms around her body.

Squinting, I studied her carefully. I didn't understand. She was beautiful. She was perfect. She was my dream girl come to life.

"What are you talking about, baby?" I asked.

Turning around, she moved her hair from her back over her shoulder, revealing the zipper down her dress.

I let my fingers brush against it and tugged it down. A large scar was on her shoulder blade, and covering the scar was a tattoo. One that wasn't there when we were together. It was a dandelion, petals, and Estelle's name.

Tracing it with my index finger, she turned and looked over her shoulder.

"Was this from..." I didn't know how to even say my brother's name in the moment. He was in prison, but I so desperately wished I had buried him in the ground.

"Yeah..." She exhaled sadly.

"I guess we both are covering pain from our past

now." She turned toward me and peeled my leather jacket off, then tossed it to the side. Taking her hand, the pushed my sleeve up and looked at my arm.

"It's not just the scar I'm talking about, Damien. I had a baby."

"Our baby," I corrected.

Laughing lightly, she nodded. "Yes, I had our baby. It was a tough pregnancy, and an even tougher delivery. It changed my body." She shrugged and everything started to piece together.

Tugging her dress down, I let it pool by her feet. She was wearing a nude bra and a black thong. She had curves she never had before and small stretch marks lined her hips. Looking at the ground, her cheeks flushed.

Dropping to my knees in front of her, I traced the marks before letting my lips touch them, kissing every single one while she gasped.

"Damn, mama." I rasped.

"Damien..."

"You're right; you do look different, dandelion." I looked up at her. "You've never been more beautiful than you are in this moment. These..." peeling her thong off, I kissed where the material had covered, "these marks that you may not like are all mine. They are from when you carried my child. They make you even more perfect." I kissed each line that dug into her soft skin.

"Now lay down and spread your legs for me, baby... Let me show you just how beautiful I know you are." I took my shirt off and threw it to the ground as Sophie eagerly got onto the bed.

Grabbing her knees, I pushed them apart and moaned as soon as I had a full view of her perfect pussy.

"All mine?" I lowered my gaze at hers. She licked her bottom lip and nodded.

"Good girl." I unzipped my jeans and took them off quickly.

Letting my cock spring out of my briefs, her eyes dropped to it and widened. "I forgot how..."

Leaning down, I planted my hands on both sides of her, unsnapping her bra and relishing with my view.

Grabbing her fuller, bigger tits in my hands, I looked at her. "Finish what you were saying."

"I forgot how big you are." She flicked those beautiful brown eyes up at me.

Laughing, I let my lips crash into hers as I teased her nipples and she moaned into my mouth.

"You think your body changing is so bad. Fuck girl, I wish you could see what I do." Kissing the side of her neck and biting into her soft flesh, she began to squirm.

"Damien..." she pleaded, and I knew she wanted my cock inside her, giving her a release she desperately had missed.

Pulling away, I moved up higher on the bed and laid down on my back. She immediately jumped up and looked my way.

"Do you want me to get on top?" she whispered bashfully.

"No, baby. I want you to sit on my fucking face so I can taste every part of you." Her eyes shot wider as she took me in.

Crawling up toward me, she stopped and tugged the sheet over her stomach, which I yanked off her. "Don't you dare deprive me and my eyes of looking at the most beautiful woman in this world." She swallowed and lifted her leg over my chest. Grabbing her thighs, I moved her up on my face.

Licking, and gently tugging, on her soft flesh, she groaned loudly in appreciation. She was just as sweet as I remembered and drenched for me.

Waiting for me.

"Damien!" Sophie screamed out as I flicked my tongue on her clit before sinking my teeth in.

Moving off my face, she slid down me, panting as she looked at me wildly.

"What do you want baby?" I teased.

"Damien, it's been over two years. I want you to fuck me like it's the last thing you'll ever do," she said confidently.

Groaning, I gripped her hips as she knelt to slide onto my cock. Her lips parted and a look between pain and pleasure painted across her face.

"Is this the last thing I'll ever do?" I held her gorgeous, curvier hips in my hands as she looked at me.

"Make me come, and I'll make sure it isn't." She pursed her thick pink lips at me, fueling a fire inside me. Her pussy stretched around my cock, and I rocked her over and over as she tossed her head back.

Flipping her over, I hovered above her before plunging deep inside.

"You are so tight for me, sweetheart." I kept my thrusts slow and steady at first because of the way her face strained. "Soph, is this okay?" I asked gently.

"If you stop, I'll tell you to leave." She cracked a small smile.

"There's my spitfire." I pulled out but let the tip of my cock stay inside of her. In one swift motion, I plunged back inside her, causing her to cry out as I repeated the motion.

"Yes!" she screamed as my strokes in and out of her grew harder and faster.

Sliding out from her, I grabbed her hand and she followed me to the over-sized mirror that was standing in the corner of her room.

"I want you to watch me fuck you. I want you to see

what I see. The most gorgeous, sexy woman in the world. I want you to watch yourself come all over my cock when you scream my name," I whispered into her ear from behind her. She was looking at me through the reflection, as I wrapped one arm around her perfect tits, and the other bending her leg up over my forearm, leaning her slightly.

"Damien! You're going to drop me," she said with worry.

"Never, baby. I'd never let you fall," I growled as I pushed inside her. The sensation was completely different for her as her back arched and she sucked me in.

Closing her eyes, she moaned my name. "Open your eyes, Sophie. *Now*. Eyes on me." She flung them back open and watched herself as I fucked her harder.

The sound of our skin slapping together filled the room as I picked up my pace and kissed her shoulder and neck from behind. She dropped her gaze and I tilted her jaw back up.

"Baby, watch yourself be free and own me." I breathed out as my orgasm threatened to end this perfection. The steam from her breath began to fog the mirror in front of us, and just like that, I felt her muscles tighten around me and the scream that came from her mouth as she came all over me put me over the edge.

Coming inside her and filling her with every last

drop of myself as she folded over my arm was a feeling I'd never forget.

Lifting her, I carried her to the bed and laid her down before falling beside her.

"I can't believe that's what I've been missing for the past two years." She ran her hand through her hair with a smile.

Turning my head to face her, I studied every bit of her beautiful face carefully.

"What?" she whispered, looking back at me with a curious grin.

"I'm trying to memorize everything about you again. Things start to fade after a few years, and I don't want to forget anything." I brushed my hand against her cheek.

"Where are you going?" Her forehead creased as concern grew within her words.

"Sophie... as much as it hurts that I didn't know about Estelle, and as much as I feel loss for the past two years, you did the right thing. You protected our daughter from a monster." I paused and turned away, staring up at the ceiling. "Me."

"Damien, is that what you think? That I didn't come back or tell you about Estelle because I thought you were evil or bad?" Sophie sat up and gripped the blanket around her.

I didn't reply to her question because there were no

words for me to say. My heart had never felt both happiness and sadness in a moment until this one.

Being reunited with Sophie and meeting my daughter brought so much happiness, but also knowing it was a fleeting moment was devastating.

Sophie reached over and turned my face to her. "Damien, I found out I was pregnant after Ashton attacked me. Kane had killed Carmen and was lurking out there. I had to go. I had to protect her from *them*, not you."

"I wondered every single day how you were. Where you were. If you were happy..." I loosened my shoulders as her eyes went to my lips.

"I wasn't happy, Damien. I was just... living. Living for our daughter. How could I ever be happy when half my heart was in Chicago and the other half was with Estelle?" She bent down and planted her lips against mine. She was kissing me in a way that made me think she knew our kisses had an expiration date. Our kisses weren't going to last a lifetime.

CHAPTER 41

Sophie

The scent of syrup and coffee grazed my nose. I stretched my arms over my head and flung my eyes open.

Sunlight poured in from my curtains, and I grabbed my phone. It was almost eight! I couldn't remember the last time I had slept in this much and...

"Estelle!" I shouted and pushed the comforter off me. Sprinting out of my room, I froze.

Estelle was seated at the table, watching cartoons on our small TV and eating strawberries and waffles.

Everything was cut up in small pieces, and I couldn't help but smile when I saw Damien's head pop out from the kitchen.

"Good morning, beautiful." He smirked at me with a spatula in his hand.

"Mama!" Estelle scrunched her nose excitedly.

"Good morning..." I said with hesitation.

Walking past Estelle, I kissed the top of her head and headed into the kitchen.

"I thought you had left." I pressed against the counter and watched as Damien scrambled eggs casually.

"Did you want me to leave?" Damien turned and paused. His V-neck was fitted over his muscles, the outline of his bicep and muscles bulging from the fitted short sleeve. My eyes fell on something that made me grow closer.

It had been such a blur last night, I didn't realize his newest tattoo.

My name was tattooed on his arm.

"I never want you to leave. It hurts too much to be apart," I whispered, tracing my finger across my name.

"I had them tattoo it exactly where you come up to me in height. Where your head would always rest when you'd be in my arms, and I felt like I had the entire world right there," Damien said taking me into his embrace.

My heart raced as I inhaled him.

"How are we going to protect her?" I rubbed my cheek against his chest, not wanting to move from this moment.

"Kane's dead, but he's got his men everywhere.

Chicago isn't safe, Soph. Not for you and Estelle to be around me." Damien picked my face in his hands.

"Dental school..." I started.

"Baby, I can find you a new one anywhere. I will. But only if you want to be with me. I just know staying here is a death sentence for us... as a family. I can't lose my girls. I'd burn the entire world down and kill everyone in it if something happened to you or Estelle. No one deserves to breathe if my girls aren't." Damien kissed my forehead.

"I'll go wherever, as long as we're together." I nodded. I knew my future was important. I knew I wouldn't give up my dreams of securing a career and the education I needed, but ultimately it was true... Being in Chicago meant not being with Damien.

But one mattered more.

Him.

Us.

Our family.

I could find a way to finish school or maybe get a job with my college degree, but I wanted our family to be together.

"Mama! Juice!" Estelle's sweet voice broke us out of our thoughts.

"I'll get it for you, sweetheart." Damien quickly ran to the fridge. I couldn't stop watching him weave his way around the kitchen, making sure his daughter had whatever she wanted.

For two years I carried Damien in my heart, but through Estelle, I carried him physically. I thought that would have to be enough, until now... Feeling his touch, seeing him, I realized I couldn't breathe without him anymore.

I wanted him. I needed him.

"Damien, how'd you know we'd be at the Ferris wheel last night?" I asked as I took a bite of the eggs he had made.

"Ezra told me I should go. But what he didn't know was that I've gone there every year since I recreated our meet-cute. I just never in a million years thought my meet-cute would be with my daughter this year." He broke into a sexy smile as he looked at me.

Laughing, I bit into a strawberry and smiled. "Our meet-cute was technically at Le Petit Bistro where you were the biggest asshat." Scrunching my nose, I busted into laughter as Damien parted his lips in disbelief.

"Sophie Shah, watch your mouth around our baby girl," he said teasingly.

"I think I need you to spank me, daddy." I winked at him as he came back toward me and lifted me up on the counter, spreading my legs so he could stand between them. Thankfully, the kitchen wall separated Estelle's view.

"You're such a bad girl..." He wrapped his hand around my throat. "Such a bad, bad girl." He leaned in, leaving only a small gap between our lips. "I think your mouth needs something to stop those bad words from coming out. Maybe it needs to be full of my cock." He pressed his lips against mine, and I let out a long moan.

"What's clock?" A small voice echoed behind us.

Jerking back, Damien flung around. "Estelle!" He looked back at me as I began to laugh so hard, I couldn't speak.

Hopping off the counter, I sank to the floor at Estelle's eye level. "Clock is something you tell time on, right, babe?" I looked over my shoulder at Damien, whose face was bright red. It took a two-year-old to make Damien Moretti blush, and I was here for it.

"Estelle, baby... I want to finally introduce you to someone very special." I stood and held my hand out to Damien. Last night we hadn't had a chance to truly talk to Estelle since she had fallen asleep as soon as we got home.

"Sweetie, this is Damien. Damien is your daddy." I had told her all about him. She knew he was a superhero, fighting the bad guys to keep us safe. But she always asked when she'd see him, and that was a question I never could answer.

I opened my hand for hers and she took it. Looking curiously up at Damien, she let go of my hand to hug Damien's leg. "Hi, dada."

In that moment, I don't know who started to cry first, but there were so many tears that all the thoughts about my future blurred, because now, I was more focused on *our* future.

The rest of the day flew by in a blur. We curled up on the couch with Estelle in between us, watching Disney movies and stealing glances.

How did we get here, and where were we going? All I knew was that as long as we were together, everything would be okay.

We'd figure this out.

My phone began to ring on the dining table, so I got up. I glanced over my shoulder, smiling at how comfortable Estelle was with Damien and how comfortable he was with her.

Without even reading the caller ID, I answered cheerily. But that cheer dissipated from my body as soon as the other voice shrieked into the call.

"Amira?" My chest constricted as she cried and slurred her words.

"Amira? I can't understand..." I tried to interject. I couldn't make out what she was saying. Damien stood and looked at me with concern.

"He's dead! Ezra! They killed him!" she screeched so loudly and in such distress, that my entire body felt like it was cracking into pieces in front of me.

"What?" I asked stupidly. Maybe it was the fact that shock had over taken my body. Or the fact that I didn't know how a human could have their heart pieced together and then, in the next moment, have it shattered into shards that would never be able to be whole again.

"He's dead. He was shot on his way to the office. He's gone, Sophie. He's gone!" Amira sobbed so loudly but everything around me grew quiet. My phone slipped out of my hand and shattered to the floor below me.

Everything grew fuzzy and suddenly, right before my body slammed into the ground, Damien came running and grabbed me.

"Sophie!"

Everything went black.

The soft buzzing woke me from a deep sleep, and I smiled as I opened my eyes. I needed to get up and make Estelle some breakfast before classes.

Except, I wasn't home.

The fluorescent lights above me had my hand shooting up to cover my eyes.

The wires attached to my hand slapped against the bedrail, forcing me to look down.

"Baby..." his voice trailed, and I was terrified. I was terrified that if this wasn't home, and if this wasn't a normal day, then the screams of Amira's voice would have been real.

It would mean my brother, my older brother who dedicated years of his life to raise me and care for me, was gone.

"Soph, baby." His fingers feathered against my arms so softly, I knew he thought I'd break if he touched me with any more pressure.

"I need to talk to Ezra." I slowly turned my head, my throat completely dry from the hospital air.

"Sweetheart..." His chest rose and fell rapidly as his brows furrowed.

"No, get away from me, Damien. Ezra doesn't even like you. He doesn't trust you. I need to talk to my brother," I shouted and swatted his hand off me.

"Where's Estelle?" Fear rose inside me as I jerked my head around in all directions.

There she was deep asleep on the small pull-out in the corner of my room with a pillow blocking the edge so she wouldn't fall off. Exhaling, I sank back into the bed.

"Give me my phone." I couldn't look at him. I just couldn't. Ezra was shattered when he found out about me and Damien. And he was terrified for a good cause. When he found out I was pregnant with his best friend's child, he dropped everything to get me away from danger.

I just never realized danger was Damien.

Without words, Damien handed me my phone. His face was covered in pain as he walked away and sank into a small chair next to Estelle.

I called Ezra, but his phone kept ringing, over and over again.

Ending the call, I hit his name again and let it ring.

"Come on, Ezra... I need you," I whispered as the ringing started to haunt me.

I repeated the action over and over until tears began to blur my eyes. I called Amira, and one ring later, her shaking voice answered, "Sophie."

"I need to speak to Ezra." I puffed out a breath of air as I waited patiently.

"Sophie, I'm so sorry I called you the way I did. I shouldn't have. Are you okay?" she said, masking the fear in her words with forced composure.

"Amira, please let me speak to my brother." I cleared my throat as I felt Damien's steady gaze on me.

"Sophie, he's gone... He's really gone." She began to cry softly, yet I swore I could feel her tears on my own face.

She was so close to having their baby. My brother was so close to becoming a dad and experiencing a love like no other.

"How?" I asked as my eyes stung with tears.

"He was shot while walking into his office. It was one of... it was one of Kane's men." She sobbed loudly.

"Sophie, make sure whatever you do, you do not go anywhere near Damien. You haven't gone near him, right? Sophie, I think you and Estelle and I need to leave. We've got to move again. Please, Sophie." She was choking on her words.

"You haven't seen him, right?" she asked again with fear laced into her voice.

"No. I don't want to be around a man that Ezra never trusted." I looked into Damien's moistened green eyes—the eyes my daughter carried. The same eyes that promised me the world, yet only took it from me.

"I can't believe he's gone." My chest felt even tighter

as the realization began to sink into my body. "I have to go, Amira. I'll call you tomorrow when we find a flight. I love you. I'm here. You're my sister. I love you. I love you so much." I began to cry as I thought about my brother's wife, pregnant and alone.

Hanging up the call, I watched as Damien brushed Estelle's hair from her face.

"Don't touch her," I fired out.

Damien stood and walked toward me without a second thought.

"My brother is dead. Your best friend is dead. Estelle's uncle is dead." I began to cry in my hands, and Damien sank into the small space on the bed beside me.

His arms wrapped around me and I cried even harder.

But this time, I was crying because I knew I'd be mourning two losses.

Two of the most important men in my life.

Ezra's one wish for me was to stay away from Damien because he knew trouble would follow him. He may have left the gang, but there was no such thing as a clean break in that world. But then, why did he tell Damien I'd be at the Ferris wheel? Did he do it so Damien could meet his daughter? Did he do it knowing I'd be running again?

After he killed Kane, Damien became a snitch, a

threat. The attorney that made sure to clean the streets of Chicago. And now Damien was carrying a target on his chest.

But now, I knew. It wouldn't be long until it was Amira, or me, or worse, Estelle. I had to protect her. No one knew besides Amira and Ezra about Damien being her father.

We'd have to leave here.

I looked at Damien. His eyes were closed and a single tear made its way down his beautiful tanned face.

I had to let Damien Moretti go.

Forever. Ezra gave Damien the greatest gift, which was meeting his daughter, and what did he get in return? Never being able to meet his own son.

CHAPTER 42

Damien

I once read somewhere that the two most powerful forces in life are love and grief. Because once you've experienced both, you know what true pain is.

We got back to Sophie's condo and she didn't say another word to me. She busied herself with packing and slamming things into boxes.

Estelle seemed anxious, so I tried to color with her and sing to her while her eyes followed her mom.

Thankfully, at two years old, she didn't really notice much, especially when I handed her a cookie after she finished her meal. I changed her clothes and tucked her into bed. Slowly, closing the door behind me, I walked down the opposite hall to Sophie's room. She was on the floor, lying on her side and crying softly. Black makeup streaks raced down her face as she stared at a small picture in her hand.

I sank next to her on the floor and wrapped my arms around her from behind. She started to cry harder.

Peering over her shoulder, I saw the small image.

It was a family picture. Ezra, Sophie, and their parents.

Old and worn and well-loved, the image oozed happiness.

She had lost everyone in that picture.

"Baby... I'm so sorry." I said the words I knew held no meaning. I had my private investigators look into what happened and who was responsible. Because I swore I'd rip them in half.

They took one of the greatest men I had an honor of calling my best friend. They took the love of my life's brother and last remaining blood relative beyond our daughter away from her.

"He died because he loved you. He died because he knew you." Sophie started to hyperventilate as tears soaked into the sleeve of her hoodie.

"Sophie..."

What could I say? She was right. Because of me, Carmen was murdered and now, Ezra. Who was next?

"I hate you." Three words that came out of Sophie's

mouth that I never realized could hurt me physically. Three words that were daggers to my heart.

Nodding, I moved off her small frame as she sat up and looked at me with bloodshot eyes. "I wish I never met you." She began pounding her fists against my chest and sobbing unconsolably while repeating the sentence over and over again.

I closed my eyes, letting her hit me.

Standing, she opened her door and I pulled myself up.

She started screaming and crying as she pounded into me angrily. I didn't move, I didn't block her. I waited and let her do what she needed to until she stopped and cried into her palms.

Pulling the chain I had worn around my neck for decades, I handed it to Sophie. "Maybe one day you can give this to our daughter and let her know her dad loved her and her mom more than all the stars in the sky." Sophie took the necklace from me, her pink lips quivering as she gripped my chain in her hands.

My breathing quickened as I ran my hands through her hair and pulled her face upward as I leaned down and crashed my lips against hers before she could protest. I needed one last taste of her, I needed to feel her. This would have to be scorched into my memory for all of eternity.

Slowly breaking away from her, and leaving my heart in her hands, I looked her in the eyes. "No one will hurt you and Estelle. I give you my word. No one will hurt Amira and her baby. I give Ezra my word. I will destroy anyone and everyone who even mutters your name. I promise you, Sophie. It ends here; it ends now. I promise you, this will be over. All the pain. No one will hurt you." I pressed my lips against her forehead.

"Your promises are empty, just like your heart." She shoved me away and walked down the hall to the kitchen.

What she didn't know was that she couldn't be further from the truth. My heart was consumed by her and Estelle, and for the rest of my days, that would have to be enough. I swiped away a tear that fell, thinking about my daughter growing up without me, thinking about my girl being without me.

I vowed in that moment to destroy every single person who dared to cross the paths of my girls.

"Get the fuck out of my house and my life, Damien. I hate—"

Anger pooled inside of me, fury raced through me, heartbreak rippled through me, and suddenly, who I used to be plunged into my soul. I took huge steps to get to her and cornered her into the wall.

"Say it. Tell me you hate me. Tell me you fucking hate me…" I planted my hands on both sides of her face, leaning in and feeling the warmth of her breath on my face.

Leaning in, I kissed her hard. Fast. Possessively. She bit into my bottom lip, but kissed me right back until she stopped and shoved her hands into my chest.

"I hate you. I'll always hate you." She breathed out, her eyes on my lips.

"Good. Hating me is easier than loving me. Keep hating me, dandelion. You're safest that way." Pushing myself away from her, I left. But I didn't just leave.

I was leaving my heart and soul behind.

Two days later, I had made sure Sophie and Estelle boarded a private jet to get to Amira in a safe place. Although Amira didn't want to, she accepted my call. I had to explain things to her. I had to apologize. I had to make amends. But most of all, I had to make sure they were all taken care of.

I set up an account for Amira and Sophie. Ezra was smart with his money, so Amira would have his life insurance and money, but Sophie had nothing. She was leaving school and moving with Estelle to keep her safe.

I wired money for her, enough to last her a lifetime and more. Enough for Estelle to do whatever she wanted, without any worry in her mind.

Everything was taken care of.

I just so badly wished I could be there to take care of them in a different way, too.

Instead, I had begun to draw in my men. The ones who left the gang. The ones who had my back from the beginning. I obsessed and lost sleep, trying to make sure I found who had blood on their hands.

Each and every last one would be taking their last breath this week.

I didn't care what it cost me. I had already lost everything.

Sitting in the chair at the tattoo shop, I was adding Estelle's name next to her mom's and two dandelions twirled together—one with the yellow leaves and the other with the white. I hoped Sophie knew how badly I wanted to make her wishes and dreams come true.

My moon. My stars. My sun.

I'm so sorry, I failed you.

CHAPTER 43

Sophie

If someone told me when I first moved to Chicago, eager to start college, that I would instead be living in a small Italian village with my widowed sister-in-law, her child, and my daughter, I'd have maybe, just maybe, requested they seek therapy.

But here we are. Three years had come and gone. Three years of living in fear and in pain.

My brother was murdered. We weren't safe anywhere in the United States. And then when I thought that I was already numb, I found out Damien was dead.

He was gone. Forever.

He died in a blood bath. He was in the crossfire while taking out the man who was looking for me, for Estelle. The man who would have killed us both. Even though no one knew about Estelle, they'd have seen her with me. They'd have known exactly who she was.

Damien had multiple men locked up for life. But this man was Kane's right-hand man, and he wouldn't have stopped until he killed me and Estelle.

So, Damien killed him.

But in the process of doing so, he was shot from behind and left to bleed to death alone in an empty warehouse.

I didn't know when it happened. In some selfish way, I was thankful I didn't. It allowed me to live a small amount of time in some demented form of bliss thinking he was out there living and breathing and so were we. That although we couldn't be together, we were still watching the same sun rise, the same stars twinkle and the same moon alter an otherwise darkened sky.

We had no connection to anyone, not even Amira's family.

Not until we knew we could.

Reese told me. My college best friend who I had sadly drifted apart from as I ran for my life had found a way. She mailed the newspaper article to the local library and put a note on it for me.

She knew where I was because Damien had finally told her the village name just before he left. He knew she'd be the last connection I had back home. He knew he was probably going to die.

Knowing he wasn't in this world left me crying myself to sleep every night. My heart ached how the last words I said to him were ridden with hatred. I saw him in every mischievous grin on Estelle's face or the way her eyes twinkled. I felt him when I walked through a field of dandelions and a cool breeze would ripple through as I brushed my fingers across the blooms.

That's where we went today. Our small village had the most gorgeous field of dandelions. They'd start of bright yellow, scattered happily through the grass. Part of me wondered if Damien had put us here for that reason. So, I'd always know what I meant to him.

Today I was walking through a field of the dandelions as puff balls. I hadn't made a wish in three years. I also wasn't sure if I blew the petals they'd all go together.

Damien was dead. There was no man in the world left who loved me unconditionally.

Plucking one up, I held it high as the sun beamed down on me. The glow and warmth relaxing me.

Taking a deep breath in, I closed my eyes and blew.

"I wish you knew how much I love you. I never hated you, and I never will," I whispered as I opened my eyes and saw every last petal had flown off the stem at once.

Tilting my head, I watched as they fluttered away.

"You didn't have to waste your wish on me..." a voice that sent chills up my spine radiated from behind me. My breathing hitched as I slowly shook my head.

I turned swiftly, but there was no one.

Letting out a soft laugh, a tear escaped. Three years since I last saw Damien. Three years since my brother died.

"You ready to go, sis?" I opened my eyes, and Amira was standing, holding hands with Rian and Estelle.

Between our two children, Damien and Ezra lived on. Rian was my brother's twin. Somedays it hurt to look at him... which I knew sounded awful, but he was so much like Ezra and I know how much my brother would have adored his son. How much he deserved to be here.

"I'm ready." I nodded as Estelle grabbed Rian's hand and raced back to the car.

We came here often and would sit in the field of dandelions. I'd lay down in the middle, surrounded by bright yellows and angelic whites, and stare up at the sky. Here, I felt the closest to Damien.

I had so many regrets. I regretted not telling him how much I loved him. How much Estelle would love him because she'd know her dad fought until the end to protect us.

Damien wasn't some knight in shining armor or prince charming.

He had done a lot of bad things before he turned his life around. Partially, thanks to my brother.

That's what mattered to me. The fact that he wanted to be good. He tried to be good and he left the gang behind. He left the darkness behind. While he thought I was his light, I think he was mistaken. He had found light on his own.

He died thinking I hated him, and that's something I'll live with for the rest of my days.

But I hoped that the way I felt him meant somewhere, he felt me, too.

In the way the stars and moon lit up the dark night sky. Or the way the sun shimmered along the deep blue sky.

Or in our daughter's laughter and smile.

I grew up with fairytales convincing me that I needed this perfect hero. But what I didn't know until I met Damien was that I never needed a hero. I was always the girl who wanted the wounded and misunderstood villain. The man that I didn't have to feel suffocated with because I needed to pretend to be someone I wasn't. The man that I could show my jagged edges to and he'd know, they'd still fit with his.

I draped my arms around myself as the wind rippled through the field and petal fluttered around me. A field of wishes. Endless wishes that unfortunately would never come true.

Closing my eyes, another tear dribbled down my cheek.

"You okay?" Amira looked over at me as she drove us home.

"I don't know if I'll ever be okay," I answered honestly. "You?" I kept my voice to a hushed whisper as Estelle and Rian sang songs in the backseat.

"Ezra wouldn't want me to be sad, and he wouldn't want you to be sad. He'd want us both to live and give the kids all the happiness in the world." She took a deep breath in. "I don't blame Damien." She made a turn, and I looked at her in shock.

"How can you not? He's the reason Ezra is gone." Rubbing my face, I hated that this conversation was coming up. The words I spoke didn't match how I felt anymore.

"Sophie, when Ezra met Damien, he was in a terrible place. He was figuring out how to balance being a student, becoming successful, and worrying about you nonstop. Damien saved him in a way, too. He forced Ezra to stop worrying about things outside of his control. Damien is the reason you got that scholarship to Jesson."

"What?" I dropped my jaw.

"Damien created that scholarship. Ezra wouldn't accept financial help from him. Between all of Ezra's student debt and saving up for his firm, he knew he couldn't afford tuition for you, but he also didn't want you to worry about debt." Amira wiped a tear from her face.

"Damien sent me the scholarship information. He knew if you got the full ride, you'd come to Chicago, get free tuition, and Ezra would be able to take care of you closer to us instead of flying to Texas so often. He made me swear not to tell you or Ezra. So, I sent you the scholarship and you filled it out. Really, it was Damien just making all of our lives easier. That's what he did. He wanted to do good and be good. Damien grew up in a terrible environment, Sophie. He got into the wrong crowd, and he carried a lot of burdens. Unlike us, he didn't have a support system, yet he was supporting all of us in his own way. His past wrecking his present and destroying a piece of us all isn't fair, but why should his past destroy his future?" Amira parked in the driveway.

I was looking forward as tears fell down my face.

"The last thing I said to him was that I hated him." I sniffled as the pain in my chest grew deeper.

"He knew that wasn't true. He knew you loved him, Sophie." She patted my hand as I unbuckled my seatbelt.

"No, he didn't. He thought I hated him. He thought I never wanted to see him again, and he made that happen, too." I shut my door and opened the back door to get the kids out. Hopping out of their car seats, they raced to our home.

"Sophie, do you believe in second-chances?" Amira gripped my arm before I went inside.

"Yes... I think so," I replied, completely confused.

"You know the old Ferris wheel in Florence? The one they still run in the evenings?"

Nodding, I shielded my eyes from the sun that was beaming on me.

"Go there. Go there tonight."

"Why? Amira, what is going on?"

"Sophie, I don't know what I believe anymore. I don't know if I've just lost my mind, but this letter came in the mail. It wasn't addressed to either of us, so I opened it." Amira handed me the small, cream-colored note.

"I'm going to go inside." She gave me a quick hug before I sank down on the small stoop.

Opening it between my trembling fingers, I let out a small gasp.

While hating me may easier for you... loving you will always be the easiest thing I do. Every time, I'll choose you. Fight for you. Love you. Wait for you. I want you. I need you. I crave you. Only you. Because when love breaks us, it also reminds us that sometimes, the broken pieces are worth mending together. And you, dandelion, are always worth breaking for. A thousand times over.

My lips quivered as I re-read the note. An address in Florence was scribbled below. It must be where the Ferris wheel was.

Racing inside, I looked around as the world spun around me.

"Amira..." I started, my voice shaking as tears filled her eyes. If she gave me any form of a signal that what my next decision was would hurt her, I wouldn't do it. I'd stay here.

"Go, Sophie. Go. If I had another chance with Ezra, I'd let the world crumble around me. You have to go." She nodded as we both stared at one another in disbelief. This was really happening. Running up to her, I hugged her tightly.

Grabbing my purse and keys, I jogged outside and opened the garage. Throwing my leg over my motorcycle and sliding my helmet on, I sped out. The wind picked my hair up as I sped as fast as I could to get to the small Ferris wheel I had taken Estelle on countless times.

Just to feel closer to him.

CHAPTER 44

Damien

People have this deep-rooted fear of death. For me, the moment Sophie said the three words I never wanted to hear, making it known that I had to walk away from her and my daughter, were worse than death.

It took me three years. Three years full of death, violence, bloodshed, and hell to end a brewing war between Kane and me. The gang and me. It took three years of knowing I had to do whatever it took to ensure my girls would be safe forever. Especially since I had signed my name under the grim reaper's wrath.

I killed the man who took my best friend's life. I shot to disarm, not to kill. I wanted him to rot in prison, but when he laughed about the fear in Ezra's eyes before he killed him, and how he pleaded for his life so he could meet his unborn child... Well, that fueled the side of me I had buried away.

I shot him right in the fucking heart. I watched him bleed and sputter pleas to save him. I walked to him slowly as he dropped to his knees, and I kicked him in the center of his chest.

A year later, after nothing else happened, I knew I had to see her.

Really, it felt like five years had gone by without skipping a beat, because it had. In the past five years, I had one night with Sophie. I had one night to meet and know my daughter.

I didn't expect much when I sent the letter to Sophie. I expected her to shred it the moment she figured out who it was from. I expected her to continue to hate me.

Yet, here I was, standing outside of a fifty-year-old Ferris wheel in Florence, Italy, praying to a God I didn't think existed that she'd come.

I clutched the collar of my leather jacket and straightened it out. An hour had passed by and tourists flocked around with their gelato, taking selfies. Laughter taunted me and lovers kissed.

The sky grew darker as another hour flew by, and I was certain she wasn't going to come. The lights began cutting off as the vendors wrapped their carts up and began to leave. The Ferris wheel attendant shouted for the last ride. Standing, I squinted, disheartened. But just as I was about to leave...

There she was. She was sitting on the Ferris wheel, looking straight ahead, not at me. Picking up my pace, I walked over and quickly handed the annoyed teenager who clearly wanted to go home all the euros from my wallet and slid next to her. My heart beat grew faster as I looked at her, a sweet, familiar smell bringing out infinite memories.

"Um... can I help you?" She raised her hands and widened her eyes at me that brimmed with tears and disbelief.

My stomach knotted as the past five years disappeared and took me back to Le Petit Bistro.

I shook my head and crossed my arms, leaning back into the seat.

"Okay... so I'm not sure if you're just new around here, but when someone is sitting in a certain place, like the seat of a clearly empty Ferris wheel, it means that seat is taken, and if it's empty, that means you ask if you can sit there."

Turning toward her, I watched her jaw clench as those big, brown doe eyes that would forever remind me of melted chocolate looked straight into my eyes.

"I don't ask for anything." I lifted a brow as she tried

to bite back both tears and a smile. "Except for today. Soph..." Raising my hand to her cheek, she pressed into it as tears fell into my palm.

"How are you even... alive?" She began to sob lightly.

"You kept my heart beating..." I started. "Forgive me. Choose me. Hate me. Love me. Whatever you give me, I'll take, as long as I have a chance to be in your heart and your mind. Because, Soph, I'll choose you every damn time." I swallowed as she sobbed softly into my hand and the Ferris wheel moved slowly. Each creak aligned with the beat of my heart.

"You never left my heart or my mind, Damien." She threw her arms around me, gripping my jacket as she took me in.

"But how? How are you here? I saw the obituary. I saw the death certificate. We got wired millions of dollars. Deeds to all your homes. This... What is happening?" she asked in disbelief.

"I had to disappear. I had to make sure that if I ever came back to you, I wouldn't be putting you or Estelle at risk." I hesitated, but wrapped my arms around her as she pressed into me.

"I don't hate you," she whispered against my chest.

"It's okay if you do." I rested my chin on her head. "I hate myself."

"Don't. Please don't," she said in an even lower

voice. Pulling her head off me, she brushed her hand against my face. "I hate that he's gone. I hate that your past caught up to us. I hate who you were forced to be. But I don't hate you; I could never hate you, Damien. I'll always choose you. Always."

"You deserve a better man." A statement that pained me to say but held so much truth.

"If you think that, then become better. Because the only man I'll ever want is you." She breathed out.

I brushed my fingers across her lips. "I love you, dandelion." Drawing her face to mine, I crashed my lips to hers. If there was anything I had learned in life, it was that I wasn't going to waste another second.

"I love you with all that I am," I whispered into her mouth as I pushed my tongue into hers, and she let out a soft moan that set fire throughout my body.

"I love you. I'll always love you." She gripped my face and kissed me back harder. Our tongues were swirling when suddenly, a voice cleared.

Sophie pulled away and looked at the teenager who was rolling his eyes. Laughing, we lifted the bar and slid out.

Walking away together, she slid her hand down, lacing her fingers into mine. Lifting it up, I pressed my lips against them.

"How's our daughter?" I asked as we walked quietly.

"She's perfect. She's so perfect." Sophie smiled up at me.

"How's Rian?" I asked nervously.

"He's Ezra's reflection. He's smart, and funny, and... an overthinker." Sophie let out a small laugh, lost in her own thoughts.

"Are you going to leave me again? Are you going to leave us again?" She froze in the middle of the small sidewalk.

"Never. If you'll have me, I'll never leave, baby." I tugged her hips and pulled her into me. My cock hardened as soon as her body touched mine.

"Okay." She bit her bottom lip while studying me carefully.

"Okay, then." I smirked back at her. "Can I see Estelle?" I asked quietly, not expecting anything in return.

"No." She shook her head, and suddenly, the air from my lungs lifted away. A small grin curved on her face. "She's sleeping."

"Do you want to go back to the place I'm staying? I'm sure you want to talk about everything, understand things better?" I rubbed my fingers across her chin, tilting her face up.

"Let's go back to your place, but I don't want to talk right now." Her chest heaved. The dress she was wearing dipped low, giving me a full view of her cleavage. Unfortunately, it gave others who walked by, including some drunks, the same view, too.

They began whistling and saying obscene words in Italian to her, and my fist immediately clenched as I flung around.

"Damien!" Sophie shouted behind me.

"Stay there," I growled as I ran to the morons who decided to look at my woman.

Gripping one of them who was continuing his rant, I shouted back in Italian, warning his friend who sprinted off into the dark alley.

The man started to profusely apologize before he sprinted away.

Sophie scowled with her arms over her chest, her tits squeezed together. Peeling my jacket off, I handed it to her. "Put this on, now," I demanded as a small mischievous grin painted across her gorgeous face.

"So damn bossy." She rolled her eyes as she put it on.

"Maybe you could wear more clothing," I said with irritation.

Rolling her eyes again, she shook her head. "I think you're right; we don't need to talk about anything tonight. I need to remind you all of these years later what happens when you roll your eyes at me." I grew closer as her breathing picked up.

"Try me," she taunted as she began to walk backward and stopped beside a shiny bike.

Throwing her leg over, she slid a helmet on and turned over her shoulder. "I'll give you a ride."

My mouth parted in shock as I stared at my sexy girl on her own bike.

"Fuck," I groaned as I slid behind her. Quickly telling her where to go, I was counting seconds until we got into my place.

CHAPTER 45

Sophie

We pulled up and I quickly parked. Damien jumped off and helped me down as I tugged my helmet off and shook my hair out.

"You are full of surprises, Miss Shah," he said in admiration.

Pressing my back against the door, I let my eyes drift from his amused face, all the way down. "It's my favorite ride."

Damien scoffed as he planted both hands by my face and leaned in. "Is that so?" His voice was dangerously low, yet made more of an impact than if he'd been shouting.

I grinned shamelessly. "One hundred percent."

"I've thought about your perfect pussy for three

years. I'm going to make sure to remind you what your favorite ride is, baby." He unlocked the door behind me.

His words caused the heat between my legs to grow rapidly.

Walking inside, I tried to pretend I wasn't affected by a single sentence he uttered, but the slickness in my panties proved otherwise.

It was a beautiful and modest house, nothing like the over-the-top, three-story villa Damien had set up for us.

Originally, I dreaded living somewhere he bought for us, but I knew I didn't have a choice. Spite and anger had no place when it came to protecting our daughter.

I knew we had a world of things to talk about; we had to work on everything. Part of me was terrified to bring him into Estelle's life again. She had met him when she was two, and now at five, she would actually remember everything.

Were there any more secrets buried? Would someone else come from his past to destroy any chance at a future we'd have together?

But right now, in this moment, that day wasn't today.

Maybe, one day, it would feel right to discuss all the pain, all the hurt, and all the anger. But today wasn't that day.

Today was ours.

Peeling Damien's leather jacket off, I tossed it on the couch and turned to face him. He was leaning against the archway, with one arm up, watching me carefully.

"What?" I asked, feeling nerves trickle inside me.

Walking slowly, he stopped. "You're the most beautiful woman in the world."

I pinched my lips to the side. "Does that work on all the ladies?"

"I don't know. There's only one lady in my life who could tell me if it worked," he replied and brushed a straggling piece of hair from my face.

"Sometimes, while hiding away, I wondered if I was worth looking for," I whispered as Damien's eyes lifted to mine.

Tracing my lips, he tilted his head slowly. "Your angel eyes saw the good in many devils, especially me. I never looked for you because I didn't want you to be scorched in my flames, but I never had to look far because you've always been right here." He dragged my hand across his heart.

Sucking in a breath of air, I exhaled slowly. "I don't want you to be gentle. I don't want you to act like I'm going to break," I said and let my shoulders drop.

Damien's jaw ticked and a vein in the side of his head grew more prominent.

"Are you sure you know what you're asking for,

Sophie?" he rasped as he grabbed my hips and tugged me closer.

Nodding, I exhaled as I felt the coolness of his breath against my face. I turned my head slightly just to breathe easier, considering I was already becoming intoxicated by him.

"Say it. Say what you want from me. Demand it," he growled as his grip tightened.

Heat rushed to my cheeks as I looked back into his stunning green eyes.

"I want you to fuck me hard. I want to feel every bit of you inside me." I dropped my head and looked away, feeling embarrassed.

Taking his index finger and thumb, he jerked my face up toward him. "Don't you dare be nervous about asking me for anything. I will burn for you. I will kill for you. I will do anything you say you want me to do. Having you spread your legs and take me in is a fucking privilege."

"Slap me." His voice rumbled.

"What?" I shook my head. "No, Damien."

"You want it rough, baby. Do it. Slap me and get the hate you feel out now. So when I fuck you, all you feel is the love from my body taking over yours."

Hesitating, I lifted my hand and slapped his perfect face as hard as I could.

"Again!" he said without flinching.

"Damien…" I repeated, but he grabbed my hand and held it in the air.

"You hated me. You felt hate in your heart for a man who hurt you. A man who broke you. Fucking hit me."

Raising my hand, I slapped Damien so hard, I swore every ounce of pain left my body when the crack of my palm met the scruff on his face.

A moment later, he left to go to the kitchen, reappearing with whipped cream.

Grabbing my wrists, he walked me into his room aggressively.

"Are you sure you want it rough, baby? You sure you can handle that?" His eyes darkened and his lips went into a straight line.

"Yes. I'm so tired of being treated like a glass doll," I whimpered as Damien peeled my dress of my body.

His eyes dripped over every bit of my body. I had changed. I wasn't the nineteen-year-old girl he fell for; I was in my twenties, had a baby, and stress, life, and fear had changed me. New curves appeared, the stretch marks deepened, and my body nowhere as tight as it was.

"So fucking perfect," he rasped as he unhooked my bra and let his eyes appreciate my breasts.

Dropping to his knees in front of me, he peeled my

thong down, kissed my stomach, kissed my pussy, kissed my inner thigh, all while I held my breath.

"Lay on the bed, hang your head off it, upside down," he said as he took his clothes off. Dropping his briefs down, my lips parted when I saw his cock. Pulsing, dripping, and so damn big. Thick, and veiny from being impossibly hard.

Sliding onto his bed, I hung my head over the edge upside down like he told me.

Leaning down, he sprayed some of the whipped cream on my chest and then licked in between my breasts in one swipe before telling me what to do next. "Open that pretty little mouth of yours."

"Put it on your cock..." I nodded at the can in his hand. Raising a brow, he did as I said.

Parting my lips, he grabbed my face in both hands and put the tip of his cock in my mouth. His pre-come oozed out and saltiness hit my tastebuds, mixed with the sweetness of the whipped cream.

He started jerking his hips back and forth as I sucked his dick and added suction. Plunging deeper, he hit the back of my throat, making me gag and choke, but he didn't stop. He kept going, and I loved every damn minute of it. His moans deepened with each stroke as I felt each pulse and twitch as he fucked my mouth.

Without even thinking twice, my fingers dropped between my legs and I rubbed my clit.

"Don't you dare touch what's mine." Damien's voice dropped and he stopped. Pulling his dick out of my mouth, my fingers froze on my throbbing flesh. Coming around to my legs, he grabbed my ankles and pulled me in one swift motion. Spreading my legs apart, he glided his eyes from my face down, pausing in between my legs.

"Spread them for me, baby." He began stroking himself as I parted my legs. Dropping down, he lifted my leg and began kissing my ankle, making his way up, where he kissed my inner thigh before his lips stopped in between my legs.

Licking in between my folds, my thighs smashed together against his face as he sucked and bit my clit hungrily.

"Damien!" I grabbed his hair in between my hands, panting as he swirled his tongue inside me.

Arching my back, a wave coursed through me as he pushed his fingers inside me, stretching me and spreading the wetness around.

"You're dripping for me, baby." He blew air against me, causing the sensation of heat and coolness to push me over the edge as he clamped his teeth against my clit, tugging it as his fingers pumped into me.

Shaking the whipped cream can, he sprayed it against my clit before putting his mouth back over me. He licked every bit up as my breathing grew shallow.

"Damien!" I screamed out as I came. He sucked up every bit of my release, then lifted his head slowly with a dark smile.

"Now you're ready for me to fuck you, baby." He planted my ankles on his shoulders and drew me down further. It had been three long years since I had felt him inside me. Nerves started to flare inside me as I watched his biceps covered in tattoos flex with his strong grip on my hips before he plunged the tip of his cock inside me.

Letting out a small cry, I covered my mouth with my arm. He was so thick, he didn't slide in easily; he had to slowly push himself in, and once halfway, he jerked so hard inside me, I had to grip the sheets tightly.

Thrusting slowly but picking up his pace, each stroke was harder and more intense than the next. His hands dropped off my hips and slid to my breasts. He pinched and played with my nipples as he balanced my legs on his shoulder.

"You're so fucking wet for me, baby." His voice was gruff and his breathing was hitched as he squeezed my tits harder.

Sliding my legs off him, he picked me up as if I weighed nothing, and flung me onto the pillow.

Taking both of my wrists in his hand, he pinned them tightly above my head as I opened my legs for him again.

"Tell me who this pussy belongs to?" He stroked his dick with his free hand as I watched him, completely drenched with another release on the brink of exploding.

"You," I whispered, looking away.

Swiping his fingers against my clit, he rubbed teasingly. "That's right, my good girl. This pussy is only mine to touch. Only mine to fuck. Only mine to ruin." Pulling his finger out, he slid it into his mouth, licking it.

"Mmm," he growled. Leaning into me, he pushed inside but this time, only halfway and then stopped. Arching his back, he grinded against me. His cock rubbed over my clit while filling my pussy, causing a sensation I'd never experienced. He looked down and watched as our bodies connected together. It was too much. He was grinding harder onto me, and rocking his dick in and out with smooth thrusts until I grabbed his arms and his lips crashed into mine, making him go inside me completely.

Crying out, another orgasm rippled through my entire body, and once my body stopped trembling, he pulled out quickly.

"Squeeze those perfect tits together for me, baby," he demanded as he pushed his cock between them. Sliding his length up and down between my breasts, he clenched his eyes shut and the lines between his brows deepened as he reached his release. His thick come shot out all over me, and tilting my head down, it splattered against my lips.

I licked my lips and he painted my nipples with his come.

"Mine," he breathed out before collapsing into the pillow next to me.

Dropping my mouth, I looked over at him. "Only yours." I leaned in and locked my lips to his.

I stayed in his arms for the rest of the night, and we talked about everything, but most of all, right as I fell asleep, I looked into his eyes and said the words I knew I would never not say to him.

"I love you, Damien."

Cupping my face, he kissed my forehead gently, "I love you, dandelion."

CHAPTER 46

Damien

Four months had come and gone. Meeting with Amira and Rian was harder than imaginable.

Rian was Ezra's twin in every sense. Guilt panged me as I watched him without a father who would have given him the entire world. Meanwhile, I was here with my daughter, learning to live.

Sophie and I were taking things slow, well... besides what our bodies were doing together. Nothing about our physical relationship was slow. I had filled her everywhere I could, and I had marked her as mine and only mine. She belonged to me and I would never let her go. Never.

I visited daily or had Estelle and Sophie over when I knew Amira needed space. She insisted she wasn't upset with me, she insisted she wanted Sophie and me to move on and be a family.

But I could see the guilt in Sophie's eyes whenever we were all together. I could see her internal battle as she couldn't decide what the right thing to do was.

Estelle was sheer perfection. My little girl was as smart as her mother, and just as beautiful, even though she favored me with her green eyes. She was kind and sweet and full of love.

She warmed up to me quickly, but didn't remember meeting me three years ago. It was starting from a blank slate five years into her life. My heart ached knowing I had missed five years of milestones and knowing I didn't experience Sophie being pregnant. But I had the chance to do life with both of my girls—something my best friend never got to do with his own family.

After much consideration, Sophie and I decided we wanted to move back to the United States. Chicago was out of the question, but we'd find home. Because, ultimately, home was wherever we were together.

Amira and Rian were going to move back to be closer to her parents. Sophie cried into my arms hours on end, feeling a sense of loss all over again.

Living with them made her feel Ezra's presence, but she also loved knowing they were okay and had a support system.

"You ready, baby?" I called up the stairs, holding Estelle's hand and a box in the other.

"Yea, I am." Sophie's voice echoed down. She jogged down the steps, and she exhaled as I wrapped my arm around her and she clung to me tightly.

Amira and Rian had left three days ago to get back to her family's house. Promises were made that we'd visit often and Facetime daily. I had set them up with an account that would ensure Amira would never worry about finances. I made her promise me that she knew I was a phone call away, and we would be there for them and Rian in any way she'd allow us to.

I'd show up. We'd show up.

Settling into our new home in Tennessee was an adjustment of its own. We knew no one, but the southern charm and joy that radiated throughout the town was exactly what we needed.

Sophie was making coffee when I came into the kitchen. I had bought us a ten-bedroom house with plenty of land and privacy. Wrapping my arms around her waist from behind, I leaned down and whispered into her ear, "Good morning, gorgeous." Spinning her around, I tilted her chin up and kissed her lips.

She looked down at the hand that was hidden behind my back, and her forehead creased. "What are you hiding?"

Handing her the brochure, I watched her read it.

She looked up at me with a confused smile. "Dental school?"

"I want to make sure all of your dreams come true. Every single one." I brushed my thumb against her bottom lip.

"Estelle's so young… I don't know if I'd have the time to balance everything, especially being a full-time student." She shrugged.

"Baby, I can take care of our daughter when you're busy. She's going to be right here. She's going to watch her mom chase her dreams. Look, we have enough money to last us ten lifetimes, so it's not for that. It's for you, my love. If this is still something you want, then do it."

"I do. I think I always felt that void. School and my own career meant so much to me. Ezra worked so hard to help me get there while my mom and dad would have been so proud. I just… You know what, screw it. I'm going to apply." An excited smile replaced any self-doubt she had as she jumped excitedly up into my arms. Swinging her around, I kissed her soft lips, feeling an enormous smile under mine.

"I love you, Soph," I whispered into her mouth.

"I love you, too."

CHAPTER 47

Sophie

"Where are you taking me?" I clutched Damien's hand tightly as we walked and he had covered my eyes with a silk tie. A door creaked opened and my feet echoed against a tiled floor.

"If this is some wild sex game, I hope you know I won't be doing it in public," I said quietly.

Damien let out a sexy laugh as we stopped. "Will you sit down, baby? I'll be right back." He helped me sit and the vinyl under me creaked.

"Don't you dare leave me here with this blindfold." I tugged it off and my lips parted.

Damien had flown us on his private jet, but didn't tell me where we were going. We stopped over in New York and left Estelle with Amira and Rian after spending a couple of days with them. They were doing incredibly well, and Amira had even started to date an amazing man. We landed in a small airport, and I couldn't tell where we were. Once we got into a limo, he had put this tie over my eyes.

My heart was racing as I looked around the empty Le Petit Bistro. It looked just the same, except my eyes stopped on the sign above the bar that used to say its name.

It was replaced with Dente di Leone Bistro. *Dandelion Bistro.*

Footsteps grew closer, and I flung around.

Damien appeared wearing his leather jacket and a nervous grin.

Dropping down to his knee, he opened a velvet black box. I held my breath as I took in the enormous, gorgeous, oval diamond ring.

"Damien..." I whispered with my hands over my mouth in shock.

"Sophie, you are my safe place and my biggest adventure. Being with you once was satisfying a craving, but now, I'm addicted to you. I need you. I *crave* you every single day, every single minute, and every single second. I love you so much, my gorgeous dandelion. I know you didn't think the first time we met was a meet-cute-worthy moment, but that moment was when my world shifted for the better. It was the moment I knew I'd never be the same. Because with you, my love, I want to do better and be better. I'll spend the rest of my life trying to do that for my girls. Sophie Shah, will you marry me and make me the luckiest man in the world?" His mossy-green eyes sparkled as he looked at me longingly. Sliding out of the booth, I fell to my knees and gripped his face between my palms.

"Yes, yes, yes! A thousand times yes. I love you; I'll always love you." Our lips crashed together and the world felt right. Tears spilled down my cheeks as Damien slid the ring on my finger, lifted my hand, and pressed it on his cheek.

"I love you," he said softly against my palm before kissing it.

Damien had bought Le Petit Bistro and renamed it. Although we weren't going to live in Chicago, he wanted to preserve the place we met. Our meet-cute. Sure, it wasn't like the movies or the love stories that made you gush. We were fighting, and bickering the entire time we first met, but it was ours. Our story. Our love.

We were back home in Tennessee with Estelle in our arms, chasing the new goldendoodle puppy she had convinced her daddy to buy her. I was going to start dental school the next year, and we were finally going to let ourselves just live the life we had always desired. The life we had always craved.

Life often doesn't end up how you wanted, how you envisioned it to be. It often ends up messier and harder.

I used to think that maybe, one day, I'd have my own happily ever after. Maybe, one day, I'd be a successful, independent woman. Maybe, one day, I'd find a man who loved me unconditionally and we'd get married, then have babies together. Maybe, one day, I'd have this life I wished for.

But maybe, just maybe, we should stop waiting for one day, because that day is today.

Sitting in the soft grass, I plucked a dandelion as Damien ran after Estelle and the puppy. Holding it up, I closed my eyes but didn't make a wish. All my wishes had already come true. But old habits die hard, so with all my might, I took a deep breath in and blew out.

Damien had come back and saw me holding the small, bare stem up.

"All the petals flew off at the same time, right?" he asked with a smirk on his face.

"How'd you know?" I asked curiously.

"Because there's someone in the world who loves you unconditionally, and that someone..." he sat down next to me and put his arm around me, bringing me in closer, "that someone is me." Pressing his lips against my forehead, I looked up at him.

"My moon, my stars, and my sun. Thank you for always lighting up my world, dandelion." Kissing him, I couldn't help but smile underneath. Wishes really do come true, but sometimes you just have to remember that your 'one day' will come eventually, and that day... that day will be everything you ever dreamt of.

Epilogue

DAMIEN

Time feels so fluid when you're not worrying about it. You end up cherishing the people and things in your life all that more.

Life was changing for us *again*. We were officially becoming husband and wife. Amira and Rian had life changes, too. Amira was married to a great guy and pregnant with another baby. She was doing well, and that meant even more because Sophie was all that happier knowing she could savor and move on to the next chapter in her life without a huge feeling of guilt.

Sophie was able to finally reconnect with Reese, who was sitting in the front row for our wedding day. Life was changing, but for the better.

Fixing my tuxedo, I waited at the end of the aisle

anxiously. My best man kept punching my leg and was whining.

"Rian, come on, dude. It'll be a quick ceremony. Your Aunt Sophie is almost coming out. She's just a little late." I glanced at my watch and looked over my shoulder at my tyrant toddler nephew who was also my best man.

"Girls!" he huffed, crossing his arms. I bit back my impending laughter as the music shifted and my beautiful daughter came out in a pale pink dress holding a basket filled with petals. Little lights sparkled all above us, and Estelle looked like an angel as she tossed flowers all around.

Reaching me, she stuck her tongue out at Rian and gave me a quick hug. "Love you, baby girl," I whispered as she took her spot.

The violinist had begun playing and my mouth parted in awe as Sophie began walking down the aisle.

My queen. She was wearing a sleek, fitted white wedding dress that hugged her gorgeous curves perfectly. Her long dark hair was pinned up with wisps falling around her face. Her gorgeous brown eyes twinkled and her thick lips were painted pink. My eyes dropped to her bouquet, and tucked in the blush peonies were bright yellow dandelions and the white puffballs. Emotion overtook me as I watched my bride come closer to me.

Exhaling, I clasped my hands together as they shook. Her beauty left me speechless.

We were getting married in a field of dandelions, in a field full of endless wishes, all of which were now coming true.

I never dreamt of this day. I never wished for this day. Not until I met her. And when I did, I begged for this day to happen.

The day where Sophie Shah, the girl I knew was off limits, the girl I knew was out of my damn league and was my best friend's little sister, became mine.

Completely mine.

Sliding her hands into mine, she looked up at me with a shy smile.

"Hi, beautiful," I said to her as pink filled her cheeks.

"Hi," she whispered back.

Lifting the dandelion up near her lips, I grinned at her. She closed her eyes and in one swift breath, blew.

Opening her eyes, her gorgeous face lit up. Every single bit of the dandelion puff had blown away.

"Someone truly loves you with all of their being." I paused. "But I know you already knew that."

Tears glazed her eyes as she squeezed my hands slightly.

I don't know what the priest said, but something about reincarnation came up. All I knew was that I started to believe in reincarnation because I hoped Sophie would let me have her in every life. Because life without her wasn't living; life without her wasn't worth it. Life with her was everything and more. She made me stop wishing for anything because with her, all my wishes became my reality.

Dipping her down in my arms, our guests cheered as I kissed my beautiful bride.

"I love you, Mr. Moretti," she said against my lips before I kissed her again.

"I love you, today, tomorrow, and forever, Mrs. Moretti. My beautiful, perfect bride."

"I thought that when I first met you was my favorite day in the world," I whispered against her face as the guests around us faded.

"Well, then, what is your favorite day?" she asked lowly.

"Today. Because today is the first day of the rest of our lives, and I get to spend every single one waking up next to you."

Her face lit up and the sexy smile on her face made me lift her into my arms and race down the aisle.

Fuck the reception. I need to have her right now. Her laughter echoed as I sprinted with her over my shoulder, grabbing that peach-ass of hers.

Once back in our hotel suite, Sophie smiled at me as

I gripped her face between my palms. Leaning down, I kissed her gently. Her plump, soft lips felt so perfect against mine, but then, in true Sophie fashion, she bit my bottom lip while tugging it between her teeth.

"I'm going to make love to my wife tonight," I whispered into her mouth.

Nodding slowly, she widened her stunning brown eyes at me as she untied my bowtie without moving her gaze from mine.

I quickly began unbuttoning my dress shirt after peeling my tuxedo jacket off, and a sexy smirk grew across her lips.

She turned around and I couldn't help but smile. Planting my lips across her exposed back, I tugged the small zipper of her wedding gown down. "Fuck..." I moaned as a thin, white lace thong was revealed. Stepping out of her gown, she turned toward me with her nipples hardened and her gorgeous body on full display. Arching an eyebrow, she planted her hand against my chest and pushed me back onto the bed.

"Damien, are you ready for the ride of your life?"

Groaning as she tugged my pants off and straddled me, I looked into my gorgeous wife's eyes. "Baby, I never got off this ride. *Never.*" Tugging her hips upward, I pulled her onto my cock, and the way she threw her head back had my entire body tighten. Being inside her was my favorite place to be, and tonight, I was going to make sure she knew how fucking lucky I felt that she was my wife.

Pumping her body up and down my length, she moaned my name but moments later, I flung her onto her back and thrusted into her with hard, long movements as she threw her arms around my neck, tugging me deeper.

"Where does my good girl belong, sweetheart?" I growled against her lips.

"On my knees or back..." She clenched her eyes shut and her back arched as she tightened around my dick.

"That's right, baby. Such a fucking good girl," I rasped, brushing my lips against her neck before dragging them over her mouth.

"Damien... I love you." She sighed with her release as I slammed my lips against hers while filling her with my warm, thick come.

"My sun, moon, and stars... thank you for being my light. You'll never know what I look like not loving you. You brought color in my bleak world. I will forever love you. Only you," I whispered into her ear as she slowly opened her eyes. I knew she saw just how much I was in love with her. And she knew I'd spend the rest of my life doing just that. Because it's true, when love breaks us, it reminds us that it's a gift we learn from, and most of all, we choose if that love is worth fighting for or not.

And our love was worth it all. Our love broke us, but it built us back up, too.

Acknowledgments

My husband and my children, Mila and Ari—you are my moon, stars, and sun. Thank you for always bringing light into my life and being the loves of my life. I love you all so much.

Elise, thank you from the bottom of my heart for loving Damien and Sophie as much as I did and for meeting them when I first finished their story. I am so grateful for you and how you understood their whirlwind love the way I intended it to be. I am so thankful for your friendship and love you!

Paige, words can't even express how fortunate I feel to call you a friend. Here's to forever oversharing, overthinking and always laughing together with endless voice notes. You just get me and I'm grateful for that and you! I love you! Spiral soul sisters forever. XO

Joss, I am so thankful for your friendship and being able to easily connect about everything with endless podcasts. Love and adore you! Thank you for always being such positive energy in my life! XO

Gabby, you know exactly where my heart is when

I'm writing these books and have been there for the ups and downs. Thank you for cheering me on even when I'm feeling like the balancing act is hard. Thank you for celebrating these stories with me. I love you, soul sister!

Jessica M., I've lost count on how many times you've made me laugh or cry through this journey with books. You always have me on an emotional roller coaster with your incredible friendship and support. Thank you for taking a chance on me when I was brand new and sticking with me. It's an absolute gift to call you a friend. Love you always, my OG girl!

Kealey, oh my girl you are so special to me for so many reasons and more but I am so incredibly grateful for how I can trust you when I first put words down on a paper and know you understand the wild ride of it all. Thank you for making me laugh and smile so much through it all. You are such a special friend to me!

Caroline, thank you for being there since my first book and always being there for me when I switch between genres. I am so grateful for your friendship, support and the years of lovely conversations.

Amanda, thank you for being a wonderful friend but also being there for each book and supporting me. I'm honored that you take the time to be on this journey with me even when I bounce between spicy romance and dark thrillers!

Cristina, thank you so much for being on this journey with me. I am so grateful for your friendship and am thankful to have you read my books early. I don't think I'll ever not ask you "are you sure this book is even dark?"

Kelly, this journey has been so beautiful in many ways but it can also be daunting. Friends like you who are supportive, kind and such a wonderful light in my life are ones I cherish the most. Thank you for reading this book early and for also taking a chance on me in both genres.

Swati and Rin, my bookies and cookies, it's an honor to call you both fellow authors but most of all, amazing friends. You both are incredible women that I adore. I'm so grateful for the laughter, the support and the friendship. Thank you for pushing me to balance romance and thriller genres and reminding me to just not kill off multiple characters in my romance.

I love you ladies so much and am grateful for each of you!

My wonderful ARC team, every book that I release is a whirlwind and can be chaos but each of you help remind me why I do this and how blessed I am to have the best ARC team an author could have. Thank you for celebrating each book, each milestone and being patient when I mood write in romance and thrillers. Adore you all so much!

To the bookstagrammers, booktokers, book bloggers that take a chance on my books and create stunning posts, videos and more, my heart overflows every single time and there aren't enough words to express my gratitude. Thank you so much!

To my readers, without you my books wouldn't see light and goodness I love sharing these rays with you. Thank you for taking a chance on my books and me.

About the Author

Monica Arya is a bestselling author of both romance and thriller novels. Monica lives in the Carolinas with her husband, two children and goldendoodle. When she's not writing, you can find her at the beach, singing slightly-off key, instigating spontaneous dance parties and chasing her children around. Monica's educational background is in Psychology, which she often puts to use in her novels. Monica absolutely loves to connect with her readers.

You can find her on Instagram and TikTok: @monicaaryaauthor

Facebook Reader Group: Monica Arya's Misfits

Website: www.monicaarya.com